PADDY HIRSCH

PRIMED

Cover Design by James, GoOnWrite.com

First edition

ISBN: 979-8-9934385-0-4

This book was professionally typeset on Reedsy.
Find out more at reedsy.com

Acknowledgments

I received an incredible amount of support from people around me, as I brought this book into being. I have a great many people to thank.

So thank you! To all the people who read drafts of this book - particularly **Don MacDonald** and **Kimberley Murray**, whose straightforward feedback kept me honest throughout. To **Nate**, for helping me navigate *The Artist's Way*, and to **Ian**, **Mac**, **Joe**, **Owen** and **Nancy** for keeping me out of the artist's slough of despair. To **Lisa Gallagher**, who got an early version to **Lyssa Keusch** at *Harper Collins:* Lisa and Lyssa's enthusiasm for the book were the mainstay of my own belief that the book was worth pushing ahead with as a self-publishing project. To fellow writers **Eric Beetner** and **Gary Phillips**, and to all the authors at *Mystery Writers of America (SoCal)*, led by **Leslie Klinger**, who've talked me through the down times. To **Nancy Silverman**, at *Sisters In Crime*. To **Jan Wilcox** and **Cindy Woods** of *Men of Mystery*, **Debbie Mitsch** of *Mystery Ink*, **Renee Raymond** at *Peninsula Seniors,* and the wonderfully generous **Janis Thomas**, who did sterling work on a late proof of the book. To **Elva**, for always being there, and most of all to **Eileen**, for being a hundred percent behind me, a hundred percent of the time.

Thank you all.

1

Belfast, Northern Ireland

Rain hammered on the windscreen and the roof of the car as it lurched over the first of three speed bumps outside the entrance to the police station. Gary Lawlor thumbed a button on the steering wheel, until Bach's Sonata No. 1 for solo violin was barely a whisper. The car in front moved up to the barrier, and a police officer leaned over, one hand on the roof of the car, rain streaming off the peak of her cap as she spoke to the driver. She wore a high-visibility jacket under her bulletproof vest and equipment belt, both of which were weighed down with gear: radio, handcuffs, sidearm, ammunition, and all the other accouterments of the modern copper.

She gestured, and the red-and-white striped barrier rose, and the car rolled forward. The barrier was lowered again, and the woman looked at Lawlor from under the peak of her cap and waved him forward.

He took a deep breath.

"Time to break the law," he muttered to himself.

And let out the clutch.

The rain gushed over the peak of the woman's cap as she leaned over to look into the car. "What can I do for you today, sir?"

"I'm from procurement. I'm here to check the purchasing paperwork for your new solar array." Lawlor reached into the bag on the passenger seat beside him. He held up a piece of paper.

"You're a wee bit early, Mister..." She peered at the paperwork. "McCarren."

"I know. I came up from Portadown. Wanted to beat the traffic."

"There's no one from accounting'll be in for at least an hour, Mister McCarren. We've no one who can escort you in."

"Ah, now." Lawlor shook his head, like a man cursing his own foolishness. "I didn't think of that. I'll go back out and get a cup of tea. Come back later."

The police officer turned her head to look at the backed-up line of cars that stretched into the street. "Do you've some ID on you?"

He reached back into the bag. There was a postcard caught inside his wallet. He took his driver's license out, and showed it to the officer. Then he slid the postcard into the inside pocket of his jacket.

The officer pushed back off the car and spoke into the mouthpiece of her radio. The barrier went up.

"Pull forward into the car park, Mister McCarren." The officer pointed. "Go to the right of the line of orange cones. You'll see a search bay marked on the ground. Drive into it. Stay in your car. An officer'll come over and check you, and then you can turn around and head back out."

"Right you are." Lawlor drove under the barrier. Eight o'clock on the nail.

2

There was a yellow rectangle painted on the tarmac at the side of the car park. Lawlor drove onto it, turned up the Bach, and watched in his mirror as the team on the gate changed shift. Led by the female officer, they ran through the car park to the main police station, all huddled over in the rain. He waited for a beat, then let out the clutch and drove slowly off the yellow rectangle and into the car park.

He slid the car into an empty space, took a laminated badge out of the bag, and hung it around his neck. He took a handgun from under the passenger seat, and pushed it into the back of his jeans. He got out of the car, turned up his collar, and walked across towards the police station, keeping level with another man as they converged on the front door.

"Nice weather for it," he said.

"If your name's Noah, maybe." The man waved his ID over the reader attached to the side of the door. It beeped, the door clicked open and the man pushed his way inside. Lawlor hustled in after him.

The man was looking at him. He was lean and hard-eyed, with a receding hairline and a thin blond beard. "Do I know you?"

"McCarren." Lawlor flicked his badge. "Facilities. Just started this week."

The man nodded. "See you around, then."

Lawlor followed the man through the interior doorway and into the station. After the rain outside, it was oppressively hot. Linoleum on the floors. Thick gloss paint on the walls. The smell of sweat and electronics, and damp clothes, steaming. There was a lift on the right side of the hallway, and Lawlor pressed the call button. The doors slid open, and he stepped inside and pressed the button for the third floor. The doors closed again, and the lift hummed upwards.

And stopped.

An alarm bell began ringing, just outside the lift, so loud that Lawlor couldn't hear anything besides his own breathing. He stabbed the buttons, but the lift didn't move.

He took the gun out of his belt, ejected the empty magazine, racked the slide and applied the lock to hold it open. He placed the gun and the magazine on the floor, and took a piece of paper out of his back pocket. He unfolded it, turned towards the back of the lift cabin and got onto his knees.

The alarm stopped. The lift started. And stopped again.

Lawlor put his hands in the air.

The doors slid open.

"Armed police!"

The lift cabin had steel bars attached to its walls at waist height. In the reflection, Lawlor saw four men pointing weapons at him, two in the kneeling position with rifles, two with handguns, one on either side of the door.

"The gun's on the deck, lads," he said.

"Armed police!" the same voice shouted again. "Do. Not. Fucking. Move!"

2

They took his possessions and his shoelaces and ushered him firmly into a cell. It was eight feet by eight, with a blinding light in the ceiling and a sleeping bench along one wall. The bench was covered by a thin, plastic-coated mattress, one end of which Lawlor rolled up to make a pillow.

But he couldn't sleep.

He took the postcard out of the inside pocket of his jacket. It was a cheap, homemade job. A glossy 4x6 print of a pretty girl, glued onto a piece of card. On the reverse, "Greetings from California!" and then, "Look who's having pizza." He had recognized the girl instantly. He'd never met her, but she was the spit of her mother. Lisa Fyffe, whose husband Jerry had served with Lawlor in 14 Company.

The girl wasn't eating pizza. But behind her, in the corner of the photograph, was a group of diners at an Italian restaurant. And in the middle of the group was a man with a head of bright red hair, who Lawlor hadn't seen in more than 20 years.

Rab Harper.

He stared at the photograph, his mind churning, the rage making his hands shake. He tried to do all the things the grief counselors had taught him to do. Breathe deep. Focus on the place where his thumbs touched. Repeat a well-worn list of affirmations.

The lock on the cell door buzzed, and the door swung open. Chief Superintendent William Carrington stepped in, arms folded over his belly, a plastic bag tucked under his arm.

"Ah now," he said. "Did they not give you a cup of tea?"

"No. And they forgot my slippers as well." Lawlor slipped the postcard back into his pocket. "Standards are slipping, Billy. It's terrible to see."

"I'll tell you what's terrible." Carrington held up the bag. Inside it was Lawlor's handgun. "Do you have a permit for this?"

"It's not mine."

"So where did you get it?"

"I drew it from the armory at headquarters."

Carrington sighed. "Do you not get it, Gary? You're not polis any more. You can't go walking about with a pistol like you're John bloody Wayne."

Lawlor didn't respond. Carrington was right: he hadn't been a police officer for more than 20 years. He'd left Special Branch as a detective inspector. A few years and a university degree later he'd returned as a civilian, to run the PSNI computer security unit. That had vaulted him over his colleagues, in terms of responsibility and access. It had made him a lot of enemies, too. He wasn't entirely sure whether Carrington was one of them.

"I should report this, you know." Carrington dangled the bag.

"You probably should."

There was silence, as Carrington considered his next move. Then he tucked the bag back under his arm. "So what about this test?"

"What about it?"

"You might have warned us you were coming."

"I did warn you, Billy. You got an email. Two weeks ago. Every division should expect a random penetration test in the next six months."

"Oh aye." Carrington nodded, grudgingly. "So did we pass, or what?"

"I walked through your front door and into the lift with an automatic weapon, Billy. What do you think?"

Carrington scowled. "I think I should have left you in here for the rest of the bloody day. But word has come down to me from on high. There's some people have flown over from London especially to see you."

"Who?"

"Americans. Very busy, I'm told. And very impatient."

Lawlor stood up. "Is there any other kind?"

3

The conference room was on the fourth floor of the headquarters building, but Lawlor opted for the stairs.

Even before he was halfway up, he could hear the sound of two men arguing. When he reached the landing, he saw Dennis Johnson, the head of the Paramilitary Crime Task Force, squared off against a civilian in a suit that looked as though it had been pulled out of the bottom of the laundry basket. The man had thin hair stretched over a pale scalp. The watery eyes and papery, red-blotched skin of a gin drinker. And the belly to match.

They watched Lawlor approach. Johnson was red in the face, smoothing the front of his starched white uniform shirt. The crumpled man was grinning.

"Everything all right, Dennis?" Lawlor asked.

"Everything's fine," the civilian said. He had one of those flat-voweled, generic accents that they churned out of classified locations in Virginia. "Are you Lawlor?"

"I am. Who are you?"

The man didn't answer. He opened one of the doors of the conference room, and pointed inside with his chin. "They're waiting for you."

Margaret Bullen, Chief Constable of the Police Service of Northern Ireland, sat at the head of the table. She was in full dress uniform, her silver hair cut in a tight bob that would have looked good on a women twenty years her junior. On her right was Davy Kilpatrick, the Assistant Chief Constable (Crime). On her left was another familiar face, but not from the police force: a barrel-chested, florid-faced, white-haired man of about sixty, dressed in a blue suit and red tie.

"Thanks for coming in, Gary." Bullen gestured. "I believe you've met Secretary Foley."

"I think we might have shaken hands once," Lawlor said. "A long time ago."

"Ninety-two." Foley had a booming, jovial voice. "I was the CIA liaison to Special Branch. And you were on the fast track to chief inspector."

He smirked.

Bullen cleared her throat. "Secretary Foley is officially in London right now. But he has been generous enough to make a detour, to pass on a briefing from the CIA office in Tel Aviv."

There was a file on the table. It was a plain, buff folder, with a thick red stripe across the horizontal and a stamp in the top right hand corner. It looked as official as a file could get.

"Davy?" Bullen said, and Kilpatrick hauled himself out of his seat, picked up the file, and walked it down to where Lawlor sat.

Kilpatrick was a big man, a former rugby player who ate and drank as though he still did scrum practice and line-out drills for two hours each day. He perched one fleshy thigh on the edge of the table, which groaned a little as he settled his weight on it.

The file was as thick as an airport novel. It was stuffed with papers and photographs, all eight inches by ten. Kilpatrick began laying them out in front of Lawlor.

A wide shot first. The shell of a car. The blast had lifted it high in the air, thrown it forward several meters, and dumped it back on its wheels. The fire had burned hard and fast, gutting the interior. But there were still several distinctly human shapes visible in the midst of the tangle of blackened steel.

Kilpatrick laid down another photograph. It was a shot inside the driver's foot well. It showed a ragged wire connected to a lever on the right side of the steering wheel. Then followed a series of shots of twisted metal. The roof, sides and engine compartment of the car. And then three photos of pieces of debris, taken from the vehicle, photographed in a lab.

The breath caught in Lawlor's throat, and a pulse began to hammer behind his right temple. He was swept away, back into the bedroom of his house, watching as his sons ran down the path to the car he had parked on the street the night before. Tommy first, eleven years old, fair hair that fell into his eyes, a lover of all things with four wheels and an engine. Andrew following, nine and three-quarters, long-legged in his short trousers, weighed down with a backpack and a music satchel, with his violin case clutched to his chest. Tommy must have taken the keys from the table in the hall, because the Saab's lights blinked and Tommy opened the driver's door and climbed in, while Andrew clambered into the back, and Lawlor saw them both there, frozen for a moment, as the clouds broke, and a pale sunrise spilled over the street.

They told him afterwards that the device was rigged to the indicator lever. Tommy must have been pretending to drive the car and pushed the lever up, they said. The initial blast lifted the Saab, and a split second later the fuel tank exploded.

A full tank, topped off the afternoon before. The car filled with flame and blew apart, and in the random way that shock waves work, the blast blew out every window in the house, except the one Lawlor was standing in. So he stood, paralyzed, as the car rose and then fell, and the white-hot flames vaporized the glass, stripped the paint, melted the tires and turned his life to ash.

"Lawlor?" The table creaked as Kilpatrick leaned towards him.

Lawlor blinked the memories away. He felt physically stunned, as though he'd been stuck with a cattle prod.

"These photos were taken in Tel Aviv last week. The car belonged to Tareq Mahmoud, the PLO negotiator." Kilpatrick stabbed one of the photographs with one fleshy finger. It was a magnification, a chunk of plastic, covered in tiny bubbles.

"This is an alloy that the Mossad labs found traces of in the steering column," he said. "Tungsten and molybdenum. In a very specific ratio. Fifty-eight percent to forty-two."

There was silence in the room. Lawlor was aware of three sets of eyes, staring at him.

"Kontimax," he said. "Rab Harper."

"You remember."

"I'm not likely to forget the chemical composition of the device used to murder my kids, Davy."

Rab Harper had stolen three boxes of a hundred Kontimax 58/42 detonators from a mining company in France in 1988. And he had used them every time he did a job for the IRA over the next four years. The 58/42 was the best in the business. But it left a residue behind after a blast. No problem for a construction company. But for Rab Harper it was, effectively, a signature. One that the bomb techs had found in the wreckage of Lawlor's car, one bright spring morning, twenty years before.

"You think this is Rab Harper?" Lawlor turned to Foley. "You think he's back in business?"

Foley shrugged. "It's a possibility, that's all. We got a bunch of data on these bombings, from the Lebanese, the Palestinians. The Israelis. We ran it through our system. It registered the unusual use of Kontimax detonators and spat out his name."

"The dets were used in every device?"

"In every highly-targeted assassination of that type in that part of the world in the last twelve months. Seven bombings. Seven kills. Mahmoud, a Druze politician, two Hamas officers, one Hezbollah general and the leaders of two Israeli settlements."

"So if it is the same guy, he's not ideological. He's freelance."

"That's how we see it."

Lawlor shook his head. "Bomb-making's a young man's game. Most of them blow themselves up before they're thirty. Rab Harper's in his fifties now. It's hard to imagine a man that age crawling around under a car with a fistful of Semtex."

"You're probably right. Still, Langley needs to take him off their list. Which means they need to run him down. And to do that, they need to take a look at his file."

"Harper's file?" Lawlor looked at Kilpatrick. "It's in the archive."

"Yeah, but we thought you might have your own file." Kilpatrick had a drinker's eyes, pale and watery. But the suspicion in them was undiluted. "Something you might have worked up in your spare time."

3

"That would be illegal, Assistant Chief Constable," he said.

Kilpatrick scowled. "Don't play games, Lawlor. I remember you finding ways to run into the search teams back then. Pumping them for updates. Looking over people's shoulders at their reports. You had your own investigation running."

"I asked for updates. Of course I did." Lawlor felt heat flare in his cheeks. "But only because I was shut out of the inquiry."

"As you should have been. Conflict of interest." Kilpatrick made a dismissive gesture. "Not that I blame you. In your situation, I'm sure I'd have done the same." He smiled and nodded. "And I'd have ended up with a file a foot thick on the fucker. So where is it?"

Lawlor shook his head, smiling at Kilpatrick's attempts at manipulation. "Why don't you stop playing the puppet master, Davy, and tell me what else you have."

"Explain," Foley said.

"You can buy Kontimax dets anywhere. So by extension, this could be anyone. What else do you have that makes you think it could be Harper, specifically?"

Foley nodded, and Kilpatrick pulled a sheaf of papers out of the file.

"These are internet intercepts made by the boys and girls at Mossad," Foley said. "They're very good at monitoring the channels used by terror groups out there. Just ahead of the Druze and Israeli settler hits, there was chatter about an Irishman joining his Palestinian brothers and sisters in the Intifada. Then they listened in on exchanges between two leaders of the New Irgun group - you know these guys?"

"Israeli extremists." Lawlor was reading the transcript.

"Yeah, real tough guys. They start talking about support from an expert they call the Red Man."

"And then there's this." Kilpatrick slid a photograph out of the folder.

It was a surveillance shot, taken in a hotel. The picture was grainy and underexposed. It showed a tall, thin man standing at a hotel counter. He was half-turned away from the camera, wearing dark trousers and a light colored shirt.

"This could be anyone," Lawlor said. He glanced at the swell of Kilpatrick's belly. "Well, not you Davy, obviously."

Kilpatrick's eyes bulged with anger. He thrust a piece of paper at Lawlor. "Surveillance report."

"Subject is approx 175 cm, approx 80 kg. Approx 50 yrs," Lawlor read. "Caucasian. Pale skin. Blue eyes. Red hair. Irish-accented English."

"It could be anyone, as you say," Foley said. "And the Irish fondness for the Palestinian cause is well documented. So that could be anyone, too. But then, the kids at Langley have a bug up their collective ass about eliminating Harper from their inquiries before they move on to other, more likely, targets."

Kilpatrick began shuffling the photos and the papers together.

"Hold on." Lawlor reached for the folder. Kilpatrick had only taken a dozen photographs out of it. It was still an inch thick. "Let me see the rest."

He flicked through the pictures to the close-ups of the interior of the car. There were more than twenty of them, all marked up with arrows that had the names of the victims written on them. The driver. Behind him, two adults. Mahmoud and his wife. And then, beside the driver, a smaller shape. Mahmoud's son, Aziz. Lawlor's eyes skittered over the photograph. The boy had been wearing his seat belt. The heat had fused it to his chest, close to his neck.

"Ten years old, in case you're wondering," Foley said.

The air-conditioning kicked in, and Lawlor felt the sweat on the back of his neck.

The next shot showed the extent of the devastation in the street. The blast had removed the driver and passenger doors, and blown the bonnet of the car far into the air. Something nagged at Lawlor's memory as he looked at the scenes, and he focused his attention for a moment, but nothing came to him.

He pulled out the last few photographs. They were individual pictures of Mahmoud, his wife, his son, and the driver. They looked like passport blow-ups. Mahmoud was a young man, Lawlor realized. He had a scrub of a beard and intelligent eyes behind round glasses. His mouth was twisted in a wry smile. His wife looked as though she was barely out of her teens. Aziz looked like his father. He looked like a boy who'd been told not to smile, but was about to burst into laughter.

Lawlor felt an intense, almost physical pain, deep inside. He closed his eyes, willing the pain away, and then something occurred to him. He shuffled back through the photos, to the wide shot of the street, and the car, with the bonnet blown off and the trunk blasted open. The jolting caused either by the blast or the car landing afterwards had bounced out the contents of the trunk, into a heap behind the shell of the vehicle. None of it had burned. There was a small suitcase that had burst open like a piece of rotten fruit. A leather briefcase, unopened. A cardboard box, one corner crushed. And leaning against it, almost out of the shot, an unmistakable hourglass shape.

The image was tiny, less than an inch long. But it was crystal clear. A protective case. Black, and glossy, with brass clasps. A little bit fancier than the generic. A little bit more robust.

Just like the one Andrew had asked Lawlor to buy for his ninth birthday.

To carry his violin.

He felt like a man underwater, struggling up from the deep to the surface, and then fighting for breath.

"He goes after them where they're softest," he said.

"That's his MO." Foley nodded. "Mahmoud. The settlers. He hit them all when they were with their families. At home. At school. The Druze hit was outside a daycare where his wife was picking up their kid. They're ruthless out there, but that's cold, even for them."

Lawlor butted the photos and papers together, and pushed them back into the file. His hands were shaking. "You really think it could be Harper?"

"Do I think?" Foley shrugged. "Not really. He's way too old and rusty, like you say. I think there are several other local guys who fit the frame, and I'd like us to focus on them. But Langley needs convincing before they move on, so I need your notes. Whatever you've got."

Lawlor shook his head. "I did search for Harper. And the Assistant Chief is right. I did squeeze people on the inquiry for information. And I spent an unhealthy amount of time online. But I never found out much. A whisper, here and there. But Harper disappeared. There was, literally, no trace of him. The search teams hunted high and low, with a lot more resources than I had. But they never found anything. Ask the Chief. She was on one of those teams."

There was silence in the room. Bullen was nodding, solemn-faced.

Foley blew out his cheeks. "Well, this is disappointing, I

won't deny it. We don't like it when there are guys out there blowing shit up without either our say-so or our know-so. And it looks like this guy, whoever he is, is only getting into his stride."

"I'm sorry we couldn't be more helpful, Mister Secretary." Bullen was on her feet, tugging at the hem of her uniform jacket.

"As am I, Madam Chief Constable." He gave her a flat smile. "It's just as well I booked a day's fishing on the Bann."

He stood up, and the door to the conference room opened. The man in the crumpled suit stepped in.

"Car's downstairs," he said, and Foley nodded, and walked out, without a word.

The man walked over to the table and began pushing the photos and papers back into the file. When he was finished, he put the file under his arm and looked down at Lawlor.

"Thanks for all your help, buddy.' He sneered. "If you think of anything, y'all be sure and give us a call."

4

Detective Chief Inspector Róisín Mackey was waiting for him at the bottom of the stairs. She wore flat shoes and a dark suit that looked a half-size too big for her. She had a leather attache slung over her shoulder, and a takeout cup in each hand.

"I figured they wouldn't have treated you to coffee up there," she said.

"Not so much as a custard cream."

"You don't like custard creams."

"They're an abomination, right enough." He took one of the cups. "But I'd have appreciated the gesture."

There was a pair of cheap saffron-colored sofas in the lobby, and a coffee table adorned with a vase of plastic flowers. Lawlor sat down facing the door.

"So what's it all about?" Róisín leaned forward. "I saw Dennis getting into it just now, with one of those Yanks."

"Yeah, they're not happy." He thought back to the conversation he had interrupted outside the conference room. The unusual sight of Róisín's ex-husband standing mute as a schoolboy in his stiff shirt. He wondered what the pasty little G-man had been berating him about.

"They think Rab Harper might be back in business," he said. "In the Middle East."

"At fifty-odd? You're joking."

He shrugged. "They found his signature in seven of those killings. The Kontimax. All car bombs, too."

"Rab's specialty." She glanced at him. "Sorry."

He shook his head.

"So there's that." He put his coffee on the table. "And then there's this."

He took the postcard out of his pocket, and handed it to Róisín. She looked at the picture, then flipped the card to read what was on the back.

"Down the bottom," Lawlor said. "There's a QR code."

"Clever." Róisín took out her phone and aimed it. She cursed.

"Problem?"

"New phone. I've not set up facial recognition yet." She punched in her code. Looked up at him. "Don't start with your head of security bollocks, now."

He shrugged. "None of my business, if you want to keep the same code you've had since the iPhone 4 came out."

"You're right. It is none of your business."

"Not very secure, though. And Andrea's birthday's a bit obvious. I'm just saying."

"Okay, Dad." The photograph popped up on her screen. "Wow. Great resolution."

"Now top right. In the restaurant."

She used her fingers to pan and zoom and focus on the group of diners. On the red-headed man in the center of the table.

"Jesus God." Her voice echoed in the wide space of the lobby.

"My thoughts exactly."

"Who sent you this?"

"Jerry Fyffe.   A pal of mine from the Det.   That's his daughter."

They were interrupted by the sound of footsteps and laughter on the stairs behind them. A group of officers, all in their early twenties, all in dress uniform. At the same time, the front door to the building opened, and a small crowd of proud parents began filing in.

Róisín stood up. "Let's go down to yours. I've something to show you, too."

Lawlor's office was a plain gray cube in the bowels of the building, two floors down behind a series of secure doors. There were no pictures on the walls. Nothing personal on the desk. Just a monitor, keyboard and mouse. A chair in front and a chair behind.

Róisín took a folder out of her briefcase. It was red, and battered and unmarked. And three inches thick. She slid it across the desk.

Lawlor looked at it. "This doesn't look very official to me, DCI Mackey."

"Nor is it. You remember we busted that network of Lithuanian brothels a while back?"

There was a sour taste in his mouth. "Underage girls."

She nodded. "We rolled up the network well enough - or most of it - but there was a loose end. They'd been making films."

"Streaming or recording?"

"We couldn't find out. No-one talked, and there was no evidence, outside of the studio they used. A right little shop of horrors, that was."

"So. Case shelved."

"Upstairs, maybe." She tapped a fingernail on the file. "But I kept it open."

They'd known each other since joining Special Branch, more than 20 years before. They were both outsiders, she as a Catholic woman on the force; he as ex-Army Intelligence. They were both resented by their new colleagues in the Branch. As such, they gravitated to each other, learned to trust each other, and stuck.

"What did you do, Ro?"

Róisín smoothed her skirt. She wore it long to cover her souvenir of their first arrest in Special Branch. A would-be INLA sniper who they cornered in his home in Andersonstown. The gunman had come quietly enough, but his wife had gone after Róisín with a kitchen knife, and left her with a wicked scar that ran from mid thigh to the top of her calf.

"You know Sean Grady? That young lad I hired a few years back out of Belfast Poly?"

"The one with the snake tat on his neck?"

"It's a rune chain, boomer. Anyway, Sean had the idea of sending some spyware to the guys we missed, to see if anything might stick. He got lucky with a suspicious wife. Got into the family PC and tacked on a nice wee program that piggybacks the spyware onto computers when they're networked."

"And this PC was part of a network."

"A big one."

Lawlor opened the file.

Sean Grady's spyware program was the beating heart of the investigation. It was like a bumper pack of drinking straws stuck into a riverbed. Some of the straws were swept away in just a few seconds, others remained in place for as much as a few months, but they all sucked up the same filth. Images and videos. A running sewer of child pornography. From all over the world.

He said, "So no one knows about this except for you and Grady?"

"We've been working on it in our own time. Filling in corners, here and there. You know how it is."

"I know how it is for a few weeks. Three years?"

"No-one wants to hear that the Emerald Isle is a child porn paradise. Not even this end of it."

"So why bring it to me? You seem to be doing well enough on your own."

"We've hit a wall. Sean thinks the dealers may be getting wise to him. His hit rate on the spyware has dropped in half in the last few weeks."

"And you?"

She smoothed her skirt again. "I kind of ran it past the ACC."

Lawlor sat back. "What do you mean, 'kind of'?"

"I told him I'd stumbled on what looked like it might be a child porn ring with possibly, just maybe, some of the players located in Belfast. I was very breezy about it, made like it was nothing big."

"And?"

"And he just turns to me and says, "I'd leave that alone, if I was you."

"Just like that?"

"Aye. I asked him why, and he comes out with some rubbish about a conflict with an ongoing investigation being run by agencies in London. And that I should steer well clear."

"How do you know it was rubbish?"

"Because I'd already cross-checked with the operations ongoing on the mainland. I've a pal in the Met, and I checked with her, too. Nothing. So either the operation he was talking about is super secret squirrel, or it doesn't exist."

He looked her in the eye.

"So you think Davy Kilpatrick is part of a child porn ring."

Her mouth twisted. "It wouldn't be the first time a copper's been caught up in something like that."

Lawlor made what he hoped was a non-committal noise. She was right, of course. And he had no love for Kilpatrick. But this was a high bar to vault.

Róisín sighed. "I don't know. Maybe he's covering for someone. What I'm sure of is that there's no other investigation. There's been no arrests made. We've seen no hint of any kind of inquiry. No approaches for liaison and support, or any of the usual. If anything this bloody network has got bigger over the last year or so. So there's something fishy going on."

Lawlor turned a page of the file. "Do you have a digital version of this?"

She held up a thumb drive.

He said, "Well, if you want my advice, I'd redact any mention of you or Sean, as well as anything that could link back to you. I'd then print the whole thing, and send it in an anonymous package to the Met. And then I'd burn the original. How's that?"

She scowled. "It's not your advice I was after."

He folded his arms. "No."

"I can't keep running this. Sean can't either. But you're on the civilian side now, so you can. Do some Mission Impossible stuff with servers in Shanghai or whatever to cover your tracks. But keep digging for me. Get me what I need, so I can build a real case."

"Sorry, Ro. The answer's still no."

She stood up. "You know this is real, right? This is kids being exploited and abused, hundreds of them, maybe thousands." She slapped the thumb drive on top of the file. "Right here in Belfast."

They stared at each other, the file between them.

The page he had turned to was a list of names. More than a hundred of them, all connected to the IP addresses of the computers in the network. Lawlor's eyes drifted down the list.

And stopped.

"Did you check any of these names out?"

Róisín leaned forward to look. "Sean ran them through the system. To get addresses and previous and whatnot. But that was all. No visits or anything. Why?"

Lawlor turned the file around and pointed. "I know that name."

"Paolo Moretti." She paged back through the file. "Looks like his computer popped up a couple of weeks ago. But just the once. Where do you know it from?"

"You remember in '92, we were chasing down a rumor about Loyalist gun shipments?"

"I remember the case. And I remember nearly freezing my arse off watching some farmhouse in Antrim in the middle of February. But I don't remember any Paolo Moretti."

"That's because his name came up while you were out. You left early for the bank holiday weekend." He looked her in the eye. "And the following Tuesday Rab Harper blew up my car."

The room was quiet. The hum of the equipment and the air conditioning in the server room filtered through the wall.

"Rab fucking Harper." Róisín held out her hand. "Let me

see that postcard again."

Lawlor handed it over.

"Kind of a coincidence, isn't it?" She squinted at the corner of the photo. "The day the Americans come asking about Harper, you get this in the post."

"It had crossed my mind."

"And?"

He shrugged. "The card was sent more than a week ago. It had to go through two postal services. Hard to predict when it would arrive."

Róisín watched him. Big eyes, as green as a cartoon cat's. "Do you think your old pal ... what's his name?"

"Jerry Fyffe."

"Do you think you can trust him?"

"I trusted him back then." Lawlor reflected. "But I've not seen him in a long time."

"What about the photo? It's digital. Could be a fake."

"I don't think so." Lawlor pulled the card across the desk. "I ran the image through some software last night. It's very high resolution, which makes it a lot harder to mess with. I'm pretty sure it's real."

"Did you tell the Yanks about this?"

"No."

"Christ." She chuckled. "How did I know you'd say that."

"They don't think Harper's their man, Ro. I told you, they think he's too old. So they'll check him out, but they won't be subtle about it. They'll spook him, and he'll disappear. For good, this time. I can't let that happen."

"So, what then?"

Lawlor stared at the card. At the pretty, smiling girl that he'd never met. At the street scene behind her. Sunshine and palm trees. A flawless blue sky.

"So now I go to California. I find Rab Harper."

He let the tip of his finger rest on the blur of red in the upper right hand corner.

"And I kill him."

5

Lawlor sat in the back of the restaurant, fighting his jet lag, toying with the wrapper of his chopsticks and watching the door.

When she arrived, he didn't recognize her. She wore tight white trousers and a short-sleeved blouse with a leopard skin print. She had blonde hair, cut in a bob, and pink lipstick that matched her fingernails. Sunglasses like the eyes of a housefly. She sashayed up to his table and sat.

"Hello Lawlor."

"Tilly? Jesus."

"It's my new look. Vietnamese tai tai. You like it?" Tilly Tran removed the glasses. Her eyes looked tired and wary. She raised a hand and called out something to a waiter.

"They do Hue food here," she said. "You'll like it."

Her phone buzzed. She checked the screen, and slid it to the side.

"So, welcome to Vegas. Or welcome back, I should say."

They had first met in 1999, at a hacker conference in the Alexis Park. A security guard had just ejected her from a corporate cocktail event. Lawlor had palmed two badges, and smuggled her back in. She had just quit Northrop Grumman with a full suite of security clearances and gone private. He had recently rejoined the police as a civilian administrator. They had both overheard about DefCon while eavesdropping in chat rooms, and decided the hacker gathering was worth a look. Their shared deception, along with the fact that, at more than thirty years of age, they were among the oldest people at the conference, was enough to get them talking.

And they had been talking ever since, intermittently. Sometimes exchanging tips online, in chatrooms, where they hid in plain sight; sometimes trading information in the dark, in coded messages sent to disposable numbers and addresses. She was far more skilled than he was: she had written a surveillance tool that he had built into every process he generated at work. It meant that hardly a day went by that he didn't find himself thinking about her.

Her phone buzzed again.

"Looks like you're busy," he said.

She shrugged. "I'm doing okay. A lot of AI-related stuff. It's kinda boring."

"What about that app you were working on?"

"The eavesdropper?" She brightened. "I figured out how to hide it in the utilities folder. You turn it on remotely and you can see and hear everything."

"If you can get your hands on the target's phone." He smiled. "And figure out their pass code."

"Details." She fluttered her hand at him. "How was your trip, anyway?"

"Complicated."

After his conversation with Róisín he had walked home, and dug his go-bag out of the back of the dishwasher. He put his Irish passport in one pocket and a brick of mixed currency in the other. Then, when it was dark, he had walked to the Port of Belfast ferry. From there he had bounced around train stations and truck stops and regional airports for two days, and finally ended in Las Vegas.

"Cash all the way? No trace?"

"Not a sausage."

She chuckled. "Whatever that means."

The waiter arrived, and placed several dishes on the table. A wide noodle, stuffed with mushrooms and pork, a mound of deep-fried rice paper rolls, a glistening hillock of fried rice, a whole steamed fish. Lawlor was so hungry his jaw ached.

"So, Captain Ahab." Tilly began putting food on his plate. "At last you get to do battle with the whale."

"Maybe. I thought I had him before. A few times."

"That time you asked me for a list of flight arrivals into Belgrade in April of 2000, was that Harper?"

"Yes."

"And the leasing documents for that apartment building in Sofia in 2012?"

"Yup."

"You could have told me it was him you were after. It's not as if I didn't know what he'd done."

"I didn't want to load you up with any more of my baggage. It was enough that you listened to me that first time." He met her eyes. "I was a mess."

She smiled. "No argument."

"I didn't think it was right to ask you to go tilting at windmills with me."

"I happen to like windmills, Lawlor. I would have thought you'd figured that out by now."

He returned the smile.

"So what do you need?" Tilly popped a morsel of spring roll into her mouth.

"I need a computer, a couple of burners. Some other gear."

"And clothes."

He looked down at himself. He was wearing the same gray suit he'd worn for the penetration test in Lisburn, nearly three days before. "I have clothes."

"How are you getting to L.A?"

"I thought maybe the bus."

"No-one who rides the bus wears a suit. You're going to stand out a mile." She smirked. "Although you probably smell just right about now."

"I defer to your local knowledge."

"Good." She scooped rice into a bowl. "What else?"

"Can you help me confirm that Harper is actually in L.A.? Run his name through Homeland Security, local police databases, property records, all of that?"

"I can do the property stuff in a minute. But the federal data will take a while."

"How long?"

"A week or more. And it won't be cheap."

"You mean, what I sent you isn't enough?"

"Sorry." She shrugged. "I need the cash."

He studied her. The lines around her eyes and mouth spoke of stress and long nights in front of a screen. Her blonde hair was a wig. The whole outfit looked like a disguise.

"Is everything okay, Tilly?"

"Yes." She waved her chopsticks, avoiding his eyes. "Let's move on."

"Okay. What about local law enforcement? Can you get anything that way?"

She shook her head. "There are a lot of police forces in L.A. County. The only thing they have in common is the jail system, if your guy even went to jail, and that's the County Sheriff."

"I would have thought everything was networked."

"You would have thought wrong. Most police and sheriff's departments don't speak to each other as much as they should. Not unless they ask real nice."

"What about the Feds?"

"Do Belfast cops talk to MI5 or whatever?"

Lawlor half-smiled. "Not without a gun to their heads."

"Right. So even if your guy has his real name registered with Border Patrol or Homeland, I don't have a quick way to find out."

"You're saying it's impossible?"

She glared at him. "Of course it's not impossible. Nothing's impossible. It's just impossible in the time you need it."

"Even at a hundred and fifty percent of the price?"

"Even then."

He sighed. "So if you can't help me with police records in L.A., what can you help me with?"

"Well," she sipped her tea, fingernail like a flag. "I can tell you the name of the restaurant in that photo you sent me."

"That's quick work, Tilly."

"Well, I didn't need to look hard." She smiled. "I've been there."

Lawlor raised an eyebrow.

"Testaccio. Italian place," she said. "And it's not in L.A., either. It's in Santa Monica. Third and Wilshire, to be precise."

The phone vibrated again. She snatched it up, and glared at the screen.

"No, bitch, you can't have it today," she muttered. She

dumped the phone into her bag, then twisted in her chair to look at the door.

"Everything okay?" Lawlor asked.

"Just a needy client." She stood up, the sunglasses already in place. They had barely eaten half of the food.

"Come on. We'll get this to go."

6

The bus to L.A. cost twelve dollars. It had WiFi and reclining seats. It was half empty. Lawlor took a seat near the back, but not too close to the toilet. He was asleep before the bus passed the Las Vegas city limits, and when he awoke an hour later, they were cruising smoothly through the desert, under stars that were bright in an inky sky.

Five hours to Los Angeles. Then a city bus to a metro station, and the light rail to the last stop on the line.

"Santa Monica."

The sky was an empty blue canvas, but it was cool in the shade and the air was salty. A clock above a kiosk read a quarter to nine. Lawlor walked up the deserted shopping promenade to where it met Wilshire Boulevard. In the center of the street was a large sculpture of a stegosaurus, with leaves for spines, set in a planter with benches arrayed around it. Lawlor sat on one and looked over the junction at the restaurant. The burgundy awnings, the crenelations around the windows. Tilly was, as always, right on the money.

He found a motel ten blocks back from the beach. It looked cheap, but cost more than a three star Belfast hotel. He cleaned up, slept, and as night began to fall, he walked back to the promenade, scanning the crowd as casually as he could. He caught the occasional second glance. Women of a certain age. His age.

There was a blare of car horns. A man was pushing a loaded shopping cart across the street. Or trying to. A wheel had caught on the rim of a manhole, and the man was struggling to stop the cart from tipping over. Traffic had come to a halt. The first car was a Mercedes. Behind it was a Lexus. The driver of the Lexus was hitting the horn, over and over. The Mercedes was giving off one long drone. People stood on either side of the street, watching.

Lawlor smacked his hand hard on the roof of the Mercedes. The horn stopped. A man got out. Late twenties. A flick of long hair over his forehead. A dark shirt with something sewn into the fabric. It shimmered in the street lights.

Lawlor ignored him, and turned his attention to the trolley. It was piled high, wrapped with a blue plastic tarp, tied down with nylon rope. Neat knots, turns and hitches.

A man's face appeared around the side of the tarp. He was short and wiry, with a beard that covered his entire face, apart from the tip of his nose and his eyes. He had a black watch cap pulled low over his forehead.

Lawlor jammed his fingers into the metal grid of the basket at the front. "I'll lift, you push. We'll take it to the curb. Ready?"

"Aye aye."

Lawlor lifted. The trolley weighed a ton. He crabbed backwards, watching for the curb, then took a long step back and hauled the front of the cart onto the sidewalk, driving rubberneckers back with his shoulder. The wiry man bumped the back wheels of the cart onto the pavement. Behind him the Mercedes roared away.

"Thanks, buddy." The man's cap had a ship sewn onto it, and the words USS Shreveport, GW1. He untied a corner of the tarp, and began rummaging. "I've got some hand sanitizer in here, somewhere. In my dopp kit. Here we are."

He held out a small tube. Lawlor squirted some on his hands and rubbed them together.

"Keep it," the man said. "I got plenty." He fastened the tarp down again.

Lawlor watched him tie a meticulous knot. "You were a sailor?"

"Ten years," the man said. He pointed at his cap. "Finished on this tub in the Persian Gulf. You're a Brit, right?"

"Sometimes."

"Sometimes. That's good." The man showed a line of white, even teeth in the bristle of his beard. "Military, too, right?"

"That obvious?"

"If you know, you know. Aw, shit. Here we go."

A bright light flashed at them from the other end of the alley. A police car was idling at the entrance, the driver playing a searchlight up and down the walls.

Lawlor eased himself back against the wall. "What are they looking for?"

"People doing drugs. Or sleeping."

"Where do you sleep?"

"Not on the goddamn street, that's for sure. I go to a shelter, down on Olympic. It's basic, but the coffee's good."

The police car had backed up. Now it made the turn up the alley towards them. The driver hit the brights, and turned the alley into a tunnel of light.

"We should maybe get moving," Lawlor said. "I don't want them thinking I'm selling you drugs."

"Okay, shipmate. You get along." The man cackled and swung his cart into the center of the alley. "I'll hold 'em off at the pass."

7

There was a bar across the street and a few doors down from the restaurant. Lawlor settled himself in the window and ordered coffee. He drank it, and a dark-skinned Hispanic man came and refilled his cup. He wore a black polo shirt and black trousers, and a small black apron filled with straws and napkins.

Lawlor pushed twenty dollars at him. "I'll be here for a wee bit. If you wouldn't mind keeping me fueled up."

The man nodded. The note disappeared.

The bar was busy. Lawlor didn't expect to see Harper, but he hoped he might see one of the other faces in the photograph. But he saw no one he recognized. Out of the corner of his eye, he watched the waiter work, moving from table to table like a dancer, quick on his feet, with the plates piled high in his hands. His eyes were tired and his expression was blank. No one paid him any attention, even when they nearly collided with him or spilled something that he immediately wiped up. Nobody said sorry or thank you. It was as though he wasn't there.

Lawlor left a twenty dollar note under his mug, and walked back to an alley that led behind the building. There was a dumpster, a reinforced door, and several cheap plastic chairs. There were cigarette butts scattered on the ground. Light came from a caged bulb, high on the wall.

Lawlor sat in one of the chairs and waited.

After about a half hour, the door opened. The waiter stepped into the alley and stretched his back. He didn't seem surprised to see Lawlor. "You want to see my green card?"

"No."

The man had short black hair and a straight fringe, as though someone had cut his hair using a bowl. The light above the door cast a shadow down the left side of his face, making his cheek look deeply lined. He dug in his pockets for a packet of cigarettes and a lighter. "I saw you watching that place across the road, I figured you for la migra. Or a private detective, or something." He had a heavy accent, but his English was fluent. Lawlor said nothing. The man lit the cigarette and took a deep, grateful inhale. "So what do you want?"

"I'm looking for someone." Lawlor pulled up the high-resolution photograph of the restaurant on his phone. Focused in on Harper.

The man took another drag. Squinted. Shook his head.

"I want to know if anyone who works over there knows him."

"So go ask."

"I don't want anyone telling him I'm asking around."

The man blew a long stream of cigarette smoke at Lawlor. "So you need a brown man to ask all the other brown men over there in the brown language about some white man, and hope that none of the other white men understand."

"Something like that."

The man dropped his cigarette and ground it out. "Cost you three hundred dollars."

"I'll pay you a hundred and fifty now. You'll get the rest if you get something for me."

The man nodded. Lawlor dug in his pocket for his wallet. "What's your name?"

"Luis."

"Do you have a phone I can send the picture to?"

"No need. I saw the photo."

"So describe him."

Luis shrugged. "Red hair, cut short. Stick-out ears. A square face. Small mouth. Little guy. Maybe fifty years old."

"He's not that little."

"Then the guy beside him is very big."

Lawlor looked, and saw Luis was right. The man on Harper's right was at least a foot taller, sitting down. He wondered why he hadn't seen that before. He pulled a hundred, two twenties and a ten from his wallet. He handed them over. "I'll see you here tomorrow, then. Same time?"

Luis took the notes and folded them into a pocket. "Noon tomorrow. And not here. On the pier. Right at the end, where the fishermen go."

Lawlor had seen the pier from the bluff that overlooked the ocean. It was as wide as a motorway, full of restaurants, stalls and amusements. It even had a Ferris wheel. It was crammed with tourists. Crowded and open. A good place to meet someone discreetly. An easy place to lose a tail.

Luis smiled slightly. He tilted his head back, and Lawlor saw what he thought was a line on the left side of his face was a long scar that ran from his chin to his eye. He saw what he hadn't noticed before, the knotted muscle in the man's forearms, and the set of his shoulders. The look in his eye wasn't tiredness, Lawlor realized. It was the thousand-yard stare of an old soldier who'd seen too much and learned how to turn himself to iron inside.

"I don't suppose I need to tell you to be careful," Lawlor said.

"No," Luis said. "You don't."

8

The motel was a squat two-story cinder block building that took up a block of Santa Monica Boulevard. To the north was a car dealership; to the south a store selling hospital supplies. The sky was the same color as the sidewalk. The morning was cool and damp. Like a summer day in Belfast.

The cinder block was in transition. Boutiques and handbag shops shared space with real estate agents and markets with hand-painted signs. It made it hard to find what Lawlor was looking for, but in the end there it was, sandwiched between a smoke shop and something called a boba cafe.

The place was packed with equipment. Boxes were stacked to the ceiling, and the floor was filled with row after row of T-shirts, jackets and trousers, all jammed up against each other. It had the same musty hessian smell of military surplus stores everywhere. There was a counter with a glass cover beside the door. A short man with thick glasses and a buzz cut stood behind it, reading a newspaper. He wore dark blue jeans, and a bottle-green T-shirt stretched tight over his belly. On it was written an Arabic word in white, and underneath it, in capitals, "Infidel."

"Good morning," Lawlor said.

The man gave him a blank look. "Help you?"

"I need a knife."

"Fixed or folding?"

"Folding."

"Spring assisted?"

"Well, I don't want something that's going to give me a surprise by opening in my pocket."

The man tapped the glass cover of the counter.

"That's what I've got."

There were perhaps twenty blades arranged under the glass. The folding knives were lined up on the right. They were all cheap, with rough plastic handles and the blades painted black.

Lawlor put a hundred-dollar bill on the counter. "I was hoping for something a little more adventurous."

The man looked at the note. He looked at Lawlor. "You a cop?"

"Not anymore. And not from here, anyway."

The man gave him another blank look. His eyes looked like tiny whelks behind the thick glasses.

After a moment, the man bent down and pulled out a drawer. He placed it on the counter, and turned away.

There were six tactical knives, all with blades more than two inches long. Three had pull-out folding blades, and a fourth was spring-assisted. Lawlor rejected them and looked at the other two. They had heavy, three-and-a-half-inch blades that opened with the flick of the wrist. The first blade was too wide. The second was more conventional and heavier, but it felt solid in his hand. He folded it and slipped it into the hidden cell phone pocket inside the pocket of his trousers. It didn't sag.

"How much?"

"Another one of those and you're good," the man said.

Lawlor slid another hundred across the counter. The two notes disappeared.

"Thank you," he said.

The man gave him another blank stare. "For what?"

Lawlor walked slowly down the center of the pier, the boards creaking under his feet, and the crowds flowing either side of him. The sea breeze, the smell of fried food, the children's laughter brought back a sudden memory, walking along the pleasure pier in Dun Laoghaire, the sun on his back, the boys running ahead, mad with excitement.

He shook off the memory.

He was nearly an hour early. There was a restaurant at the end of the pier, and a flight of steps up onto the roof. Lawlor sat on the top. He felt wrung out, a combination of the jet lag and the uncomfortable bed in the motel. It was ridiculous. He'd slept in a tree once, for God's sake. Eight blissful hours, on operations in Belize. Now he could barely get five hours' kip in a normal bed.

He took out his phone and studied the photograph. Up until the day before, he had been fixated on Harper. Now he was focused on the men around him. The big man on his right, with a bullet head and a wide neck. And on his left, standing up, a bearded man in a tight suit, holding a bottle of wine that was wrapped in a napkin. Not a guest. An employee. Possibly even a manager. Tattoos creeping out of the collar of his shirt, and spilling out of his cuffs onto the backs of his hands.

For the first time Lawlor wondered whether he was biting off more than he could chew. Harper had been off his radar for twenty years. He had disappeared without a trace. Lawlor had suspected the IRA might have killed him. The bomb he'd planted under Lawlor's car had nearly derailed the peace process. But the fact that he was alive and healthy told Lawlor that Harper was a survivor. He wondered what he was into now. Maybe he had gone straight, into real estate, like everyone else these days. But the big man beside him didn't look like a real estate agent. He looked like something else entirely.

A kid wearing faded jeans, royal blue Nikes and a silky white soccer shirt sauntered up the steps. He tapped his wrist. "You got the time?"

Lawlor looked at his phone. "Five to twelve."

The boy laughed. "English, huh? Liverpool or Manchester United?"

"Irish," Lawlor said. "And I'm more of a rugby man."

The boy tapped the front of his shirt. "Los Catrachos," he said proudly. "Honduras. We play Mexico tomorrow."

The boy put one foot on the top step and leaned forward, as though he was examining his shoes. "Luis says no one knows the guy in the picture," he murmured.

Lawlor kept his eyes on the water. "Where is Luis?"

"Gone."

Lawlor felt a tightness in his gut. "Gone where?"

The boy gave a minute shake of his head. "Away. He told me to tell you the big guy is with La Colonia."

"La Colonia?"

The boy licked his finger and rubbed at the toe of his shoe. "He said you would pay me."

Lawlor was about to argue. This wasn't part of the deal. Except that maybe it was. He thought about Luis. A hard man. Not the kind who scared easily. Not the kind that took needless risks. And now he was gone. And that told him something.

He already had the three rolled fifties in his hand. He dropped them beside his shoe. There was a blur of blue and white, and the boy and the money were gone.

The wind gusted, plucking at his shirt like a child begging him to get up and play. Lawlor shivered, the skin bumping on his arms. He had the feeling that he had turned over a stone. Now it was time to see what crawled out.

9

Róisín sat with her hands folded over the file on her lap, her back straight and head up. The chair was like a torture device. Her thighs were itchy and wet with sweat where they touched the black molded plastic; her lower back ached.

She forced herself to be still. To not look up at the bulbous lens of the camera in the upper corner of the room.

Kilpatrick was not her immediate boss, so a personal summons to the ACC's office was unusual, and her antennae were vibrating. Her unit was doing okay. It had been the subject of a very favorable story in the Telegraph about credit card theft. Twelve convictions. But that was six months ago, and she had already been patted on the back for that. This was something else.

There was a cheap pine display cabinet full of trophies and medals against the wall opposite her. Something white reflected in the glass. She realized with a shock that it was her own face. Pale as a ghost against the black of her hair and the dark wool of her suit.

Maleficent, they called her. She'd been sat in the corner cubicle in the ladies a few months before when she first heard. Two women had come in and started talking about a skinny cow with hair like wet seaweed and a whore's mouth. It was several moments before she realized they were talking about her.

"Looks like Maleficent, don't she?"

"So she does. Do you think she has a crow in a cage?"

"Aye, sure. She turns into a dragon after closing time, too." They had both cackled and before she could stop herself, her fingernail was jammed into the ridge where the scar on her leg wrapped around the outside of her left knee. It was like plugging into a live socket, a jolt that writhed up into her crotch and snapped her eyes open, all of her senses suddenly razor sharp and tingling.

She must have made a noise because the women had suddenly fallen silent and there was only the sound of toilets flushing and taps running and heels clacking as the door swung open and closed. Róisín had sat for a moment as the pain drained away and was replaced by a rank backwash of shame.

Maleficent. A cartoon witch. They'd better watch out or she would turn into a feckin' dragon, right enough, and burn the both of them to a crisp. Pair of fat heifers.

The door opened. Kilpatrick leaned in. She shuddered as his piggy wee eyes gave her the once over. Back in the old days, before the police service changed its name and cleaned up its act, he'd gained a reputation for being a little handsy. Not that he'd ever touched her. He was always scrupulously courteous. But she trusted him about as far as she could spit a live rat.

"Come on in, Róisín."

He pointed her towards an armchair and went to the other side of his desk to sit. Róisín perched on the edge of the seat. Kilpatrick released a catch on his own chair that allowed him to recline. He steepled his fingers. He smiled. "I read your quarterly report on Sean Grady. He seems a useful lad."

"Very much so, sir. We'd be way behind without him."

"I know he's not the most popular hire we've made."

Aye, she thought. Not with his tattoos and his hair and his taste in cubicle decor.

"But we need more of his type on the force."

You mean because he's Catholic? Or because he has mad hacking skills? She kept her mouth shut.

"So you be sure to keep him onside."

"I will, sir."

"Good."

He gave her a long look. Big blue eyes. Tiny red capillaries in the whites. She thought back to their last exchange, when she'd mentioned a child pornography case. "I'd leave that alone, if I was you," he'd said. When for the last three years she'd been doing precisely the opposite. Her stomach churned.

He said, "Where's Lawlor?"

She forced a frown onto her face. "Lawlor, sir? Is he not downstairs."

"If he was downstairs, I wouldn't be asking you, would I?"

"No, sir. Of course not. Sorry."

"When did you last see him?"

Something told her not to lie. "Day before yesterday, sir."

"Where?"

"Right here, sir. I popped down to his office for a chat." Shit, she thought. What difference did it make where she had seen Lawlor?

Kilpatrick nodded, and she knew her instinct to tell the truth had been right. The bastard already knew the answers to all the questions he was asking. Well of course he did. That was peeler 101.

And then her mind began to turn over the implications. Was Lawlor being watched? If so, why? Another thought: was *she* being watched?

"This is the second day he's not shown up for work, Róisín. No note, no email. He's not answering his texts or his phone. Where is he?"

The edge of the chair was digging into her buttocks. "I have no idea, sir. Do you want me to go round to check on him?"

"He's not in his flat." A definitive statement. Meaning Kilpatrick, or someone on his orders, had been in for a look.

The watery blue eyes stared. She stared back, as hard as she knew how, a substitute for hurling herself over the desk and punching him in the face.

"You think something's happened to him?"

"Do you?"

"I've no idea, sir. I've not heard from him." Which was the truth. But she could hear the worry in her own voice. And not just for Lawlor, off on his idiot suicide mission. Why had Kilpatrick ordered someone to break in to his flat?

"Did he say anything about going anywhere? Taking a trip?"

"A trip?"

"Are you going to repeat my words back to me, Detective Chief Inspector? Or are you going to answer my question?"

"No, sir. I mean, he didn't say anything about a trip."

She thought about the file she had brought down to him, two days before, and her stomach flipped. "Did something happen here, sir? I mean, is there some kind of security issue?"

"You don't consider the abrupt and unexplained absence of our head of systems security an issue?"

"Of course, sir."

"What did he say, when you saw him?"

She shrugged. "Not much. We talked about work. I asked him for some advice about the case I'm working on. The cyberbullying thing." God, she hoped they hadn't bugged his office.

"Nothing else?"

"No, sir."

They stayed that way for a few moments, he all spread out in his Aeron, she perched on the hard edge of the armchair, her feet tingling now. The muffled clatter of a computer keyboard and the wheeze of a laser printer filtered through the door.

"You were in Special Branch together."

"Yes, sir. We joined the same day."

"Did you know what he did before?"

"Army Intelligence. He said he was in 14 Company before he came over to us."

Those eyes. A pair of blue marbles in puddles of slush. The spawny bastard still hadn't blinked, as far as she could tell.

"Did he tell you much about his army time before that? His work in South America?"

She shook her head. No, Lawlor had never talked about South America, or anywhere else. She had asked him about it once, when they were sitting in a transit van, watching a UVF weapons hide. He had told her that he had two lives, before kids and after, and it was only the second life that he cared to talk about.

Kilpatrick sat for a while, letting the silence work on her. She waited him out.

"We're worried about him, Róisín. You should be, too."

She tapped her fingers on the folder in her lap. She knew Lawlor would have covered his tracks as best he could, but there was no way to avoid leaving some kind of trail, however faint. She couldn't risk covering for him. But at least she could muddy the waters a bit.

"I suppose he was a wee bit down," she said. "I mean, it was the anniversary of the bombing the other week. I think maybe it brought back a lot of memories."

Kilpatrick picked up a pencil and started flicking it around the knuckle of his thumb. He didn't glance down once. She felt like she was being measured for a box.

"Speaking of memories, did he talk about the old days at all?" he asked.

"How do you mean, sir?"

"Cases. The things you were working on back then."

"We were only working on one thing, sir. Loyalist guns."

"Ah yes." Kilpatrick caught his pencil in mid-air, and placed it carefully on the desk. He sat up. "What happened to that case?"

"Nothing," Róisín said. "After the bomb, Lawlor went on compassionate and Dennis Johnson stepped up as acting DI. But before we could get back to work, the first ceasefire happened. Word came down that there were talks on and every active investigation was shelved."

"Did you object to that, when you were so far along?"

"I wouldn't say we were that. We were still scratching the surface."

"Do you think we did the right thing back then?" he asked. "Shelving all those cases? Putting Special Branch on ice?"

She shrugged. "I can't say I liked it at the time, sir. But looking back I can see how the political situation was changing. I get how the negotiators didn't want the Branch making waves during the talks. That was the beginning of the end, really, wasn't it? Not that there was much left of Special Branch after Mull."

"A bad day." Kilpatrick nodded to himself, his eyes distant. The Aeron made a gentle creaking sound.

Róisín waited. Kilpatrick's eyes refocused.

"Very well, Detective Chief Inspector. That's all. If Lawlor contacts you, or if you see him, let me know immediately."

"Yes, sir." She stood up, avoiding his eyes, and made for the door. Head up, straight back, through the waiting room, and along the lime green corridor back to her office. It wasn't until she saw the damp print of her palm on the folder she had been carrying and felt the sticky taste in her mouth that she realized she was bathed in sweat, as though she had just run a fast 10K in the sun.

10

A bad day, he'd said.

Christ, that was an understatement. She had a vision of herself, sat on the couch, with an instant coffee on the table in front of her and News at Ten on the box. The 2nd of June, 1994. Trevor MacDonald reading the news, solemn as the grave. A Chinook helicopter had ploughed out of the mist and into a Scottish hillside. The crew and twenty-five passengers dead. Army, MI5, and ten from Special Branch.

Her bosses. Her colleagues. Her friends.

Lawlor had called then, half cut and raging. She had barely heard him. She remembered putting the phone down and going to the bathroom. Taking a towel out of the press, unfolding it and laying it on the couch. Then sitting down, bunching up her skirt, and pouring the scalding coffee over her thighs.

Lawlor had spiraled, working non-stop, convinced that the IRA had something to do with the crash. A surface-to-air missile, or a bomb in a briefcase. Something. It had taken him months to accept the official finding, that it was pilot error. The Chinook had simply flown too low in the fog.

The IRA declared a ceasefire on the 31st of August, and all

Special Branch activities were put on hold a second time. A week later, the results came in from the forensics lab, saying the residue from the bomb that had blown up Lawlor's car matched Rab Harper's signature.

And Lawlor disappeared.

It was weeks before she heard, and she only heard fragments. A operations team had been called to a remote security force base on the southwestern border, a place called Clonatty Bridge. A Lynx helicopter had been dispatched to fly two men to Belfast for treatment at the Royal Victoria Hospital. She had checked the records. No flight plan had been filed. There was no patrol record for the ops team. And there was no admission paper at the Royal. But a nurse on duty that night identified Lawlor as one of the men.

A week later, she heard he'd handed in his papers.

Special Branch had been effectively dismantled in the weeks after. Every serving officer was either offered retirement or transferred. She'd been lucky enough to draw the short straw: computer crimes. An underfunded, unglamorous backwater unit, housed in an old, unheated Nissen hut, on the far edge of the headquarters plot at Castlereagh. It was an experiment. One that wasn't expected to go anywhere.

She thought back to her meeting with Kilpatrick. The questions he'd asked. The way that he'd sat up when she mentioned the case she and Lawlor had been working on.

She logged in to her system. Like all of the Special Branch files from before the moratorium, it had first been microfiched, and then scanned into the system. But not digitized, or rendered for search.

The idea of paging through the file exhausted her. She remembered how thick it had been. Two files, stuffed with paper and photos and cuttings.

She began paging through the file, and felt the memories wash over here. The nights she and Lawlor had spent sitting in cars and in bedsits, juggling long-lens cameras and notebooks and two-way radios. Banging on doors. Working the phones. Talking to people. There was no CCTV to rely on. No social media profiles to trawl. Back then, investigation was a contact sport.

She paged through to a long list of names and license numbers, typed out in Courier font on a series of pages of old school computer paper, the edges perforated for use on the old VENGEFUL printer. She and Lawlor had spent hours going over those lists; whole days, underlining names to check, making calls, and then highlighting the names in different colors to designate their intelligence worth. Pink for high value. Green for follow up. Yellow for no connection established.

There were thousands of names, but even now some of them jumped out. Most of them high-lit in yellow. Charles Cross, a butcher in Lisburn who became one of the best sources they had. He'd been stopped at an Army checkpoint after visiting his mistress. Eddie Greavey, a heroin dealer, who'd been kneecapped by the UFF and died of blood loss. Tom Leeson, a rumored UVF man who had said nothing when she'd doorstepped him, but pinched her bottom when she turned to go. She had made a fast turn and kneed him in the balls for that one. She smiled at the thought.

Ronan Moran. Car thief. Haircut like one of the Human League. No connection established.

Bobby McEwan. UDA member. A beer belly like a space hopper. No connection established.

Her eyelids were heavy. The yawn, when it came, was so

wide it made her jaw ache. She clicked the file shut.

Whatever it was that had piqued Kilpatrick's interest, she would have to look for it later.

She laughed to herself.

Maybe it would come to her in a dream.

11

The restaurant was full. Every table was taken. There was a line of people waiting, sitting on chairs in the foyer of the place, and standing in ground outside.

Lawlor edged past the line to the hostess. She was a dark-haired, dark-eyed woman of about twenty. She gave him a fast once-over, her eyes taking in the cheap shirt and trousers he had bought in Las Vegas.

"The wait is about an hour, sir. Would you like to put your name down?" Something in her voice saying she'd rather he didn't.

He smiled. "I'm waiting with a party. Can I just use the toilet?"

She looked uncertainly at him. He was gambling. He had already seen that clothes sent mixed signals here. Some of the people he had seen, it was hard to tell if they were hipster or homeless.

She decided. "Past the bar to the left, sir."

The bar was a crowded sweep of polished teak, staffed by two men in beards and waistcoats rattling cocktail shakers and pouring wine. There was a tray holding glasses and another holding sets of cutlery wrapped in starched napkins.

He slid one of the cutlery sets into his pocket. Then he took a breath and staggered into a hallway, past a trio of women waiting in line. There were three doors, one marked PRIVATE. He dropped to his knees outside it, and rolled onto his side, groaning.

One of the women squealed, and for a moment he was alone. And then there were voices, feet around him, hands on his shoulder, turning him onto his back. He let them prop him up against the wall. He kept his mouth shut.

"He doesn't look so good."

"Someone better get Grisha."

He stayed still. He kept his eyes open. Moved his head around a bit. Let them know there was no crisis. No need to call emergency services and disrupt things with an ambulance and a stretcher. Not good for business. He was just a guy who'd slipped and fallen. But one who wasn't getting up in a hurry.

Crisis over, the crowd of waiters began to thin out as they went back to work.

He sat, breathing shallow breaths, waiting. It was a few moments before he saw out of the corner of his eye what he wanted to see, a familiar man with a shaved head and a black shovel blade of a beard. A tight-fitting suit, but not bespoke. Not tailored to hide the bulge from the hardware under his left arm. The man squatted down. He waved a hand in front of Lawlor's eyes.

"Sir? Are you okay?" A slight accent. Eastern European, maybe. Or Russian.

Lawlor nodded. "I'm okay. Sorry. I have low blood sugar. I just need to sit for a while."

"You can't stay here, sir." Annoyance in the man's voice. And then a decision.

"You can sit in my office." To the waiters: "Help him up."

He unlocked the door marked PRIVATE. Put the key back in his right pocket. The waiters grabbed Lawlor under the arms, hauled him to his feet and maneuvered him through the door. Lawlor gave them a little help, but not much.

Inside the office there was a desk with a chair on each side, a pair of bookcases, a safe. The waiters lowered him into the nearest chair. The man with the beard sat on the desk. He undid his jacket. "I'll sit with him. You guys get back to work."

The waiters pulled the door closed behind them.

"I just need a minute," Lawlor said. He rubbed his face.

"Take your time." The bearded man checked his watch, and Lawlor saw the tattoos on the back of his hand. Blue, blurred and faded, the kind made with a spike of metal and ballpoint pen ink. The kind made by men with lots of time on their hands and not much to do. Like during a long spell in prison.

"I'll just call my wife. Let her know ..." Lawlor took the phone out of his pocket and held it up. The man nodded.

Lawlor tapped at the screen. Brought up the photo. Pinched and dragged until Harper's face was centered and clear.

"You're Grisha, right?"

"Ya."

Lawlor held up the phone. "You recognize this guy?"

The bearded man's eyes did no more than flicker. And then his right hand darted up and left, under the open flap of his coat. Lawlor was already on his feet, stabbing at the man's throat with his right hand, driving the tips of his stiffened fingers into his trachea. The man reared backwards, choking, clutching at his neck. Lawlor crowded him, pressing him against the desk, forcing him on his back while he reached inside the jacket. Felt the butt of a pistol. Pulled out a Ruger

9mm.

He fingered the safety, dropped the gun on the floor and leaned forward, putting his whole weight on the man's chest. He felt in his pocket for the fork in the cutlery set.

The bearded man was catching his breath. Lawlor leaned close. They were nose to nose. Lawlor smelled brandy on the man's breath.

He pressed the tines of the fork deep into the soft skin under the man's left eye. "Don't move, Grisha." Little more than a whisper. "Don't make a sound. Or I'll take your eye out."

He pushed the tines deeper and the man froze. His eyes stared.

Lawlor pushed the phone into his face. "I know you recognize him, Grisha. Very quietly, tell me what you know about him."

The man went to shake his head, but the fork was dug in too deep. "I don't know him," he said, voice like a pepper grinder.

Lawlor leaned harder, grinding his hips and chest against the man. "Do I seem like a serious man to you, Grisha?" He pushed the fork so that the tines dragged the man's bottom eyelid down.

The man's Adam's apple bobbed. "Yes. You are a serious man."

"Good." Lawlor kept his voice low and level. "Because I want you to believe me when I say that if you don't tell me what I want to know I will take your eye out. And then I'll shoot you in the kneecaps. You'll never see straight and you'll never walk again."

The tines of the fork were sunk deep into the man's skin. Sweat was oozing through the mustache of his beard. "I do not know him. But I recognize him. He was a customer here.

But only once." The accent strong now.

"When?"

"A month ago. Maybe less.

"And who was he here with?"

The man was pale, his eye bloodshot and staring. "I cannot. I ... I cannot."

Lawlor tutted. "Say goodbye to your eye, son."

He dropped his phone on the desk and clamped his hand over the man's mouth. He reversed the fork, and jammed the end of the handle into the bottom of the man's eye socket. The scream was muffled by Lawlor's hand. The man bucked and writhed. He beat his fists on Lawlor's back. He was younger and stronger, but Lawlor had twenty pounds on him, at least, and Grisha was trapped on his back.

Lawlor flipped the fork and rested the tines back against the soft skin at the bottom of the man's eye. He pressed his mouth to the man's ear. "That was a trial run, Grisha. Just to show you I'm as serious as the boys who gave you that gun. Now I'm going to take my hand off your mouth and you're going to tell me who this man came here with. Then I'm going to get up and walk out of here, and you're never going to see me again. You understand?"

He pulled back far enough to see the nod. And then he took his hand away.

"Ovian." Grisha's voice was hoarse. "Artur Ovian. He owns this place. This man was his guest. Ovian said they worked together."

"Doing what?"

"I don't know. I swear."

"What about this other fella, the big one?"

"I don't know him. The only one I know is Mister Ovian. It

was his party. Some kind of a celebration. Ovian, this man, and a group of Latins. Two or three top guys. Four or five men."

"Did they say what they were celebrating?"

"I didn't ask. I never ask. My job is to run this place and that is all."

"Alright." Lawlor nodded. "I'm going to let you sit up now, Grisha. And then I'm going to walk out of here. I'm going to take the key and the gun with me. I'm going to lock the door, and I'm going to put the key on the bar. You can call one of your guys to let you out after I'm gone."

Lawlor pushed himself off the desk. He kept the fork where it was. "Nice and easy, now."

He bent and picked up the Ruger as Grisha sat up. He racked a round into the chamber.

"I don't want to use this, Grisha. I don't want to make a noise and I don't want to shoot you. I really don't. But I am a very good shot and I will kill you if I have to. Am I clear?"

Grisha nodded. His fingers fluttered around his damaged eye.

"You're fine. A wee bruise, that's all. No damage. Now take the key out of your pocket and hold it out. Stay sat on the desk."

It took a moment for Grisha to fumble inside his tight trousers. Lawlor reached forward and took the key. "Where's your phone?"

"Here." Grisha motioned at his right breast.

"Take it out. Then take out the battery. Put the parts on the desk."

Grisha did as he was told. But reluctantly. Lawlor could see his fear wearing off. His anger beginning to kick in. Lawlor knew he had only a few seconds before Grisha decided to go for him.

He backed towards the door, the Ruger leveled.

"Drop your trousers."

"What?"

He flicked the safety off. "Your trousers, Grisha. Do it."

Grisha fumbled at his belt, and his trousers slid off his hips and pooled around his ankles.

"Now your jacket. And your shirt."

Grisha did as he was told. As he undid his shirt, he revealed a chest and torso covered in tattoos. A cross, draped in a tricolor flag, a pair of crossed daggers. An eagle's head. A letter L intertwined with an A. An A intertwined with a P. He dropped his shirt on the floor. His eyes screamed murder.

"That'll do." And then Lawlor was out and in the hallway, the door shut and locked; the gun made safe and deep in his pocket. He put the key on the bar and headed fast for the exit, through the wash of restaurant noise and out into the cool, sea-salt night.

12

The woman on the night shift at the motel was Hispanic, short and stocky, with long, dark hair, one wing of a butterfly tattoo peeking out from under the collar of her dress. She was on the phone, and when Lawlor pushed through the door she looked up, and a flicker of surprise showed briefly in her eyes.

She ended the call. Lawlor came to the desk. "I'm staying in Room 12. Jones. I left a dark green backpack with the clerk this morning. It's got a tag with my name on it."

She looked under the counter.

"It's right here." She slid off her chair. "Are you on vacation?"

"What makes you think that?"

"Your accent. Irish, right?" She hefted Lawlor's backpack onto the counter.

"Sorry. Not even close." Lawlor took the bag. "South African."

He smiled at the woman, slung the bag over his shoulder and walked away, down the hall, towards the rooms. As soon as he turned the corner and was out of sight of the desk, he quickened his pace, past number 12 and down to a fire door. A sign in red and white warned that an alarm would sound if he opened it, but he slapped the bar and pushed through it anyway, and strode into the street.

He walked quickly down to a junction, crossed with the light, and began a fast loop that would take him back through side streets, to a cafe diagonally across from the motel. It was still open, and he ordered a small brewed coffee. He sat beside a pillar that cast a shadow on the window and allowed him to see into the street.

For five minutes, vehicles passed the motel in both directions. Cars, buses and trucks. Lots of trucks. Then a long, low-slung, boxy car jolted into the parking lot. It was painted a dark shade of red, and had some kind of icon on the bonnet, like something from a seventies film.

Two men got out. They were dressed in baggy jeans and loose, white T-shirts. They had shaved heads and tattoos that covered their arms to the wrists. They sauntered into the motel. Ten minutes later, one of the men came out. He got into the car and drove away.

Lawlor sat in the cafe for another half hour. When the second man didn't show himself, he finished his coffee and left.

He walked south, not sure where he was going, zig-zagging through the neighborhoods and staying away from the wide boulevards. He was thinking about the look in the woman's eyes when he came into the motel. The questions she had asked. She had been given a description. Look out for a big white guy, more than six feet tall, short gray hair, blue-gray eyes, fifty-ish. Long arms, big hands. Irish accent. The men who had come hadn't known he was staying there: she had called and told them. Which meant whoever was looking for him had cast a wide net. They had sent out his description to every hotel and motel in the city.

But who was looking for him? He thought about the two men. They didn't look black or white or East Asian. Probably Hispanic. And a Hispanic crew sounded a lot like La Colonia. Which meant maybe Luis hadn't got away after all.

He walked down an alley behind a car parts store. There was a large dumpster, with a black plastic lid, propped open by a pile of cardboard. He took the gun out of his waistband, popped out the magazine and stripped the weapon down. He tossed the parts into different corners of the dumpster and walked on down to the end of the alley.

He stopped. A billboard loomed over the street. Remembering the Armenian Genocide. A hill of skulls, ten feet high and twenty across. The sky behind the hill painted red, blue and gold; the same colors Grisha had tattooed on his chest. AP. for Armenian Power.

He was halfway across a wide boulevard before he read the street sign. Olympic. He remembered the homeless man with the cart, who said he went to a shelter on Olympic Boulevard. And a shelter might be a good place to hide for a night, to get his bearings. But which way?

Away from the beach, most likely. He turned left, and passed a light rail station and a cluster of industrial-looking buildings. On the next block was what looked like a sports center, with a curved roof, several stories high. It had an entrance hall with floor-to-ceiling windows, and Lawlor could see people moving around in there. They all wore baggy jeans and sweatshirts, and had the stolid look of veterans of a thousand AA meetings.

When Lawlor knocked, a big man broke away from the group. He had a wide, flat nose and a large gold stud in his right earlobe. He waved Lawlor away, mouthing something and pointing at a sign on the door. Lawlor read, 'Shelter Hours: 6 pm to 10 pm'. A clock on the wall in the foyer behind the man read ten to eleven.

Lawlor turned away and looked down the boulevard towards the ocean. He could smell the sea. He felt alert and focused, as though the ozone was sweeping his tiredness and his depression away. But it wasn't ozone, he knew; it was adrenaline, and it wouldn't last. Things weren't going well. Some things were happening too quickly; others were happening too slowly. He was old and rusty. He needed sleep, to rest his body and his mind, if he was going to keep hunting Harper. If he wasn't to make a mistake and get himself killed.

"Hey, shipmate."

A short man was standing in the doorway. It took Lawlor a moment to recognize the ex-sailor he had met the day before. He had taken off his watch cap, and his hair stuck out at all angles, like a scarecrow.

"Thought that was you, man," the sailor said. "What you doin' here?"

"Someone told me the coffee here is worth crossing town for."

The sailor grinned. "Come on in, then."

The hallway smelled of stale sweat and old clothes, mixed with the greasy odor of frying oil and over steamed vegetables. There was a long desk in the middle of the room, and a wide door that led into the large building behind. In front of the desk was a big plastic bin, three-quarters-full of dented cans and bottles, not all of them empty.

The men in the foyer stared at Lawlor.

"Don't look at him like that," the sailor said. "He's a veteran, same as us."

"That right?" The man with the stud in his ear looked him up and down, bloodshot eyes in a dark face. "You been drinking?"

"Not a drop in twelve years," Lawlor said.

The man nodded slowly. "He's your responsibility, Willis."

"I'll take care of him." Willis handed Lawlor a paper cup of coffee. "You need a place to stay tonight?"

"I do."

"Well, I got you. You missed chow, and you're too late for a bunk, but there's some old mattresses, you don't mind sleeping on the deck."

"I don't mind."

"That's the spirit." Willis slapped the key bar on the doors and pushed them wide. The building was what it looked like, a converted sports center, with a vaulted ceiling, fifty feet high. The space was big enough for a full-size basketball court and seating, but now it was packed with rows of bunk beds. The smell was intense, a sour, musty reek, stale sweat and unwashed clothes, like a gym locker full of old socks that had been festering for a week.

Willis closed the door firmly, and led Lawlor down the center of the hall. They walked along a corridor created by two ranks of bunks. Clothing and bags of possessions hung from the frames; heavy packs and brimming trash bags were stuffed under the beds.

"Head." Willis pointed to a row of six Portakabins, squatting at the back of the hall. He walked to the far end of the row, reached behind the last one, and pulled out a mattress, six inches thick and sheathed in black vinyl. He thrust it at Lawlor. "Here you go. You might find a spot down there in the corner."

He fumbled in his pocket, then tossed something at Lawlor. It was a packet of earplugs. "Industrial grade. Construction guys use 'em."

There was a row of mattresses laid out on the ground behind the toilet block. There was just enough space for Lawlor to squeeze his mattress in beside the wall.

"You goin' freeze there, man." A man dressed in a grubby white singlet and long black shorts was standing in the entrance of the Portakabin, buckling his belt. He was short and wide, with a head like an egg and a huge handlebar mustache.

"I'll be alright."

"You ain't got no coat, man, and it's cold down there. There's gaps in the joins. The wind comes through like a goddamn knife." He grinned. Big, yellow teeth, like a horse's. "Gimme ten bucks and I can get you a blanket."

"No thanks."

"Five, then."

"Leave him alone, Garza." Willis pushed past. He had a blanket over his shoulder. "Here." He handed it to Lawlor. "You'll need this. It gets cold in there.The wind comes through the joins."

"I just told him that," Garza said. His grin widened.

"Leave him alone, man," Willis said. "He's with me. okay?"

"Okay." Garza looked Lawlor up and down, a flat look in his eyes. "If you're cool with Willis, you're cool with me. What's your name?"

"John."

Garza waited. Lawlor said nothing. Garza smirked. "Alright John. John it is. Just not John Doe, right?" He punched Willis lightly in the shoulder. "Sleep tight, Willis. You too, John."

He turned away.

"Don't worry about him," Willis said. "But keep your stuff close. And keep your shoes on. Not everyone knows you're with me."

He nodded and walked away. Lawlor lay down. He put his backpack under his head like a pillow and wrapped the blanket around him. It smelled strongly of cleaning fluid and faintly of vomit, but it was thick and wide, and long enough to cover his toes.

A toilet flushed. He took the earplugs out of his pocket, rolled each one tight and stuck them into his ears. He closed his eyes and listened to the roaring sound of his own breathing until he fell asleep.

13

Lawlor snapped awake. Someone was fumbling with his right shoe. He kicked hard, and connected with something soft. At the same time, he sat up and saw a shape go sprawling against the wall of the hut. But there was no sound, just the hammering of his blood in his ears, until he remembered the earplugs.

He pulled them loose and got to his knees. He slung his bag. The man got to his feet, rubbing his chest. It was Garza.

"The hell you do that for, man?" he whispered. "I'm tryna help you!"

"I thought you were after my shoes."

"I was tryna wake you, man. Damn. You got a kick like a mule."

The hall was quieter now, filled with the sound of three hundred sleeping men. They snored, belched, farted and called out in their dreams. Lawlor fumbled for the phone in his pocket. Ten past three.

"Where's Willis?"

"He told me come warn you. Some guys are here, asking questions."

"Why didn't he come himself?"

"He's in the back, man. He's handling it. He told me to show you the way out."

The lights in the hall had been dimmed. Everything was drenched in a yellow glow, as though the whole place had been irradiated. Garza's jittery shape was a dark hole in the yellow. Lawlor could feel the danger like an itch. He pushed the blanket off, and stood up, pushing his arms through the straps of the backpack.

"Where?"

Garza jerked his head. "Follow me."

"I have to pee."

"Well hurry up, man!" Garza was hopping from one foot to the other, rubbing his hands like a kid waiting his turn at a fair ride. Lawlor smelled the sweet, chemical stink of his breath, and the alarm in his head went into overdrive.

He went up the steps into the toilet hut. It was a low-ceilinged building, built against the inner wall of the hall. It had three toilet stalls, all with the doors removed. There were two urinals at the far end, and a pair of basins. Above them was a small louver window, with three plastic panes. It took Lawlor a few seconds to remove them. He tossed his backpack up onto the roof above, and then struggled through the opening. He dragged himself onto the roof, pulling his knees up and rolling over.

He waited, lying on his back, looking up at the high ceiling of the sports hall. He was covered in dust and filth and drenched in sweat.

Garza entered the room beneath him. Let out a stream of curses. And hurried out, and into the hall. Lawlor chuckled to himself, counted to a hundred, grabbed his backpack and lowered himself off the side of the roof. He looked around the side of the hut. Garza was gone.

He caught his breath, and slipped down one of the long tunnels made by the bunks, moving towards the entrance to the hall.

The door to the hall was wide open. Lawlor could see into the street, where a car idled, its headlights shining into the foyer.

He thought about the door. Willis had made a point of keeping it closed. The people who were after him must have wedged it open, so they could keep an eye on things in the hall. They had deployed the big gray plastic bin full of confiscated bottles of booze that Lawlor had seen in the lobby. They had dragged it into the hall, and used it to pin the door against the wall.

Lawlor eased back along the row of bunks, squeezing the pockets of the coats and jackets on the beds, until he felt the small, square shape of a matchbook through the lining of what looked like an old army overcoat. The matchbook was more than half used. More than enough. He crept back up the line of bunks, easing a half-discarded blanket off one of the beds, and then stepped quickly across the open space between the bunks and the end wall.

There was an opening between the door and the wall, just big enough for him to disappear into. He stepped into the slice of darkness and peered into the plastic bin. It was three-quarters full of bottles and cans. He could see the top of the bottle he wanted, a red cap with a logo of a black bat, but it was jammed down the side, and wedged in with several other empties.

Crouched in the narrow space, he began removing bottles, one by one, and setting them on the ground. It was nearly ten minutes before he was able to ease the bottle he wanted loose. The muscles in his legs were screaming at him. But it was worth the effort. The bottle was half empty. The contents smelled like paint stripper. He sprinkled the liquor over the blanket, then stuffed it into the top of the tub. He used one match to light the rest of the book, then tossed the whole lot into the bin.

The liquor fumes caught fire immediately, burning with a clean, blue flame, and Lawlor hurried back to the bunks to watch. He needed flames and smoke, but the liquor was burning too clear, and the blanket was not catching. He looked around. The man on the bed beside him was snoring. Under his bunk was a heap of plastic bags, all tied together. Lawlor grabbed the bundle, walked over to the bin and threw them in.

It was like throwing water on an oil fire. The plastic caught immediately, and there was a huge belch of smoke that rolled up to the high ceiling.

"Fire!" Lawlor yelled, walking backwards behind the bunks. "Fire!"

For a moment, there was nothing, and then the alarm, shrieking, the sound bouncing off the walls and the floor.

Men fell out of their bunks, shouting incoherently, scrabbling for their belongings. The narrow corridor between the bunks and the wall was suddenly crowded with people, foul-breathed and wide-eyed. Lawlor pulled a blanket off a bunk and let the crowd carry him. His eyes stung. The bin had begun to melt, and the plastic was throwing off great billows of black smoke. The crowd changed direction again, towards the doors at the back of the hall, and Lawlor felt himself being swept sideways, almost losing his footing. The smoke was like grit in his mouth, and acid on the back of his throat. He felt a jolt of panic, and then a swell of relief at the sensation of cool air on his face. Someone had opened the doors.

"Hey."

The voice, like a frog croaking, came from over his left shoulder. Its owner was lying in the top bunk. He had a face like a pickled walnut, and a faint froth of hair over a pale skull. He smelled like rubbing alcohol. His eyes were bleary. "What's all the goddamn noise?"

Lawlor helped the man down. He wore so many layers he was as big as the Michelin Man, but he was as light as a child, and Lawlor imagined he could feel the man's bones under the clothes. He grabbed the man under the arm and hurried him towards the back door.

Most of the men were already out, and Lawlor ducked his head under his blanket and hustled out with the crowd, the man still tucked under his arm. A fire truck pulled up, and as the crew rushed through the door, Lawlor slid to the side.

The man grabbed at him. "What about my stuff, dude?"

"It'll be fine," Lawlor said. "It's more smoke than flame in there. But it's the smoke that kills you."

"That right?" The man's eyes glittered in the lights from the fire truck. There was a slight smile on his ravaged face and Lawlor realized he was much younger than he appeared. He backed away and raised his hand.

"Hey man! Come back!" the man croaked.

But Lawlor was already moving.

14

The shelter was part of an industrial complex, a collection of squat, utilitarian buildings clustered around a wide junction. Most of the homeless men had crossed the street, and were huddled by the fence of the opposite building to watch the show. Lawlor kept his head down as he moved to join them, the blanket pulled over his head like a monk's cowl as he scanned the crowd.

There were two watchers, positioned with their backs to the fence, on a small berm that gave them a degree of elevation. At first glance, they looked a lot like the homeless men. They had scrubby beards and wore knit watch caps and baggy jeans. But their clothes were clean. Their boots were new. And their eyes were constantly scanning the crowd.

Lawlor was walking directly towards them when he spotted them. He fought the urge to turn aside. An ambulance arrived, lights like a circus ride, drawing the attention of the watchers. Lawlor ducked his head and walked past them.

"How we supposed to find this guy now?" one said.

"You got his photo, don't you?"

"Sure, but it's dark out. And he's gonna be dressed like a mendigo. You can't tell 'em apart. Are we even sure he's here?"

"The little dude with the hair all over his face said he was."
The second watcher chuckled. "But not until Fermin cut off
three of his fingers."

"Three? Damn!"

"Dude didn't make a sound the first two. Just stared at
Fermin like he was going to kill him. Then Fermin did his
thumb and he fainted. He gave it up after that."

"The thumb? Ey. That's cold. He use the big shears?"

"Nah. The pruning ones." He laughed.

Lawlor felt a flare of anger. Willis had helped him, even
though he was the one who needed help. And now he was
suffering for it. He toyed briefly with the idea of taking the
laptop out of his backpack and using it to break the necks of
the two La Colonia men, one after the other.

And then he let it go. Killing these two wouldn't help Willis
or himself. And it would damage the laptop.

The second watcher took a call. He said yes and no a few
times, and then yes again, like a man confirming things and
taking orders. Then he put the phone away.

"Our guy got loose," he said. "He started the fire inside.
Poured liquor on something and set it alight. Used the smoke
for cover."

"Shit." The first man shuffled his feet. "He coulda walked
right past us."

"You'd better hope he didn't. Fermin will cut your pecker
off. He's been looking for this motherfucker for nearly a week,
and he's pissed about it."

"So what do we do?"

"We check these guys out."

"The roaches? All of them?"

"That's right."

"Damn." The watcher hawked and spat. "We'll get their stink all over us."

"It's either get a little stink on you now." The man waggled his fingers in the air. "Or sew one of these back on later. Up to you."

The watcher swung around to look behind him but Lawlor was already gone. He had ditched the blanket, and he was drifting along the fence line, fading away from the larger knot of homeless men gawking at the fire engine. There was a flurry of movement as two paramedics wheeled a gurney up to the ambulance and loaded someone on board. Willis, maybe.

He reached a junction and turned left, off the street and out of the light. It was little more than an alley, with several big metal trash skips on one side, and cars parked nose to tail on the other. The street smelled of urine and rotten food, and was loud with the sound of the freeway close by.

As he walked, he thought about this man, Fermin. Was he a boss for La Colonia? It seemed likely. He wondered how much experience he had at hunting people.

He reached a junction, bathed in yellow light from the street lamps. He stepped off the sidewalk and onto a weed-clogged bank that ran up to a low fence. He squatted down to catch his breath, willing himself to wait. The urge to keep moving, to take full advantage of his momentum, was almost overwhelming. But the trained part of him knew that momentum without caution could propel the hunted man into a trap.

A vehicle pulled up an alleyway opposite him and turned slowly into the road. It was a nondescript, dark pickup, not clean, not dirty. In the back there was a rack full of shovels and rakes and brooms. In the front there were two men, faces made pale by the streetlights, scanning the road as the pickup made the turn.

Which suggested that Fermin had thrown up a loose cordon around the shelter, and was using mobile units to patrol the area. Good for Lawlor, in a way, because it made the cordon easier to penetrate, but bad because it was less predictable. There was a big risk that he would run into another mobile unit if he kept using the streets.

But Fermin couldn't patrol the freeway.

Lawlor waited until the car was gone, and then he climbed over the fence. It ran along the spine of a man-made berm that fell steeply to the freeway. There was a ditch at the bottom of the slope that looked like dead ground. The car headlights swept over it like beams from a lighthouse. Beyond was the shelter of a bridge.

The ditch was deeper than it looked from the top of the embankment. And it was full of trash. Empty drink cans, fast food wrappers, dirty nappies, abandoned clothes. At least it was dry. He edged along in a crouch, keeping his head down until he reached the bridge and the deep shadow of one of the big concrete uprights. Everything hurt. His knees, his lower back. He had pulled something in his right shoulder. He held up his hands in the light from a passing car. His fingers twitched like a cat's whiskers. He clenched his fists and pain flickered up his forearms like he'd stuck his thumbs in a light socket.

There was a voice in the back of his head, whispering. He was old. He was tired. Whoever Harper was involved with, whatever he was into, it was too much for him to be tangled up with. It was going to get him killed.

Cars and trucks roared by, just a few feet away. The noise was deafening. He was shivering now, and not with the cold. Delayed shock, another, more distant voice told him. He closed his eyes. He felt like a man in a shallow trench with a tank about to roll over the top. His teeth chattered. He cringed. The ground was shaking, the tank coming closer, its tracks chewing up the mud.

And then there was a squeal like the sky tearing and a horn sounding, as loud as a ship coming into dock.

Lawlor's eyes snapped open.

A car was broadside across the center lane, a huge truck heading straight towards it. The truck driver sounded their horn again, and the car slewed onto the hard shoulder, just a few feet from Lawlor. The truck blew past, and the car straightened up and drove away.

Lawlor's heart was pumping hard, but the panic was gone, like a mist swept away by the wind. His mind was clear. And it was telling him something didn't add up.

The big man in the photo with Harper was with La Colonia. Lawlor had assumed that Luis asking about Harper had triggered La Colonia's hunt for him. That Luis had been caught, and given them a description that they had circulated to the motel. That the photograph the watchers at the shelter had mentioned had been pulled from the security camera in the motel lobby.

But then the watcher said Fermin had been looking for Lawlor for nearly a week. Even though Lawlor had been in California for less than 36 hours. Which meant Fermin had started the hunt while Lawlor was in transit from Belfast. *So who had told them he was coming?*

Lawlor stayed in the ditch and followed the freeway down to the beach, where it curved north behind a row of narrow houses built right on the sand. A curved footbridge took him over the road and up onto the palisade, and then he walked into the town.

There was a Starbucks open, already busy, and he used the cover of the morning traffic to sneak into the bathroom.

The man in the mirror could have spent the night on the beach. If he had also rolled into a fire in his sleep. His clothes were filthy. His face was smudged with soot. His eyes were as red as a five-day drunk's. His hair looked as though a madman had tried to tear it out in tufts.

He washed in the sink and did his best to brush the dirt out of his clothes. Then he plastered his hair down, and went to stand in line.

Fortunately the rush had died down, and there was only one person in front of him. The barista had spotted him, and looked on the point of calling someone to throw him out when he took a ten-dollar bill out of his wallet and made a show of pushing it into the tip jar on the counter. After that, ordering was a breeze.

He got a large drip coffee and two bran muffins. Then he settled into a corner that was out of sight of the door, opened his laptop and logged on.

He had no mail.

But there was a draft message in his account. No subject. Just a link to a chatroom.

Tilly.

No-one else knew about the account. No-one else knew the password. It had to be her. But was she alone?

He ate the muffins and drank half of the coffee, thinking

about how agitated Tilly had been in Las Vegas. The wig. The glasses. The demand for more money.

They had known each other for a long time. He had trusted her with details about himself that he had not told anyone before. Not Róisín. Not even his ex-wife. He had told Tilly about his boys. About his own childhood. About the things he had done in the service. About the things he wanted to do to Rab Harper. And unlike everyone else in his life, she had understood. She had helped.

But she had not trusted him. She had been a good listener, but she hadn't shared much in return. He knew she had spent some time in government service, although she was never too clear about exactly what that meant. She had never married, or had kids. She liked to dance. She didn't like drugs. She liked being alone. She didn't like strings, either in her work or her personal life.

And that was all he knew.

He stared at the link for a little while longer. Finished the coffee. And clicked.

A cheesy site popped up, reminiscent of MySpace circa 1999. A private room. A winking cursor.

And then ...

<Where are you?>

He typed, <Why do you ask?>

<I had the other faces in that photo IDd. Not good.>

He was more certain now. But not a hundred percent certain.

<You mean the photo I showed you at the Turkish restaurant in Orlando?>

And then, without hesitation, <You mean the Vietnamese in Vegas. You loved the banh cuon.>

He felt a swell of relief. <And the company.>

<:-) I need to deliver some information to you. If you're still in the LA area.>

<I am.>

<Location?>

He hesitated for a second. <Santa Monica. Third and Arizona.>

<Perfect. Wait ten minutes. Someone's coming to pick you up.>

It was a white hybrid with a ride share logo on the windscreen. It had mouse-fur seats and a green magic tree swinging from the rear-view mirror. The driver wore a monk's tonsure and a black and gold aloha shirt. He said nothing to Lawlor, and Lawlor said nothing to him. They drove for five minutes with the ocean on the left and a scrubby cliff on the right. Then the driver turned right up an incline and into the long-term parking basement of a hotel. He pulled up at an elevator bank and pointed at the door.

"Number 1817."

The hallway on the 18th floor was cluttered with room service trays. Lawlor realized he was still hungry. He took an uneaten dinner roll from one and stuffed it in his mouth as he walked along the line of doors.

He counted down to 1817. He stopped outside the door. It was made of a varnished pine. The numbers were black metal in a copperplate font.

His mouth was dry, and there was a pulse in his throat. The whole way, he had been asking himself questions. Was that really Tilly on the other end of the message app? And if it was, was she alone? What was the information she had sent for him? Who was the driver she had dispatched to pick him up? Who was in room 1817? Why was he trusting her?

Because he had always trusted her in the past.

But could he trust her now? He thought about the disguise she'd worn in Las Vegas. He looked at the varnished pine of the door. When the door opened, he might find anything behind it. Whoever answered might usher him in and give him a drink. They might open the door for him and walk away. They might shoot him in the face.

He shrugged off his backpack and placed it carefully on the floor to the side of the doorway. Then he took a deep breath.

And knocked.

15

The phone rattled on the kitchen counter. Róisín flicked her thumb over the screen. "Dennis. Hi."

She imagined him in the parlor of the big house in Armagh. On his grandmother's couch, with its worn damask fleur-de-lys and the old-lady smell of lavender. Looking out of the big windows, over an emerald acre of lawn. The family seat.

He said, "Will you be down tomorrow?"

She closed her eyes. How long had it been? Three weeks. No. Four. A month. Where did the time go? "I'm sorry, Dennis. It's been busy."

"I'm sure it has. But it's not me you need to apologize to."

He was frowning, she could feel it. Those heavy jowls, speckled with a persistent shaving rash that made his cheeks look like slabs of raw pork. The small, bright blue eyes. The plume of gray hair, like the frizz on an ancient coconut shell. He'd be wearing his old brown cords and an Aran sweater with a striped shirt under it, the collar frayed. He was one of those policemen who looked a decade older in civilian clothes.

"I'll be down tomorrow," she said. "I'll take her up to the Discovery Center."

"She's fifteen years old, Róisín. She doesn't want swings

and seesaws."

"Craigavon then. I'll take her to the shops at Rushmere."

There was a rasping sound, and she knew he was rubbing his hand over his chin, the way he did when he had something awkward to tell her and was thinking about how best to pitch.

"She wants to go to Belfast," he said.

"Rushmere's just as good as Belfast."

"I'm not talking about going shopping, Róisín. I mean she wants to stay in Belfast. With you."

"Stay?" Her mouth made a sticky sound. "Here?"

"The summer holidays are coming up. She's bored down here. She wants to live with you for a while."

"But that's not the agreement." Róisín's eyes flicked around the studio, panic rising in her chest. She suddenly saw the place as a visitor would see it. The bare walls and the drab carpet; the vacant living room, the single bed. The sparse kitchen. Neat. Tidy. *Empty.*

He sighed. It was like a train rumbling past her ear. "I won't say I like the idea, either, but she's insisting. She says if I don't let her, she'll run away to Belfast anyway. And she will, I know it. She's as stubborn as you."

"I don't have a spare bed."

"Then get one. Go to IKEA. Have them deliver it."

Her panic curdled into anger. "I don't live in a bloody country mansion, Dennis. I live in a bedsit."

"Get a foldout sofa then. This is your daughter we're talking about, for heaven's sake. Could you maybe try not to be like your parents, just for once?"

She leaned back, held the phone out in her outstretched hand and screamed silent curses at it.

Then, as calm as she could, "Punching a bit below the belt

there, Dennis."

"I'm only saying, Róisín." The warning in his voice.

"What? Mammy was a lush and Daddy was a shag-about and I turned out to be both?"

"That's not what I mean, at all. Just that neither of them were there for you when you needed them. And that you don't have to repeat the pattern for your own child."

"Repeat the pattern? What kind of books have you been borrowing from the library? You sound like a bloody shrink."

"I'm just trying to bring our daughter up to be a whole person."

"So I'm only half a person, am I?"

"Jesus Christ, Róisín, would you ever stop?"

She laughed. "Now now, Dennis. Taking the Lord's name in vain?"

"Don't you dare make fun of my religion."

"Oh, I wouldn't dare. Especially not if it's helping you bring up our daughter as a whole person. Someone who's caring and tolerant and open to other points of view on things like, oh, I don't know, gay marriage? A woman's right to choose?"

There was a long pause. Then, "I know what you're doing, Róisín. You're trying to hurt me because you're in so much pain yourself."

"Oh, sod off."

"It's obvious from the way you live. The long hours. The running. Your diet."

"What do you know about my diet?"

"I know you've not been eating properly. Your clothes were hanging off you the other day."

"So? Maybe I don't want to be a fat aul' cow like the rest of them around that place."

"It's just another way of hurting yourself, you know." He stopped.

She braced herself, her fingers white where they wrapped around the case of the phone.

"You aren't doing that again, are you?" He sounded tentative.

"How dare you?" She couldn't stop her voice rising. "How dare you ask me that? After what you did ? What right have you to ask me something like that? What bloody right...?"

"Stop it!"

His shout brought her up short.

"You can't go on like this Róisín. You need to see someone. For your own good. And for Andrea ..."

"Oh yes!" Her face was burning. "You'd like that, wouldn't you? Have that on my record so you could wave another piece of paper at the judge, telling him I'm unfit so you could have full custody."

"Well, why not grant me full custody? It's not as if you ever come to see her on the days you're supposed to."

"She's my daughter!"

"So be a mother to her. Spend some time with her. Starting this weekend."

Róisín now screaming inside her head. Leaning over the counter, the phone clamped to her ear. *Breathe. Breathe. Jesus Christ, breathe before your head splits wide open and your heart bursts.*

"I can't, Dennis." Mumbling. "I have work."

"You won't have to take any time off. Grosvenor has a summer school. I'll arrange it all. All you have to do is be her Mum. What about that?"

Her rage was gone. All the fury blown away, like steam off

a pot. And what was in the pot was pure panic. She looked around the bare flat again. This was where she hid herself. And how could she do that with Andrea here?

She squeezed her phone hard, driving the edge into the muscle at the base of her thumb, searching for the digital nerve. A throb of pain ran up her forearm, like touching an electrified cattle fence. A brief respite.

"What about her weekends? I work on the weekends now."

"Well maybe you should stop. Give yourself a break. Cut back on the running and explore the city a bit with your daughter. See the place through her eyes."

Her eyes. Róisín imagined her daughter, standing in the bare, narrow space, looking around. Those big eyes. Seeing everything. *Knowing. Judging.*

She put the phone on speaker, placed it carefully on the counter top, leaned forward, slid a drawer open. She took a table knife, ran her thumb over the lightly serrated edge. She dropped to her knees, pulled up her skirt, and placed the rounded point of the knife against the base of the purple worm of scar tissue where it passed over a tight band of tendon in the joint of her knee.

"Róisín?"

She closed her eyes, held her breath and thrust the knife home.

It was like smashing a mirror. The world around her seemed to disappear. She had an image of herself plunging into a glacial lake, turning over and over in the water, the shock of the cold numbing her senses, whiting everything out.

A long, shuddering exhale. A slick warmth on her fingertips. She had dropped the knife. The blood slowed, slipped around the back of her knee and dripped onto the floor. She watched it, dully, as though it belonged to someone else. The blood. The knee. The floor. The life. She wanted to curl up on her side on the floor and go to sleep.

"Róisín?" Her ex-husband's voice like a fly in her ear.

She reached up and pulled the phone off the counter top. "I heard you."

"And?"

She smeared blood across the screen of the phone. Zig-zags and swirls, until it dried. "I'll see you tomorrow."

16

Gravel crunched under the wheels of the Mini as Róisín swung between the lichen-wrapped gateposts and up the drive. A quarter-mile of sunlit lawn stretched either side of her, and she felt as though she was being watched by the four big windows set into the facade of the old red-brick Georgian perched on the top of the hill.

Andrea was standing in the door to the house. She was as dark and pale and tall and slim as Róisín. Only her eyes were her father's, brilliant blue, and as blank as a freshly-painted wall. She wore faded jeans and an over sized maroon hoody with the Royal School coat of arms on her left breast.

Róisín spread her arms. "Give us a hug, then."

Andrea smelled of Imperial Leather soap and cheap shampoo. Her hug was limp.

"Sorry I've not been down," Róisín said. "Work."

"Dad has work, too."

"Your Dad's a Chief Superintendent, love. He gets to order people about and go home at five every day. I'm one of the peons who actually has to do the grafting."

She sniffed. "I heard you caught those scammers. Dad showed me the story in the paper."

"Did he now?"

"He says you won't let me come and stay with you over the holidays."

"Do you really want to?"

She sulked. "It's boring here."

"It's even more boring in my flat. I don't even have a telly. You'll go mad staring at the walls. "

"Dad says there's summer school."

"There is. But the Grosvenor pool isn't heated. And they don't have horses. So you'll miss your riding."

Andrea sighed.

"Well, I'm here to talk to your Dad about it. Where is he?"

"In the kitchen."

"And your Gran?"

"In her room."

"How is she?"

"Bloody awful. She has this wee bell that she rings, and I have to run up to her, like straight away. I have to bring her tea and help her to the bathroom. One time she made me cut her toenails, the smelly aul' cow."

"You shouldn't talk about your Gran like that."

Andrea slid her arm through Róisín's and put her head on her shoulder. "Sorry," she whispered, not meaning it, and Róisín smiled as they walked around the back of the house.

He was sitting at the kitchen table, an array of tiny bits of metal and plastic fanned out across the table in front of him. A cup of tea by his right hand. And a scowl on his face.

"You're late."

"It's a good thing you've something to keep you busy, then." She nodded at the parts. "Are you back to building your wee cars again?"

"It's the dishwasher control panel. A wire in the connector box burned out." He poked a scorched piece of plastic with a screwdriver. "I'll have to solder it."

"Is there any tea in the pot?"

"It's stewed now."

She helped herself anyway.

"Look," he began. "I know you're under a lot of pressure right now. With your caseload like it is."

"What do you know about my caseload?"

"Only what I read in the weekly briefings, like every other Chief Super on the force. Twenty-three open investigations? With your team as small as it is?"

"My team is entirely capable, thank you very much, Dennis."

"Fair enough." Dennis held his hands up. "I hear that young fella Grady's a bit of a star. Where did you get him from?"

She sipped her tea. It was lukewarm and tasted of rust. "Yeah, Sean's great. He was teaching computer science at Coleraine when he came over to us."

"He's not from Coleraine though, is he? I thought he was a Belfast lad."

"He is. From Ardoyne." She stared. "I hope that's not a problem for you, Dennis."

He looked solemn. "Not at all. I'm all for integration, as you know."

"Uh huh." She swigged the rest of the tea.

The silence filled in around them. The room was warm and stuffy, the air filled with the dust from the worn furniture and the ragged carpets that hadn't been cleaned since Dennis' father had died.

"So," Johnson said. "Did you go think about what I said?

About seeing someone?"

"I did not."

"It's just, if Andrea's going to stay with you for more than a few weeks ..."

"Do you want me to take her or don't you?"

He sighed and shook his head.

"Are you seeing someone, Dennis? A woman, I mean."

His cheeks turned a mottled pink. "Seeing someone? Me? No."

"It's just, all this fancy language you're using. The welfare of our child." She made comma marks with her fingers. "My 'deflecting,' or whatever you called it on the phone. It sounds like you're going out with a psychiatrist."

"I'm not going out with anyone."

"She's probably a copper, now I think about it." Róisín let the scorn seep into her voice. "That'll be why you were all gussied up in your uniform the other day."

"I had a meeting, actually." He stared at her, his eyes narrow. "A VIP visit."

"Aye, I saw you in the car park."

"Oh, you did?" He was very still.

"Aye, with some fella in a flasher's mac. Looked like he'd just been dragged out of a snug in the Crown. Who was he?"

"He was one of the VIP's staffers. Why?"

"Well it looked like he was giving you orders, Dennis. Sticking his finger in your chest."

"He's American. He was just making a point."

"Your face does this thing when you lie, Dennis." She pointed to the corner of her mouth. "There's this wee muscle tightens up and twitches. I remember from when you used to come back from the races, or the card clubs, or wherever it

94

was you went to throw away every penny we had. Telling me you'd been on operations, or out with the boys. You're doing it now."

"You're one to talk. Sneaking about with all your secrets. The things you do to yourself. Your family." He spat the word out as if it was something rotten.

When she was thirteen, Róisín had gone on a school trip to the University swimming pool. She had been astonished by the height of the high diving platform, looming over them like some kind of cartoon monster. It had acted like a magnet. She had slipped away from the group and begun climbing the ladders that linked the three tiers of diving boards. She had just begun ascending the third tier when someone noticed her. By then it was too late. She had made it to the top and was standing on the edge, shivering in her flimsy factory shop swimsuit when the lifeguard made it to the top tier. She remembered the terrified look on his face and then how small the pool looked below her, like the tiny envelopes they stuck on the bunches of flowers at her mother's funeral. All the faces looking up at her from the poolside, like little pink cherry blossoms fallen on wet pavement. She remembered thinking it was a long way down, and she'd be a long time under the water, so she'd better take a deep breath.

She had the same feeling now, the distant sensation, looking at her ex-husband from a long way away. The faint idea that she was about to explode. And then his head turned towards the door, and she saw Andrea there, and the air hissed out of her, like she was a punctured balloon.

"Why are you fighting?" Andrea said.

"We're not fighting," they said, in unison. And then they exchanged a glance, half amused, the kind of non-verbal exchange they used to have when they were married. *Like, you think this is fighting?*

"What does he mean, that you hurt yourself, Mum?" She was hugging herself, her eyes big.

Róisín opened her mouth, but Dennis spoke first. "I'm just saying that your Mum makes choices that I don't agree with."

"Like what?" Andrea asked.

"Like working too hard, for one thing." Dennis looked Róisín square in the eye. "And not eating properly. I get cross with her because she has to look after herself, so that she can look after you."

Róisín stood up and went to the window. It looked out to the side of the house, towards the old stables that Dennis had shut up when they sold the horses. Her throat had closed up. She wanted to punch him in his hypocritical mouth, but she had seen the expression on her daughter's face, and recognized the same feelings she had felt once, watching her mother shake the last drops out of one bottle of gin and twist open the cap of another.

She exhaled, her breath condensing on the glass. Dennis was many things, but he wasn't a drunk, thank God. He was in fact, she had to admit, a good father. A loving constant in her daughter's life. Good with the homework and the extracurriculars. The desk drawer in his office was full of Andrea's rosettes from gymkhanas and riding competitions. Not so great with the emotions or the empathy, mind you. But he was a male of the species, and this was Northern Ireland, so what could you expect?

She said, "School breaks up in two weeks, doesn't it?"

"It does," Dennis said.

"Well, I'll need some time to clear my desk and get the flat in order. How about you stay down here through July, Andrea, and come up to me for August. I'll see about taking a couple of weeks off."

Andrea was beaming. "Really?"

Róisín felt her heart lift. "Absolutely. It's not as if I don't have the time coming to me. We'll maybe go to the beach for a few days, or something."

"She'd like that," Dennis said. "Wouldn't you Andrea?"

"Yes."

"Me too." Róisín realized she actually meant what she was saying. "I could use a holiday just now."

17

When Lawlor came out of the shower, Tilly was reclining on a long couch the color of a wheat field, under a window that looked out towards the ocean. She wore a sleeveless coral sundress and a pair of striped wedges. The wig was gone. Through the window behind her, the sky, the sea and the sand were three horizontal slashes, blue, green and tan, like a child's painting.

He sat down on a chair opposite her, pulling the too-short terry-cloth hotel robe over his knees, so that he didn't embarrass them both. There was a tray with a pot of coffee and two cups. He poured one for himself and sucked half of it down.

"How long have you been here?" he asked.

"Not long." Tilly curled her feet under her. "After I dropped you off, I sent that photo to a guy in the bureau who owes me one. As soon as he got back to me, I came on over."

"So what came up?"

"I asked about Harper first. But he didn't register in the system. It was the faces next to him that my source got all hot and bothered about."

She opened the file and handed him a glossy 8 x 10 of the photo of Harper and his dinner companions. She pointed to the big man on Harper's right. "Fermin Rafael Reyes. Also known as The Gardener."

"Because he uses gardening tools to kill and torture people?"

"Yes." She had turned the color of the couch she was sitting on. "How did you know?"

"Let's just say someone I know got on his wrong side."

"Okay." She frowned at the photo. "Well he may not look it, but he is a real gardener. He owns a yard work and landscaping business."

"Which includes a fleet of trucks."

"Yes. Jesus, Lawlor. How do you know all this?"

"I know because from the moment I got here, his people have been chasing me all over this city."

"How did they even know you were here?"

"Don't think I haven't been asking myself the same thing."

There was a knock on the door, and she unfolded herself from the couch. Checked through the peephole and opened the door. A hotel porter brought a pile of boxes and clothing store bags into the room. Tilly folded a note into his hand.

"What's this?" Lawlor asked, when the man was gone.

"New clothes. For you."

"You remembered my size."

"Hard to forget."

A buzzing sound brought her back to the couch. She picked up her phone. Stared at the screen, a blank expression on her face.

"You need to get that?" he asked.

She shook her head. The buzzing stopped. And then there was the ping of a voicemail.

"We can get out of here right now, if you want," she said. "You can be back in Belfast for dinner tomorrow. Just say the

99

word."

He rubbed his face. His head was ringing with tinnitus. Like a warning sign. Because she was right. He should just say the word. And not just because two of the biggest and most dangerous gangs in America were on his tail. What really frightened him was what Tilly had said about what her contact at the FBI had told her, that the picture of Harper hadn't been flagged by the system. Rab Harper was a terrorist, a bomb-maker and a serial murderer. He was sought by law enforcement, all over the world. Including in the US: the last time Lawlor had looked at the FBI Most Wanted list, Harper's photo had featured prominently.

But now, somehow, it was no longer there.

Tilly's phone pinged again. She ignored it.

"What's going on, Tilly?"

She shook her head. "It's nothing."

"Don't do that."

"There's nothing you can do, Lawlor."

"How do I know until you tell me?"

She gave him a long look.

"It's a guy who did some work for me a few weeks back. The job ended up being a lot trickier than either of us thought, and there was a lot of back and forth. Me and him. Me and my client. Anyway, it gave this guy time to figure out who my client was."

"He's threatening to cut you out."

"Worse. He's going to burn me to the client, unless I pay him double. He doesn't know exactly who I am. Like, not my name or anything. But he does know I worked for DoD. And he knows I work out of Vegas. "

"And you don't want your client knowing that?"

"The only thing I want my clients knowing about me is that I can deliver. One little bit of intel about me gets out, and that's it. Clients talk. Word gets around. People start pulling on the thread. And then I'm exposed."

She folded her arms and hugged herself.

"That's why you're here," Lawlor said. "You could have emailed me all that stuff. You needed to get out of Vegas."

"I drove out, right after I dropped you." She flashed a smile. "It was weird. I was fine until I saw you, and then, after you left, I just felt ... exposed. I didn't even go home. I just got on the freeway. I've been here longer than you have."

"And what about this guy you owe? What are you going to do?"

"I'm going to pay him." Her smile disappeared. "But I'm already running him down. I've got traces on all his accounts. When I make the next payment, I'll find out who he is. And I won't be texting him to let him know."

Lawlor looked at the set of her mouth, and the hard look in her eyes. "You sure I can't help."

"I've got it under control."

"You're making me feel a bit redundant."

"I'm sure we can find a use for you."

Her face had softened, and she was looking at him through half-lowered eyes, the trace of a smile on her lips. The window was closed tight and triple-glazed, but it was so quiet that Lawlor imagined he could hear the waves on the shore.

Her eyes were huge. Her skin shimmered in the sunlight. She said, "Why don't you come over here?"

18

For a moment he thought he was back in the shelter, the fire alarm screeching like a deranged insect. Until he remembered he was in a hotel. He sat up, trying to locate the source of the noise. An alarm, but not fire or smoke. The kind emitted by a bedside clock. But not the one on the table beside him. It read 09.19, red digits glowing in the dark. How long had he slept? The bed beside him was empty, the sheets mussed and cold. Tilly was gone.

He stumbled naked into the living area of the suite, looking for the source of the noise. The blackout curtains were drawn. The only light came from another digital clock, on the writing desk. The display read 09.20.

Lawlor felt the wall, looking for a switch.

There was a box on the coffee table in the center of the room. A large, white cardboard cube, the kind made to carry a layer cake. The lid pulsed slightly with the noise of the alarm.

Lawlor sat on the couch, and flipped open the lid.

Inside was a clock radio, the alarm turned up to max. It wasn't a sleek, gray model with muted lighting like the pair in the suite. This one looked like a relic of the 80s, a brash chunk of black plastic the shape and size of a brick, with sharp corners and bright green digits the color of nuclear waste. 1.3.94

It was like being punched in the face. He felt blazing hot and freezing cold at the same moment. The numbers were burning into his brain, like a brand, except that the scars of the numbers were already there, and the brand was just making them fresh again.

The first of March, 1994.

He saw Tommy and Andrew, running down the path. Tommy pushing away the hair that flopped into his face. Andrew hugging the violin case to his chest.

Everything slowed down. His mind seemed to separate. Part of him had the irrelevant thought that there were three clocks in the same room, all reading different times. That part of him was already commanding his arm to move, to stretch out his hand and stop the irritant noise. But another part of his brain told him that to touch the clock was to die.

The alarm stopped.

For a moment the suite was deafeningly quiet. And then a phone began to ring. A tone that you didn't hear much, any more: the telltale Nokia chime. Muffled. Somewhere close.

He turned over the cushions on the couch and found an old phone. He held it in his hand and stared at it for a moment, checking himself, noting the acid in his guts, the clear, cold feeling in his head, the slight tremble in his fingers.

He flipped open the phone.

There was a pause. The sound of breathing. Then, "Hello Lawlor."

A man Lawlor had never met. But a voice he had heard hundreds of times. Perhaps even thousands. It hadn't changed much over the last twenty years. It still had its West Belfast edge, and its slightly nasal tone, thanks to a broken nose the man had sustained in a fall as a child.

"So," the voice said. "Do you know who I am?"

"Yes, I know who you are," Lawlor said. "You're Rab Harper."

"You've a sharp mind, for an old man," Harper said. "Most people would have hit the button on that clock, just to shut the alarm off. Not you, though. I bet I didn't even need to leave you that wee clue, did I?"

Even if Lawlor had wanted to speak, he couldn't. He felt somehow separated from his body, floating somewhere just below the ceiling, watching the husk of himself, sitting naked on the couch, the phone clamped to his ear, staring into the box, at the numbers glowing green on the clock, 1.3.94.

"That's a date you're never going to forget, is it?" Harper's voice crackled on the phone. "If you'd only done what you were supposed to do that day. If you hadn't gone to bed late the night before. If you'd got up when your alarm went off, instead of turning it off and going back to sleep. If you'd have got up and gone to work on time like a good little peeler, then everything would be different, wouldn't it?"

Lawlor looked around the room. How had Harper known when to turn the alarm off? There must be a camera somewhere. He was suddenly aware of his nakedness.

"Do you like the radio?" Harper asked. "It took me forever to find the bloody thing. Thank God for eBay, eh?"

Lawlor stared at the clock. The flashing green light, the sharp, ugly corners... He had never owned a clock like this, but there was something familiar about it.

"The great thing about it is how much plastic you can get

inside it," Harper went on. "It's only C4, mind. I was after finding some Semtex, for old times' sake, but it's too much of a bother to get it over here. Still, C4'll do the job. And it *will* do the job. So you bought yourself some time. But I warn you, if you leave that room ... if you so much as open the door, I'll pull the trigger on that thing and bring the whole house down around your ears." He paused, as though he was taking a drink or lighting a cigarette. He'd been a smoker, back in the 80s. Lawlor wondered if he still was.

"Now you're probably wondering where Tilly is, aren't you?" He paused.

Lawlor didn't respond.

"We were hoping to slip this wee parcel into the room as a surprise for the both of you. But she heard my lads when they let themselves in, so they had to shut her up. She's fine now, in case you were worrying. But the lads had to take her along with. So I have her now, in case I need to concentrate your mind."

He paused again. Lawlor's eyes were still closed. His mind was spinning. Was there really a bomb in the clock? He had to assume there was. And if so, how did Harper know where to find him? How did Harper's men know he and Tilly were in bed? Was the suite bugged? Did it have cameras? He pulled the throw over his lap. His eyes flicked around the room.

"The old brain's going like a bloody whirligig right about now, isn't it?" There was glee in Harper's voice. "You're probably asking yourself, if this bastard Harper hasn't blown me into my next miserable excuse for a life by now, what does he want? Isn't that what you're wondering, Lawlor?

What the hell is it that I want?"

19

"The answer is no." Lawlor was surprised by how hollow his voice sounded in the empty room.

A pause.

"You don't even know what I want yet."

"I don't care, Harper. Even if it was just a lump of sugar for your tea the answer would still be no."

He could hear Harper breathing on the end of the line. "I think you're forgetting something, Lawlor. I've got your wee bit of stuff here, remember?"

Lawlor squeezed his eyes shut. It was like running the ball of his thumb down the blade of a scalpel. At any moment he expected to hear Tilly scream.

"I remember," he said. "So what?"

"Jesus, you're a cold one." Harper sounded disgusted. "I shouldn't be surprised, mind, knowing what you've done. But I've got a dozen lads here, too. One word from me and they'll run a train on her until she splits. And then I'll gut her like a herring and throw her in a skip for the seagulls. Do you hear me?"

"Yes." Lawlor felt cold, as though someone had opened a window and let in the night air.

"And?"

"And the answer is still no."

Harper was silent.

"You forget," Lawlor said. "I'm an old hand at this game. The only leverage you have against me right now is Tilly. You say you'll hurt her if I don't do what you say, and I believe you. And I like Tilly. She's an old friend. I don't want her hurt. But I want to help you even less. So if you bruise her, even slightly, I'll walk out of here. Maybe your lads'll shoot me, or maybe I'll get away. Either way, I'm gone. If you kill her, same thing. Holding her gains you nothing, so you may as well let her go. Now."

"I still have the bomb."

"So push the button, or pull the trigger, or whatever. You'll be doing me a favor. Then I won't have to live knowing I was responsible either for hurting Tilly or for helping you."

Harper exhaled, his breath roaring in Lawlor's ear.

"You don't know these guys." His voice was low. "They're like wolves. They'll tear her to pieces."

"So don't let them. Let her go. Put her in a car, take her to the middle of nowhere. Leave her by the side of the road."

"I can't."

"Why not?"

"I just can't."

Lawlor let his head drop between his knees. He was shaking, cold lines of sweat leaking out of his armpits and down his flanks. He thought of Tilly, shut up in a room somewhere, drugged or restrained. Men watching her.

These guys are like wolves, Harper had said.

Not my guys. These guys.

So, not Harper's men; someone else's.

He sat up. "Let me speak to the boss."

"I am the boss." Harper sounded choked.

"No you're not. You told me yourself, you can't even control your people. They weren't even supposed to take Tilly, were they? You said they improvised. Why not improvise by sticking her with ketamine or giving her a crack on the head? Why go to the trouble of taking her out of there? Because that's what they do, right? They take women. So they took Tilly. And now you've got a situation that you can't control. So let me speak to the man who can."

He snapped the phone shut. He dropped the phone on the table, as though it was alive. He stared at it, the thoughts spinning in his head. What had he done? Had he killed Tilly, or made her safer? There was no way of knowing. He closed his eyes. Rubbed his temples, felt himself crumbling inside. *What had he done?*

He stayed like that for a while. And then he got ready to move. He showered and shaved, and then he got dressed, his eyes on the clock radio. Was it really a bomb? Or was it just a piece of theater? Something about it still snagged in his memory, like a slub on a cotton sheet. It was there, and then it was gone.

The green digits on the clock face were transparencies, stuck on to the face and lit from behind. Harper had gone to some trouble. There was no reason to disbelieve the device wasn't packed with explosive, as he claimed. He was certainly capable.

The phone rang, vibrating in starts across the table.

"I'll let her go." Harper's voice was abrupt.

"Do you have the authority?"

"Yes. But it has to be a trade. You for her."

"Forget it."

"Mister Lawlor?" A new voice stopped him from snapping the phone shut.

"Yes."

"This is the only way this can happen I'm afraid." The voice sounded like something being dragged up a gravel path. The ruined voice of a lifelong smoker, with an Eastern European accent. "If you would like to live, and Ms Tran to be released unharmed, then you must come to us. To me. The alternative is death for you both. Quick for you, perhaps, but slow for her. Am I clear on this?"

The voice was emotionless and matter-of-fact, as though he was reading a list of instructions from a manual. It was the voice of a man who had done bad things in the past, and did not let his memories trouble him.

"Yes," Lawlor said.

"Good. Then I can save us both a lot of time and trouble. My men are outside. In a moment they will knock on the door. You will let them in and they will escort you to a car. You will, I'm afraid, have to ride in the trunk. They will bring you to me. When you arrive, I shall let Ms Tran go. My people will bring her back to where you are now. Then we shall talk."

"Why should I believe you? What's to stop you from killing her anyway?"

"Because I suspect that if I break my word, you will become uncooperative. And that is not what I want."

"What do you want?" Lawlor asked.

"Just to talk."

"So why not talk here?"

A sigh. "Because the authorities tend to take a great deal of interest in my movements, and I want our conversation to be a confidential one."

"And so you can kill me afterwards, quick and clean and no one the wiser."

The man chuckled. "I have no interest in killing you, Mister Lawlor. Quite the opposite, as I have said. I want you to live a long and productive life."

"In your interest."

"If you choose."

"And if not?"

"Then not. It is entirely up to you."

The line hummed. Lawlor stared at the blank computer screen, thinking about the man's proposal. A boss, clearly. A cold-blooded man, without scruples or squeamishness; one prepared to cut his losses, kill everyone and walk away. But he wanted Lawlor, for some reason, and he was prepared to trade. And it was a good trade. If Lawlor played it right, he could free Tilly and get close to Harper. Close enough, perhaps, to kill him.

Harper. He could feel his fingers tingling. Thoughts forming about what he might do when he saw him. He shook them away.

"I agree," he said. "But I want to speak to her first."

"Of course."

There was a scraping sound. He must have had her there all the time.

"Lawlor?" Tilly's voice was thin and wobbly, like a wine glass about to fall and smash. "Is that you?"

"It's me, Tilly. Are you okay? Have they hurt you?"

"No. They stuck me with something. But that's all."

"It's going to be alright. These people want to talk to me about something, and they're using you to get me to agree."

"What do they want?"

"I don't know. But don't worry. I've made an arrangement. We're going to change places. They're going to bring you back here. Once you're back, don't stop moving. Just get out."

"What about you?"

"I'll be fine. Don't worry. Take care of yourself." He paused. "I know you're angry, Tilly. I know you're thinking about a counter-strike. But just leave it, okay?"

"That's good advice, Mister Lawlor." The gravel voice was back. "If she follows it, she'll be quite safe, I promise you. I'll see you very soon."

20

The trunk opened. Two silhouettes looked down at him. A cold, artificial light behind them. His eyeballs hurt. His mouth tasted dry and stale.

"Out," one of the men said.

He stood back as Lawlor struggled out of the trunk. They were in a garage. Big enough for three cars. Shelves on the walls, oil stains on the concrete floor. A pegboard with gardening equipment and DIY stuff, neatly arranged. Screwdrivers and chisels. Several hammers. Several saws.

"Don't even think about it." The man took a switchblade out of his pocket. He snapped it open and rested the tip of it on the end of Lawlor's nose. "You gonna behave yourself? Say yes and I'll cut you loose."

"Yes."

The blade cut the plastic tie as easily as a thread. Lawlor flexed his fingers as the blood pumped back into his hands.

"Let's go," the man said. His accent was heavy. Eastern European. "Me first, then you, then him. Try anything and he'll put a hole in your spine. Got it?"

"Got it."

"Okay. Time to meet the boss."

He pushed open the door.

There was a party going on. Some kind of family gathering. A dozen women in the kitchen; about the same number of men watching football. All of them dressed as though they had all just come from a nightclub. And everyone drinking, bottles of wine and beer and shot glasses of clear liquor on every surface. The men kept their eyes on Lawlor as his two escorts led him towards a staircase at the far end of the room.

The children were tossing a ball about. One missed a catch and the ball hit Lawlor on the knee. He let it bounce, flicked it with his foot and sent it right back into the circle. The children clapped.

"What's your team?" one of the older boys shouted.

"Leeds United," Lawlor said.

They all booed.

"They're all Barca fans." The gravelly voice he had heard on the phone belonged to a slim man in a light gray suit, standing on the staircase. From a distance, it looked as though he was wearing something over his face, like a bank robber's stocking mask. But as Lawlor got closer, he saw why the man's voice sounded the way it did. Not because he was a lifelong smoker, but because he had, just once, inhaled a nearly lethal amount of smoke, and was lucky to be alive. He had been horribly burned. His features were a blur, like a painting smudged by a giant thumb. His nose was a sharp point, a ridge of flesh that only just covered the bone. He had no lips, just a gash in the lower part of his face. His right ear was intact, but the left had been burned down to a shriveled nub. His skin over most of his face, and the whole of his head looked like the scales of an animal, puckered and scarred in sloughs and channels of ash gray and livid purple. But his eyes were alert and bright, two pale orbs staring intently from their holes in the ruined flesh.

"Better Barca than Bayern," Lawlor said.

The man laughed. "And why do you say so?"

"Euro '75. Two-one on aggregate against Ararat Yerevan in the quarter finals."

"Very impressive, Mister Lawlor."

"Not really. Leeds went all the way to the final that year, so I paid more attention than usual."

"Ah. The Damned United. They lost to Bayern as well, did they not?"

Lawlor nodded. "Two nil."

"Then we already have some common ground. Even if it is merely a mutual loathing of the Bavarians."

He was high enough up the stairs to look down on Lawlor. "You know who I am?"

"Artur Ovian."

"Just so." He inclined his head towards the man with the gun. "I would like to treat you as a guest in my home, Mister Lawlor, but you have something of a reputation."

"Do I?"

"Will you give me your word that if I send these men away, you will not try to do me harm?"

"Would you believe me if I did?"

The man's eyes were the same battleship gray as his suit. "I think I would, yes. You strike me as the kind of man who keeps his word."

"I'm expecting you to keep yours."

The man gave him a detached look, like a scientist about to dissect a live frog. He started up the stairs. "Come."

The room Ovian called his study was as out-sized as the dining area downstairs. A glass coffee table the size of a barn door. Deep Chesterfield chairs. Ovian gestured toward one of them. Lawlor ignored him.

"Where's Tilly?"

Ovian took a phone out of his pocket and consulted it. "She is almost at the hotel. Five minutes and she will call."

Lawlor turned in a circle, looking around the room. There was a pressure in his ears that told him the place was completely soundproofed, the windows triple glazed. They could have a gunfight in there and no one outside would be any the wiser. His palms were suddenly damp.

"Harper works for you," he said.

"He is not called Harper anymore. He has had a different name for some years now. Rehan Markosian. Markosian is his wife's family."

"He's married?"

"In Armenia. It is the best way of creating an identity. Better than bribing some official who might talk later."

"When was this?"

"Perhaps fifteen years ago. He lived there for several years, to cement his identity. Then we moved him here."

"We."

Ovian made a half shrug. "I am part of what you might call … a syndicate."

"Armenian Power."

He grimaced. "That is one arm of the operation. But a very small part of our business interests."

"So what does Harper do for you?"

"Many things. Mostly with computers."

"He always was handy with electronics."

"Yes." Ovian touched the tips of his fingers together, like a man about to say a prayer. His left hand and wrist had the same puckering and scarring as his face. "I know all about his past. He has spoken of it often."

Lawlor felt a sudden pain in his chest. "Would he like to come out and talk to me about it now?"

"Not just yet."

There was a bottle of sparkling water on the coffee table, and three glasses. Ovian poured himself a glass, and sipped, his little finger sticking out at a right angle, like an old lady drinking tea.

His phone vibrated. He picked it up, listened, then put it back on the table and tapped the speakerphone.

Lawlor said, "Tilly?"

"I'm okay. I'm at the hotel. It's all good."

"Did they hurt you?"

"No. I'm fine. What about you?"

"I'm fine. Are they still there?"

"No. They're gone. Don't worry. I'll see you online, like ..."

Ovian jabbed the phone with a finger and ended the call. "So. Now we can do business."

"I said I'd hear what you have to say. That's all."

"That's all I want."

"And what if I refuse to do whatever it is you want from me?"

"I don't think you will. We will be keeping an eye on Ms Trang until our business is concluded. As insurance." Ovian slipped the phone back into his inside pocket. His jacket opened, and Lawlor saw the butt of an automatic in a holster under his left arm.

"Why all the theater?" Lawlor asked.

"What do you mean?"

"The bomb in the box. Snatching Tilly. It's all a bit elaborate, isn't it? Why not just send a couple of lads to break in, drug me, wrap me in cling film and bring me here."

Ovian nodded. "That is the way I would have done it. But Rehan wanted to make a point. He wanted to make you remember."

Lawlor laughed. "It's not something I'm likely to forget. It's why I came all this way."

"To look him in the eye."

"For starters."

Ovian sipped his water. "I was hoping you might give him the chance to explain."

"What's to explain? The bastard tried to kill me, and ended up murdering my children. What would you do in my position, I wonder?"

Ovian half-shrugged. "Yes. I put myself in your position, knowing what you know, and I would do the same as you have."

"You have no idea what I've done."

"But I do, Mister Lawlor. I know that you have spent twenty years of your life chasing the man you believe murdered your boys. I know what you have felt."

Lawlor didn't respond.

"Do you know anything about Artsakh? You may know it as Nagorno-Karabakh." Ovian asked.

"A little. It's a disputed territory in Azerbaijan. There was a war there, in the 80s."

"Yes. I led a small unit in the Armenian militia then. We killed Azeris and Russians, stole their supplies and sold them. It was good business. Very dangerous, but very profitable.

I made a lot of money. I bought a house." His ruined face twisted. "Which was a mistake.

"My comrades came to help me paint it. And then we got drunk. And in the middle of the night, men came. They threw Molotov cocktails through the windows. The intention was only to scare me, and to put me in my place. But the house became an inferno in seconds. My wife couldn't wake me. By the time she did, it was too late. I tried to save her..." he touched his scarred cheek, "But it was, as I say, an inferno. I escaped. Everyone else died."

Lawlor said nothing.

"I knew exactly who had ordered this." Ovian went on. "But I was a small man then, with no power. So I did what I was told. And I comforted myself in the usual ways. Drink. Drugs. Women. I was lost for a long time. I don't really know how I came back from that, but I did."

Lawlor waited, the question in his eyes. Ovian nodded. "Yes. Eighteen years later, to the day. I thought revenge would taste sweet."

"I don't care what it tastes like."

"Of course not. You are a man of principle. I expect you have considered ending your own life. I know I did, many times. But you will never do this, because you cannot die before you have avenged your two boys."

"So bring the bastard in." Lawlor's mouth was sticky.

"Trust me, my friend, when I tell you that if I had the man who killed your family, I would do exactly that. But I do not have him."

"You're talking in circles. It's irritating."

"In that case, let me be direct. Rehan Markosian, or Robert Harper, if you prefer, did not put the bomb under your car. He did not murder your children." Ovian's eyes were like chips of gray stone in his ruined face. "But he can tell you who did."

21

"Seriously?" Lawlor laughed. "All the effort you've taken to get me here. For that?"

Ovian lifted his hands. "I know I am challenging every assumption that you have held about this matter for twenty years, but please listen to me, just for a moment."

"They're not assumptions. There was evidence."

"Yes. Evidence that led you directly to one man, correct?"

Lawlor could feel the pressure stoking inside his chest again. He said nothing.

"And you never considered another suspect."

Lawlor toyed with the idea of going for the gun in the holster under Ovian's left arm, but the Armenian was quite ready for him. He sat upright, his hands on his knees, his jacket open. He would have the weapon out and firing before Lawlor was on his feet.

"There were no other suspects. He left a forensic signature."

"Evidence can be fabricated."

"Not this kind."

"I would like you to entertain the possibility that this was." Ovian held up a finger. "Just for a moment. And then think about the rest of the scene: the target, the type of device. If you did not have the forensic evidence, would your prime suspect have fit the frame?"

"This is a waste of time."

"Please. Just listen to him. And then decide."

Lawlor looked at his hands. They were shaking slightly, and he could feel the sweat on his palms.

"He's here?"

"He is outside the door."

Lawlor took a breath. His heart was racing. Twenty years. He thought of Andrew and Tommy, their arms around each other. Laughing. Alive.

"Okay." He breathed out. "I'll listen."

Ovian made a gesture, a flick of his hand, and the door sucked open and a man walked into the room. He was tall and slight, with a frizz of red hair over a high, pale forehead. He looked exactly as he had in the photo Jerry Fyffe had emailed Lawlor, just a few days before.

Robert Aloysius Harper.

Lawlor felt as though a giant was leaning one hand on his chest and using the other to crush his windpipe. He wanted to launch himself out of the chair, but the gun in Harper's hand kept him in his place.

"Put the weapon away." Ovian's voice was cold.

"I'm taking no chances," Rab Harper said. His eyes and mouth were small and pinched, clustered tight around his nose, like the three holes in a bowling ball. The gun was in his right hand. The cake box was tucked under his left arm, along with a thick folder, stuffed with papers.

"I will not. Ask you. Again." Ovian was the kind of man whose voice got slower and quieter the angrier he became, and now he was speaking very softly indeed. There was a click as

Harper thumbed the safety on the automatic. He sat down on the couch, the gun on one side and the cake box and the file on the other.

Now was the time. Lawlor's heart was going like the drive shaft on a train engine. His palms were soaked. Twenty years he had been chasing this man, and here he was, less than five feet away.

But Ovian was ready for him. His jacket hung open, his hands tense on his knees. He would put a bullet in Lawlor before he'd even laid a finger on Harper, let alone killed him.

Lawlor had to wait.

Harper had thickened in the usual places, around his waist and his face, but he still managed to look scrawny. His hairline had receded, but his Adam's apple looked the same as it had in his arrest photos, like a chunk of concrete, swallowed by a stork. He was dressed like a tech support clerk, in a white short-sleeved shirt tucked into gray trousers. Pouches on his belt. Two phones and a multi tool.

He put the file to one side, and opened the box. He took out the clock radio and placed it carefully on the table. Then he sat back and folded his arms.

Lawlor looked at it. He looked at Harper. He looked at Ovian. They were both staring at him, expectant. He looked again. At the chunky, old-fashioned box. The hard edges, the slanted digital display. And the same feeling he had in the hotel room crept up on him, like something walking up his spine. A memory, a bad one, but just out of reach.

"Remember now?" Harper's voice was hard.

Lawlor didn't answer. His mind was turning in a circle, revolving around the shred of memory, expanding slowly. A clock radio, just like this one. On top of a pile of household items. In a cardboard box. In the boot of a car. In the dark. In the rain...

And then it all came back in a rush.

"Now he remembers."

But Lawlor didn't hear him. He was twenty years younger, standing in the middle of a road in South Tyrone, soaked to the skin, with the rain coming down in sheets. There was a man on his knees on the blacktop in the middle of the road, a soldier either side of him, his hands on his head, his hair plastered in hanks like strips of orange peel over his high, pale forehead.

He'd been drinking, Lawlor remembered that now. Five pints - maybe six - in the lounge at Whitesides in Clogher. Cosying up to the target the whole time. And then a suggestion. A wee place close to the border, a place where they specialized in a certain kind of entertainment. Then out to the street, the target's yellow Astra, and then on the road. Giving directions down the narrow lanes in the heaving rain, towards a place Lawlor knew, nice and quiet, just north of a closed crossing point that made the road a dead end. Perfect for an interrogation.

Except the troops were out. Four Royal Marines on the road, which meant eight more hidden in the hedges and up on the high ground. A red torch cycling up and down on the outside of a bend; the target panicking, braking hard, then out and running into a ploughed field, Lawlor after him, slipping and sliding in the furrows. And then four marines, rising up out of the mud, weapons up and screaming at them to get on the ground.

The marines had dragged them both back down to the road. Put them on their faces on the wet tarmac as they popped the boot open and searched the car. Lawlor had fumbled the ID out of his wallet, thanking God he'd not drawn a weapon from the armory.

Then he was back on his feet, his head fogging with the whiskey, looming over the target.

"Where is he?" Screaming the question, over and over, pushing the corporal away when he tried to grab his arm.

The target, Patsy Harper, had looked up at him through a sheet of rain. In the wet and the high-powered torchlight, his hair looked the color of blood.

"I hope they suffered," he said. "Your two wee, precious boys. I hope they squealed while they burned."

The rage took him then, and he reached into the boot of the car, grabbing the first thing to hand. Hard plastic, a square shape. Smashing the object into Patsy Harper's face. Plastic splintering, blood like a fountain out of his left eye. Screaming. And then again, over and over, the electrical lead whipping back and forth as he battered the clock radio into the man's head, until one of the marines stepped forward, rifle butt swinging, and all the lights went out.

22

"Remember now, don't ye?" Rab Harper said.

Lawlor didn't reply. His face throbbed. He knew the taste of whiskey in his mouth was his imagination—he hadn't had a drink in a dozen years—but his nose and the back of his tongue seemed to burn with it. Ghost liquor, the whiskey called it. He clamped his jaw shut, sure that if he even opened his mouth to breathe, he would vomit.

"Patsy has a glass eye now," Harper said. "He takes it out at night. Keeps it in a wee plastic box. And his speech is off. Some kind of lesion in his brain. Makes him slur like he's drunk. The kids rag him about it. Used to be you look twice at Patsy Harper and he'd break a piece of you. Now the kids kick his stick away and push him about the place until he tips over."

Lawlor looked away.

"You didn't really think my own brother'd tell you where I was, did you? Even if he knew, he wouldn't have said."

"I know."

Harper's face went white, then red. Then he took the multi tool out of the pouch on his belt and picked up the clock radio. His fingers were long and slim, like a musician's. They fluttered over the device, touching it here and there with the tool, and a moment later, the radio was in pieces on the table. Most of the electronics had been removed from inside. A small white brick filled the space, along with a tiny cell phone. A rainbow of wires was wrapped around them. Harper held up the bomb. "Would you have known which wire to cut?"

Lawlor didn't answer.

Harper tugged on the wires, poked with the scissor, and pulled out the detonator, a small, copper-colored tube. He set it down carefully with a tiny click.

"I've been watching you. These last twenty years, I've watched you online, and I paid people to watch you in real life. So I know how it is for you. I know how much you want your revenge. But you won't find it here. Not in this room."

Lawlor felt as though he had detached from himself. Part of him wanted to smash Harper's face into the glass coffee table, over and over until his nose burst and his head split. But another, cooler part of him was curious to see what the play was here. And what Ovian wanted.

"I don't believe you." He was surprised at how level his voice sounded.

Harper glanced at Ovian. "Aye, well I can't say I expected you to up and take my word for it. But will you listen for five minutes at least?"

"So you can manipulate me into doing whatever twisted thing that it is you or your boss want done? Fuck you."

"Aye." Harper's face was suddenly bright red. "Well I am fucked, if you hadn't noticed. I'm a marked man, wanted for murder, which means I am stuck here, with no way back, because someone put me in a frame that your pals were only too happy to pull off the shelf and hang on the wall."

Lawlor was silent.

Harper picked the folder up off the chair and placed it on the table. Squared it off with the edge of the glass. Placed the detonator carefully on top.

"I always loved these dets," he said. "You know why they're branded 58/42, right? The alloy ratio?"

"I've read the forensics report on the murder of my children, yes."

"Yeah. Okay." Harper licked his lips. "Well, those numbers are rounded. The actual ratio in the dets I stole was 57.6 to 42.4. But in 1990, the company changed the alloy composition. Just a wee tweak, to 58.2 to 41.8. That still rounds to 58/42, you see?"

"I'm not here for a fucking chemistry lesson, Harper."

"Just listen for a second. Your techs found the alloy in the wreckage of your car, and they tested it like they always did. But when they filed their report, they rounded the numbers. Just like the company did. Just like every tech team did in every investigation report that they put together on all the work I'd done in the past. Which meant that anyone reading the reports would think that the detonator used in your car was the same as the detonators I'd used before."

He waited for a reaction. When none came, he shook his head. "You can pull the files yourself. It's easy enough: I already have."

He placed his hand on the file. "I have them right here."

"Aye, right." Lawlor sneered. "You probably just mocked up a couple of website pages and printed them out five minutes ago."

"You can call Kontimax in Hamburg. They'll tell you."

"You've had twenty years to set this up, Harper. I don't doubt you've done a grand job of it."

Harper shook his head. "What about the trigger, then? Every other device I placed was detonated with line of sight. Radio frequency transceivers and infra-red, right?"

"So what?"

"So the device in your car..."

"The bomb."

Harper flinched. "Okay, then. The bomb. It was detonated by a power surge from the battery, triggered when the ignition was turned. Passive. Not remote controlled. Not line of sight. I never made a device ... a bomb... like that. You've read my file enough to know. I was careful. I never killed anyone. Not one person. Thirteen devices. Thirteen bombs. But all commercial targets. Never against people. And not a single death. Not one."

Lawlor turned to Ovian. "Is this what he's been spinning you? That he's a peaceful man who never hurt a soul? He must not have told you about his work in London, then. About Brenda Sullivan. Or Richard Hunnicutt." Lawlor spat out the names. "Thomas Chilton. Tina Johnson. Lorna McDermott..."

Ovian was staring at Harper, his face like a stone.

Harper shook his head. "I never killed anyone."

"You think you have to kill someone to take their life?" Lawlor kept his voice level. "Lorna McDermott can't eat, drink or defecate unless it's by way of a tube. She can't speak. She can't hear. She can hardly see. She may not be clinically dead, but she's barely living."

"She wasn't supposed to be there," Harper muttered. "We didn't know she'd stayed late."

"And the rest of them? Hunnicutt lost an eye. Tina Johnson is still in a wheelchair. Brenda Sullivan took her own life. And Chilton died last year, did you know that? A wee piece of metal they never found worked its way into his brain and killed him."

Harper's hands were clasped tight. "I'm not saying I wasn't responsible. I'm not saying I didn't make mistakes..."

Lawlor turned to Ovian. "We're finished here. This man has lied to you, and he's lying to me now. I don't know what it is you wanted me to do for you, but the answer is no. So you have a choice. You can take me out of here and kill me, or you can give me that gun and leave me in here to do what I came to do. Either way, one of us isn't leaving here alive."

They all looked at the weapon on the couch. Harper's hand twitched.

"Give it to me, Rehan." Ovian held out his hand.

Harper picked the gun up by the barrel and handed it over. Ovian checked the safety, and cocked the weapon. He removed the magazine, and set it aside. Then he placed the weapon back on the glass table in front of Lawlor, the barrel pointing at Harper.

Harper was staring at the gun, as though his legs had been cut from under him and lain in his lap.

"You lied to me, Rehan," Ovian said. "You made me believe that no one was hurt in your bombings. I took you at your word. I hid you. I kept you safe. I made you part of our family."

"You can't." Harper's eyes glistened. "If you do this... You know... If this..."

"Be quiet."

Ovian turned to Lawlor. "I considered this man to be one of the most trustworthy in my organization. A mistake, it turns out. So now it is up to you to decide whether he lives or dies. I understand a blood oath and I will respect your decision, Mister Lawlor, whatever you choose."

He took the magazine from the table. Slipped it into his

pocket. And then stood up, and walked out of the room.

23

Lawlor picked up the gun. It was a Beretta nine millimeter. It felt comfortable in his hand. It was slightly nose heavy, because there was no magazine, just the single round in the chamber, so he tilted it up so that it pointed at Harper's chest.

"It wasn't me." Harper's voice was a whisper. All the color had drained out of his face, so that with the frizz of orange hair over his head, he reminded Lawlor of a painting of Queen Elizabeth the First. "I swear on my mother's life. It wasn't me."

Lawlor was aware of his heart, pumping hard and fast in his chest, sending vibrations into his neck and his groin and his temples. His breath was shallow and high in his throat. He felt intensely alive, and hyper-alert, the way he'd felt, far in the past, in the fractions of a second before violence had broken out: an armed arrest. A fight. A street riot. A shooting. His whole being was concentrated in the breech of the Beretta, melted down and compressed into the shape of the bullet in the gun.

He thumbed the safety off, and slid his finger into the trigger guard.

Harper groaned. "Please. I have a child. A girl. She's only

twelve. If I'm gone, God alone knows what'll happen to her. And to Seda. My wife. They'll put them on the street. Both of them. Please."

Something uncoiled inside Lawlor's guts. He thought of the photos in the file Róisín had shown him. The shabby rooms, the harsh lighting.

He pushed the thoughts away. "You didn't give a damn about my family. Why should I care about yours?"

"It wasn't me. I keep telling you." Harper's eyes were wide, the pupils dilated so much they were almost black. "And if you kill me, you'll never know who it was."

"I know."

"You *don't* know." Harper placed his hand on the file. "Twenty years. All that time you spent looking for me, I spent looking for who really did it. And I found him."

Lawlor shook his head. He wanted to take up the pressure on the trigger of the gun in his hand. Squeeze, and feel the power of the automatic jerking in his hand.

But something stopped him. It had snagged in his mind, the moment Ovian had said it. That the inquiry had focused on Harper from the beginning. And that no one else had even been considered as a suspect. The chemical signature had sent the police after Harper, naturally enough, but there should have been other lines of inquiry. Blind with rage and grief, and half in the bag most of the time, he hadn't seen it then. But looking back, Lawlor realized the investigators' vision had been tunneled from the jump.

It was like a tap being turned off inside him. The adrenaline drained away, and he felt suddenly ten years older, shaky and breathless. And torn in two: part of him was screaming at himself to do what he had come all this way to do, while another part, detached and curious, wanted to know what Harper would say, and how it would play.

He said, "You found who?"

Harper gaped, relief flooding his eyes. "Bobby McEwan."

The idea was so absurd that Lawlor laughed out loud.

"Nice try. Bobby McEwan was UDA. And he wouldn't have known a detonator from his dick."

"He was a handyman."

"Handy? He could just about paint a fence, if he was sober enough."

"He still had enough nous to strip a few wires and hook up a battery. It's not rocket science."

"Building a bomb's a bit more complicated, wouldn't you say? Bobby McEwan wouldn't have had the first clue."

"That's exactly what I'm saying." Some color had come back into Harper's cheeks. "He didn't make the bomb. He just planted it."

"And who would want Bobby McEwan to plant a bomb in my car?"

"I don't know. But I think it had something to do with some kind of arms deal he was involved in."

Lawlor felt suddenly cold, his skin bumping on his arms and his back. "How would you know that?"

"He told me."

"Did he come to you in a vision? Bobby McEwan's dead. His house burned down, twenty years ago. With him in it."

"That wasn't him."

Lawlor felt almost disappointed. "Is that really the best you can do?"

"I'm telling you." Harper eyed the gun. "McEwan's alive. And you might think about what day it was his house burned down, by the way. Four days after your car blew up. He told me himself, he went for a carry-out, came back with the beer and found the place in flames. He's not the sharpest tool in the shed, but he knows how the game's played. He turned around and went straight to the docks. Got on the next boat out."

"So whose body was in the house?"

"A mate of his. Or not so much a mate, but some guy he'd met at the Linfield Rangers supporters club in Glasgow. He was over for the Glentoran match that weekend. But they all got so plastered after the game, he stayed an extra day. I tell you, McEwan's a lucky skite. There was no forensics. Your lot just assumed it was him."

"What do you mean there was no forensics? There's always forensics."

"Well, there would have been, had they anything to check against. I read the report. They found teeth, but they had nothing to compare them to. Bobby McEwan never went to the dentist. Not once, even when he was a kid."

Lawlor shook his head. "I don't buy it. If some guy had gone missing on a football trip to Belfast, we would have had the Glasgow police on the phone. We would have connected them."

"Except nobody missed this fella. He was an ex-con. He had no family. Wasn't married. No kids. Lived alone in a room in a squat. Lined up for the dole every week like half the men in Scotland back then. When he never came back to the squat, people just thought he'd moved on. No-one asked any questions. And you know what it's like in places like that, no one goes to the police about anything."

Lawlor weighed the Beretta in his hand. Harper was looking at him, his eyes wide, not blinking. He hadn't shown any sign that he was lying, but after more than twenty years of living under a false identity, Lawlor had to assume he was well-practiced at it.

The hard part of him was urging him to end this farce, to shoot Harper and walk away. Harper was a talented hacker, who Lawlor was sure could have tweaked police records in the past. But talk about an arms deal was different: *that* wasn't in the records. And Harper was on the wrong side to have been told about a loyalist paramilitary deal at the time.

So how did he know about it now?

"So where's McEwan?" Lawlor said.

Harper shrugged. "I can't tell you for sure. I found him online. Not in the real world."

"Okay. How?"

"I just stumbled on him. A few years back. I was trawling a bunch of nationalist chat groups. It's where the Huns all hang out online. All these fat, pasty guys getting drunk and spouting off on a Saturday night. He was banging on about this and that, one-upping other guys talking about how they'd beat up this guy or kneecapped that guy. Then he said something about planting a bomb in a peeler's car. I pressed him, but he shut up pretty fast. Then he disappeared. And I had to wait for him to resurface. You know."

Lawlor nodded. He had spent the best part of twenty years looking for Harper. He knew.

"I got lucky on the eleventh of July a few years back. It was a Saturday night, and he was steaming drunk. We were swapping stories about escaping from the law. Next thing I know, he's posted an old clip from the Belfast Telegraph, a story about a house burning down. "I'm a ghost," he says. Lucky for me, I screenshot it. I ran a quick search and found out it was McEwan's house. I knew who McEwan was, and at first I thought that maybe this guy had killed him and burned his house down."

"But that didn't fit with his story about being a ghost."

"Right." Harper bobbed his head, his eyes darting from Lawlor's face to the gun, and back again. "Exactly. So I focused everything on him. Eventually I found a way into his computer. His antivirus killed it pretty quick, but I did get a photo of him, from the camera. Ran it through the PSNI database and there he was. Twenty years older, and twenty pounds heavier, but no hint of a doubt."

"And so you called him back and told him you recognized him, and he just told you he put the bomb in my car." Lawlor's voice was acid.

"That was more than a year later. He was drunk, as usual. Some guy in the chatroom was moaning about how the leaders of groups like his were always making mistakes. Next thing I knew, he's blabbing about being given a bomb to hit a target and ended up killing a couple of kids instead. Blamed his bosses. Didn't name names. But it all fit. It was him."

Lawlor's mouth was dry. "What else did he say? Did he say anything about the person who gave him the bomb? Who his bosses were?"

"I went back at him a bunch of times, different identities, different angles, but he never mentioned it again."

"What about this arms deal? How did you find about that?"

"The same way. Drunk web heroes arguing about weapons and bragging about glory days. McEwan comes out with a story about how he was part of a UDA squad that hijacked an IRA shipment once, up in Ballycastle."

Lawlor's fist was tight around the grip of the gun. The rivets were digging into his skin. "Did he say when?"

"Ninety-one. January. There was a detail about them having to wait for five hours in a van by the side of the road. Said he nearly froze his bits off. Which sounds about right for North Antrim, that time of year."

"Anything else?"

"Not right then. I got him to re-tell the story again a couple of months later. Like, 'Tell me how you pulled one over on the IRA.' He was even more hammered than usual. He starts going on about how the boat the guns came in on was one of those big motor yachts, the kind you see girls with bikinis on. Only there was no way anyone was wearing a bikini anywhere near that boat it was so bloody cold. He was cracking up telling the story. Then he starts on about the fella who ran in the guns. The IRA called him The Sicilian, after that Mario Puzo novel that was big at the time. McEwan's joke was the guy wasn't from Sicily at all, he was from Milan, and you couldn't call him The Milano, because that's a kind of biscuit. Ho, ho, ho. Plus, he wasn't an assassin, He was a hairdresser."

Lawlor felt as though he was about to throw up. "Did he have a name?"

"Oh sure." Harper smirked. "Another big joke. McEwan was on about him having a great head on him, being a hairdresser, and all. That and his name was Moretti. You know. Like the beer."

24

For twenty years Lawlor had been certain about Harper. But now that certainty had evaporated.

Because Harper was telling the truth: he had always hit commercial targets. The people his bombs had hurt were only in the area by chance. He had always used vehicles, yes, and he had always used the 58/42 detonators, but he had only ever used remote detonation triggers that gave him line of sight to the target. No booby traps, like the one used in Lawlor's car. That alone was a glaring deviation from his M.O., one that Lawlor and the investigation team had seen at the time, but dismissed when the test results came in. The telltale presence of the alloy, the definitive Rab Harper signature, swept everything else away.

Then there was the story about Bobby McEwan. It was insane. And yet it made a certain kind of sense. The IRA had no motive to kill another policeman back then, not while they were in negotiations with the British Government. The bomb nearly derailed the entire process. The leadership was furious. But the other side had every reason to keep the Troubles stoked: loyalist paramilitaries depended on the chaos and the threat of violence for recruitment and money. As for the guns,

Lawlor was sure that if the UDA high command thought he was getting close to finding their arms caches or disrupting their supply lines, they wouldn't hesitate to kill him. But the real clincher was the name Harper had given him. Paolo Moretti. The same name he'd seen in the unmarked, red-jacketed file that Róisín had slid across his desk in Belfast just a few days before: a name he hadn't seen for more than twenty years, but that still rang as loud as a fire alarm in his head.

"Tell me about Moretti."

Harper's face folded in on itself. "Nothing to tell. Never met him. McEwan mentioned the name once, that's all."

"What else did McEwan say about the hijack?"

"Just that they hit a van coming from a boat in Ballycastle. But I remember the UVF got serious firepower right after. All those pub shootings. They were spraying rounds about like Scarface. I remember the panic in the newspapers."

Lawlor nodded. The forensics had told the story: NATO brass at Loyalist shooting scenes until 1990, then suddenly 7.62 casings everywhere, like the aftermath of a Red Army Faction hit. Then a spate of Czech AK variants turning up in Protestant housing estates. The obvious conclusion was that the UDA had managed to arrange a shipment of former Warsaw Pact weapons.

"You believe me." Harper leaned forward, eyes bright. "This fella Moretti - you knew the name. You were after him."

Lawlor kept his face neutral, but Harper was already connecting dots.

"Makes sense. Who else would they trust to investigate Loyalists? You'd have had to be an outsider."

He was right. For most of Special Branch, there would have been too much danger of digging up a name they might know.

Lawlor had been weeks from promotion when Dennis Johnson handed him the case. *For the experience.*

Not that he cared, at the time. To him, the paramilitary groups were little more than criminal gangs. But many of his colleagues saw it differently. That became clear when his requests for any kind of assistance, from forensics to photocopying, were automatically slotted to the bottom of their inboxes. He'd been shunned and isolated. Just him and Róisín, drowning in paperwork. Then that Thursday before Easter - a call from a Garda contact in Galway. A busted customs officer trading information about men with Northern accents moving crates from a boat registered in Algeciras to a yacht flying a British ensign.

The *Swallowtail.*

Lawlor's eyes searched Harper's face now, for any hint that he might be feeding him a line. "Did McEwan say what the boat was called?"

"No. Just that they hit a van coming from Ballycastle harbor."

Lawlor shook his head. Harper wasn't lying. But this still didn't feel right. "We would have heard about a hijacked IRA shipment. The high command would have kneecapped everyone involved."

Harper shrugged. "Gerry McKee ran Antrim Brigade. When he said shut up, people shut up."

"McEwan's crew would have bragged."

The words triggered something. A memory: some drunk in a burger bar, talking through a straw about the Red Hand Commando hitting an IRA shipment. Lawlor had laughed it off. Made a few calls. Got nothing. Never filed a report.

Harper caught his expression. "Twenty-twenty hindsight?"

Lawlor didn't answer. But his brain was boiling. He'd been so close. After the Galway tip, he'd spent hours tracking the yacht through ship registrations and radio licenses until he found a vessel called *Swallow Tail*, berthed in Ballycastle Marina. It was a dinghy, not a yacht, and it had no registered owner. But a security guard checked the slip's paperwork and found that it was paid for by a credit card owned by one Paolo Moretti.

The database had given him the rest. Forty years old. Dual national. Single. Hairdresser. Owner of a new Ford Cortina and a business on the High Road in Ballycastle. He had the same home address, which meant he lived above the shop. The photo on his driver's license showed a narrow-faced man with a sharp chin and a feathered haircut, like an aging pop star or football player. Sharp eyes and a trace of a smile. His record showed he'd never had any kind of interaction with the police, not even a speeding ticket. There was no record of him owning a boat.

It was thin. No criminal connections, no link to Republicans. Just a hairdresser with a boat slip. But Ballycastle was right on the coast, near the border. perfect for smuggling. Lawlor had wanted to drive up that night. But it was two in the morning, Easter weekend coming. Róisín was away. His family had plans.

Paolo Moretti could wait.

25

The door opened, and Lawlor started. He felt as though he'd been woken from a dream, but he hadn't slept. Just drifted, as the sun had tracked shadows across the room.

Ovian was standing in the doorway.

"Leave," he said, and Harper picked up the cake box and the file, and hurried from the room.

Ovian picked up the Beretta, cleared it, and put the ejected round in his pocket. He holstered the gun.

"So." He sat down. "Do you believe him?"

"It's not as simple as that."

"He either did it, or he didn't." Ovian crossed his legs, plucking at the crease of his trousers. "And from what I have learned about you, you have a knack of knowing whether a man is telling the truth. Do you think Rehan is telling the truth?"

Lawlor wanted to ponder the question. But the lizard part of his brain was far ahead of him. "I do."

"And just like that, your world has been turned on its head."

It was exactly the way that he felt. In twenty minutes, everything that he had believed for twenty years had been flipped, as though the picture of the world he had held in his head had been a negative, all this time. He had seen Harper as the enemy, as an evil entity. Now he saw him for what he really was. A scapegoat. An easy target. And what did that make him? He felt his stomach twist.

"It's a lot to take in," he said.

Ovian smiled at the understatement.

"Will you able to clear his name?"

"Me? No. But if he can get the right man in a box with the right people..."

"Perhaps you could help him with this."

Lawlor shook his head. "It's something I used to do. But a long time ago."

"The kind of skill a man doesn't forget."

The door opened and a woman came in, carrying a large platter of food. She was about forty, with long black hair and wide-set eyes, dressed in a crimson shirt that matched her lipstick. She placed the platter carefully on the table.

Ovian waited until she was gone.

"There are men who can break other men, but I have plenty of these." He forked some of the food onto a plate. "Some of them know how to do it without leaving a mark. But you, I'm told, can break a man without laying a finger on him."

"Harper is prone to exaggeration, as you know."

"Oh no." Ovian wagged his fork. "This is not from him. This is from your own people. From your own files."

"You don't have my file."

"I said files. Plural. Your police file and your army file. Both. As I told you, Rehan is a highly resourceful man. Although he will be the first to admit he has not been able to find a way into your headquarters since you set up the system there."

He began to eat. Lawlor watched him, trying to decide how

deep the bluff went. It was entirely possible that Harper had hacked the police database, which had leaked worse than a bullet-riddled colander before he took it over. But the MOD was a different matter.

He forced himself to pick up a fork. "Even if he did get my files, they're redacted." The darker parts that Ovian was referring to, anyway.

Ovian dabbed at the corner of his mouth with a paper napkin. "As I said, Rehan is very talented in some ways. I will let him explain it to you himself, but essentially your file was redacted using software, and he developed an AI program to remove the black lines. So, thanks to him, I know all about you, and your unique capabilities."

"And that's why you agreed to help him. Because you want me to help you."

"Exactly."

Lawlor stabbed his fork into one of the pastries. It shattered, and crumbs spread across the table.

"Hard to eat these things without making a mess," he said.

"Impossible," Ovian nodded.

"Same goes for questioning a man. Even if you don't lay a finger on him. Do you understand?"

Ovian nodded. "I understand you might be reluctant to go back down that path. But what if it turned out that our aims happened to coincide, and we both want answers from the same man?"

"And what man would that be?"

Ovian smiled. "Fermin."

Lawlor felt like a man with a bad hand in a million-dollar poker game. It took everything he had not to react. But of course Ovian knew about Fermin. Lawlor had a photograph of Fermin and Harper together on his phone, and because Harper was Ovian's man, that meant Fermin and Ovian were in business together. Or, more likely, in competition, given their ethnic and tribal loyalties. The meeting was probably some kind of truce talk, a regular rendezvous to settle turf issues and make trades. Ovian would almost certainly have sources in Fermin's camp, which meant he would have heard about Fermin's hunt for Lawlor, maybe even before Lawlor was aware he was being hunted.

"Do you know what they call him?" Ovian asked.

"The Gardener."

"A sick joke. His landscaping business is fully legitimate. Bonded, pays taxes, everything. But some of the crews aren't yard workers, they're assassins. They attract no attention when they park out front of a target's house. When they're finished, they transport the bodies in those big bins they use to pack yard waste. Then they put the bodies through mulching machines and bury the debris on the properties that the legitimate crews maintain."

"Efficient."

"Very. And in a city as thinly-policed as Los Angeles, when you leave behind neither a body nor any other evidence, it makes it very difficult for the authorities to conduct an investigation."

"Why is Fermin after me?"

"I do not know. All I know is that you are important to him. Very important. He has every one of his people out looking for you. Men, women, children. The whole city."

"And why do you want him?"

"That is my business."

"It won't be after I question him, so you may as well tell

me."

Ovian's smile almost reached his eyes. "It seems our interests do align, then."

Lawlor nodded. "It seems they do."

Lawlor had not seen a camera in the room, but there must have been one, because when Ovian made a gesture, the door opened and Harper came back in to the room. His high forehead shone, as though he'd been caught in the sun.

"He has agreed," Ovian said.

"So you believe me?" Harper looked like a small child, hoping for a present.

"Let's just say I'm open to the possibility that not everything you've told me is a crock," Lawlor said.

Harper looked relieved. "So when does it happen?"

Ovian stared at him, and Lawlor felt the tension between them.

"When I decide," Ovian said. "In the meantime, take care of Mister Lawlor. Make sure he rests. And wait for my call."

Harper waited until he was gone. And then he sank into the couch, in the same position he had been before. Legs splayed, hands clasped between his knees.

"Jesus," he said. "Thank fuck that's over."

Lawlor said, "Well now we're all pals, you can tell me how you found Tilly."

Harper rubbed his face. He looked exhausted. "Who says it was her and not you?"

"Your boss said you haven't found a way into my office yet, and that's the only place I ever contacted her. I know you didn't track me into the country, so it must have been her you were onto."

"You're half right. I've been on her for more than five years now. I saw you together in Vegas in '05. It took me a while to break into her systems, but I got there."

"So you were on me from the start."

"Just from when you landed at McCarren. And then we lost you when you got off the bus in L.A." He smiled. "You've not lost your edge."

Lawlor didn't respond.

"We had a couple of guys on Tilly, too," Harper went on. "They tailed her to the hotel here. Put a camera and a bug in her room. And then you showed up."

The sound of men shouting from downstairs filtered through the door. Maybe an argument over the football. Maybe a full-blown fight. Harper didn't appear to notice.

"You look how I feel," he said. "And you heard Artur. You might want to get your head down for a bit. He's the kind who likes to keep his plans all wrapped up and go at a moment's notice."

Lawlor nodded. He was thinking of Tilly, wondering how she was going to get away from the men who were watching her. Not that he was too concerned. She was a resourceful woman, and judging from the way she'd had him picked up and delivered to the hotel in Santa Monica, she had local talent to call on. But he couldn't help worrying.

"So, interrogation." Harper leaned forward over the table. "Is that a skill that atrophies? Or is it like riding a bike?"

Lawlor had learned his craft at the School of Intelligence in Ashford. The old, bloody methods first, and then the newer ones that didn't leave a mark. He had been fascinated, even compelled, but he had recognized the central weakness in all of them: they were unbearable. Much better to have the subject open up before the punishment even began.

There was an art to getting inside another human's head. Probing like a scalpel blade in an oyster, looking for the muscle that holds the shell closed. Lawlor had been good at it. It was like solving a puzzle. And this was the problem. He had derived immense satisfaction from his work, and felt pleasure when the puzzle was solved and the "client" began to talk.

Put simply, he liked breaking people.

And he knew that if he opened that door, even a crack, and felt the old fascination and feelings, it might be impossible to close it again.

And then he might be lost.

But there were things he wanted, too. He wanted to know why Fermin was after him, and who had set him running. He wanted to know who had hired Fyffe and taken Harper's name off an Interpol list. He wanted McEwan. He wanted to know how much he had been paid and who had paid him. He wanted all those things.

So in the end, he realized, he really only had one choice. Because to stop, to go home, to lose himself in a bottle, was to die. And he wasn't ready to die just yet.

He looked Harper in the eye.

"Sleep sounds like a good idea," he said. "Let's go."

26

Lawlor was a guest.

Except that he wasn't. He might be able to leave, but how far would he get, without help? He had no idea where he was, and Fermin's people were still out there, looking for him. Busboys and hotel clerks and traffic cops and security guards and drivers all over the city would have been asked to keep an eye out. If he decided to run, he'd be lucky to make it to the airport. It would be a miracle if he made it on board a plane.

He showered and shaved, but sleep eluded him. Closing his eyes was like running an old newsreel in his mind, flashes of black and white that jabbed at his brain. Harper's brother Patsy, in the bar, in the car, in the road. On the ground.

There was a knock at the door. Harper stood in the hallway, shifting from one foot to the other.

"Thanks again for hearing me out." Harper flashed a grin. "And thanks for not shooting me."

"Don't think I won't change my mind."

Harper's lips pursed. He was chewing on the skin inside his cheek. With his high forehead and his crown of curly red hair, he looked like an overgrown child. Lawlor felt something twist inside him.

"Look, I'm sorry about your brother," he said. "I wasn't well at the time."

"You might say."

"It's not an excuse. What I did was wrong. But I wasn't in my right mind."

"I can't blame you for that." Harper was fidgeting, glancing down the hall. He jerked his head. "I want to show you something before dinner."

Lawlor followed him to a stairwell, but instead of going downstairs, Harper led them up. He stopped midway and held up his hand.

"No cameras here," he said in a low voice.

Lawlor waited.

Harper sagged against the wall behind him. His face was gray in the half light.

He said, "You can't trust Ovian."

"Who says I do?"

"I'm just saying. He's evil. Smooth as silk on the outside, but a raging beast underneath. That story he told you about taking revenge for his wife? He left out the part where he did twenty guys before he got to the right one. People in this community whisper his name, when they say it, because of what he got up to during the war. Ethnic cleansing, systematic rape, targeted assassinations. The burn scars he's got? He could get surgery, get a new face – I mean, we're in L.A. for God's sake. But he won't do it, because it scares the hell out of anyone who meets him. He likes it. That's the kind of man you're dealing with here."

"Why tell me all of this?"

"I thought I should warn you."

"About what?"

Harper looked away. "Your friend Tilly. She's not safe. Ovian's guys are watching her. I heard him give the order. Once your business with him is done, he might decide she's a loose end. And that's if you get him what he wants. If you don't..."

Lawlor felt a hollow in his guts. "Tilly can take care of herself. What about me? Will I be a loose end?"

"If you can't get a name out of Fermin, definitely."

"And if I do?"

A shrug. "He's not exactly predictable."

"Great." Lawlor glared at him. "So what? We're pals now? What do you want from me?"

"I was hoping you might give me a way to contact your pals back in Belfast. Have them turn over a stone or two. See what crawls out. See if I can't get myself off the hook."

"This is in the event your boss decides I'm surplus to requirements and puts a bullet in my head?" Lawlor laughed. "Jesus, man, but you've some balls on you."

Harper looked at the ground.

"Why the hell do you want to go back there anyway?"

Harper frowned. "Because it's my home. And my ma's there. She's got cancer. Lungs. She could last a while, right enough, but there's no one to look after her but Patsy, and he's next to useless."

"So bring them over here. I'm always hearing how America has the best healthcare in the world."

"They won't leave. And even if they did, that'd be a red rag to the spooks to come after me. MI5, FBI, all the rest of them. They'd love to cross me off their lists."

Lawlor stared at him in the gloom of the hallway. "But you're not on their lists."

"Aye right." Harper laughed. "I've been on page one of the lot of them for twenty years now. It's why I have my wee pink palace up the coast and why I hardly ever leave it."

"You went to dinner in Santa Monica the other week."

"I'm not a hermit. I can go to the cinema or the theater or a busy restaurant. So long as I stick to places where there's a low likelihood of law enforcement looking about, I'm okay."

"Well, you don't have to worry. You're not on anyone's list anymore. Not on the Interpol Red Notice. Not on the FBI's Most Wanted. Not even on the NCA."

"Since when?"

"Since the other day. Look for yourself."

Harper pulled out his phone and began tapping. "Jesus." His face was luminous in the half-light. There was a half-smile on his face. "Well I never."

Then he scowled. "None of that'll stop me from getting lifted back in Belfast though, will it? I bet I'm still on their bloody list."

"I'd say you were."

They stood for a moment in the stairwell, Harper tapping at his phone. Sounds from the kitchen filtered up the stairs.

"What exactly do you do for Ovian," Lawlor asked.

"I help him steal."

"Steal what?"

Harper gave him a sly look. "Information, mostly. Property records, bank transactions. Pretty mundane stuff, but put it all together the right way and it can be dynamite."

"You're talking about bribery."

"I'm talking about leverage."

Lawlor chewed that over. "You're pretty valuable to Ovian, aren't you?"

152

"I make sure I am. I'd be dead otherwise."

"He seemed happy enough with the idea of me shooting you earlier."

Harper shrugged. "He's a gambler. And he bet the right way, didn't he?"

A door opened below them.

"Rehan!" A woman's voice. "Dinner is ready."

"Down in a sec, love," Harper answered.

"Was that your wife earlier, brought in the food?" Lawlor asked.

"Seda, aye." He grimaced. "Speaking of leverage,"

"I don't know what you expect me to do for you," Lawlor said. "I'm not a miracle worker. And I'm not a copper any more. Even if I told the chief constable it wasn't you, that wouldn't be enough to get you off the hook. They'd need solid proof it was McEwan and not you."

"A confession."

"That's what it would take, yes. And you don't have anything close to that."

"What if I could deliver him, and you could get the confession out of him?"

"You said you didn't know where he is."

"Well, it's hard to be a hundred percent certain when you're only on the Internet." He smiled slightly. "But if I did get you a confirmed address, maybe you could pay him a wee visit..."

Lawlor shook his head. "Don't even think about it. Like I say. I'm not a copper anymore. If I even touched him I'd be poisoning the tree. You'd need to get him in a room with a couple of real police."

"Like your pal Róisín."

Lawlor tensed, and he felt the heat in his face. "What about her?"

"Relax." Harper held his hands up. "I just know you're mates. And that she's quite the sudoku fan. And a good Catholic girl."

"You hacked her."

Harper shrugged.

"I warn you. Leave her out of this." Lawlor's voice was cold.

"I'm just saying. She's the one you'll work with on this, right? I mean, when you get back."

Lawlor stared, and Harper shrank away. "I'm just saying. I need your help to get back home. And I know things. If you leave me and I go down, I'm not going down alone."

"I don't know what you're talking about, Harper." Lawlor crowded him against the railing. He jabbed his finger into Harper's chest. "But you stay the fuck away."

27

The water dispenser in the ACC's outer office made a sound like Poseidon belching. Róisín felt eyes on her, Kilpatrick's assistant measuring her up as she listened to the phone. Her name was Annabelle. She was a doe-eyed woman in her late twenties, all short skirt and low-cut top, like she'd just stepped out of an eighties music video. She put the phone down carefully and looked at Róisín through her lashes. "You can go in now."

Kilpatrick was sitting behind his desk. It had nothing on it, apart from a phone. "Anything from Lawlor?"

It was their new routine. Róisín reported to him every morning before work, and let him know if there had been any progress in locating Lawlor. Which there had not been, of course. Lawlor did not want to be found, and Róisín didn't want to find him.

"Nothing, sir."

The last several times she had made this fruitless report, Kilpatrick had dismissed her with a wave. Today he nodded to a chair.

Róisín sat, her insides feeling like a plastic sauce bottle being squeezed. She assumed they were up on her phones. Work, home, mobile. Her internet, too. Everyone in the family, most likely. A waste of time. And money. She wondered if Kilpatrick had thought to put anyone in the post office.

He took a thin buff file from a drawer and placed it carefully in the exact center of his desk. "You told me Lawlor didn't talk much about his past. Did that include his childhood?"

"He didn't talk much about that either," she said. "He said once he was from near Portadown. His parents sent him to boarding school. Campbell, I think. Then he went into the Army."

Kilpatrick shook his head. "I'm sorry, Róisín." But his lips had twisted into a hint of a smile.

She stared at him, a hole opening up inside her. It was the same feeling she had, two years into her marriage, when Dennis had confessed about his 'wee habit'. "What?"

"He's from Lurgan, originally. His father ran a tractor dealership. Quite successful. Both parents were killed in a boating accident on Lough Erne. There was a collision. Lawlor was ashore with some friends of the family. He watched it happen."

"How old was he?"

"Six."

Her compassion and her sense of betrayal were tying knots inside her. She fought to keep her voice level. "So what happened to him?"

"Both parents were only children. There were grandparents on the father's side, but they were already in a home. Some cousins, but no one would take him. He became a ward of the state. He was fostered for a while, but nothing took. In the end, social services put him in care."

Róisín felt panic rise up inside her, squeezing her chest and

156

closing her throat. "Where?"

Kilpatrick placed a palm lightly, carefully on the closed file. His eyes were like marbles. "Kincora."

She had wrapped her arms around herself, and now she held herself tight, the way she'd held women who'd been beaten or raped. The betrayal was a shock. But, just like when Dennis had told her how many thousands of pounds he'd lost on the horses or the cards, or whatever, there was another feeling with it; the sense that she already knew. There had been signs with Dennis: the way he was so controlling about money, and secretive about what he did with his time. She'd felt it from the very beginning, but she'd just ignored it, let work and life and the kid and the booze and the pain and finally the running wash the feeling away.

It was the same with Lawlor. She wasn't lying when she told Kilpatrick that Lawlor had rarely talked about himself. She had done most of the talking. She had made a lot of assumptions. They'd been in East Belfast one day, and she'd asked where he'd been to school, and he'd made a vague gesture, and said something like, 'I was a boarder in a place around here.' She'd assumed he was talking about Campbell College, it being the only boarding school in the area. But he'd been talking about another place entirely. A place where kids did board, and were schooled. But not a boarding school in the sense that people usually meant when they put those two words together.

Kincora. An orphanage. Where dozens, possibly hundreds of kids had been lent out for systematic sexual abuse by the wealthy and powerful in the seventies. Right when Lawlor would have been there.

"Here." Kilpatrick was standing in front of her. Somehow

he had left the office and returned without her registering it. There was a mug in his hand. "Two sugars, right?"

The tea scalded her mouth.

"Bit of a shock, I should imagine," he said, eyes off to the side.

"A bit."

"There are also a few things about his military career that he wouldn't have told you."

She said nothing. Her jaw ached. Her tongue was pressed against the raw skin on the roof of her mouth.

"Lawlor left the home when he was sixteen." He was back behind his desk now. "Joined the Army as a junior leader. Did very well. Transferred into Intelligence. Specialized in interrogation. Spent time with 14 Company, with MI5 and SIS. He worked all over. Here, the Mediterranean, South and Central America. Africa. The Gulf. It's a long list." He looked up. "Did he ever talk about any of that?"

"I told you already." She had to force the words out. "No."

"You should think very carefully about that." Kilpatrick closed the file. "Because I'm not going to be the only one asking you. Lawlor is a government servant. Has been for more than thirty years. Because of the nature of his work, his security clearances go all the way to the top. And because he has continually been employed by the Crown in some respect, those clearances have never lapsed or been revoked. Add to that the level of access he has enjoyed because of his work here, and you can understand why I'm under pressure to locate him."

She nodded. She was numb.

Kilpatrick folded his hands together. "We have a window, Róisín, but that window is closing. If he comes in now, if he gives a full account of what he's been up to and why, then all will be forgiven. We'll call it a holiday and be done with it. But if he stays out there, if we don't hear from him, we're going to have to assume the worst."

"The worst?" Her face was hot.

Kilpatrick tapped a finger on the file. "This is not some low-level data entry drone we're talking about here. Lawlor had long-term access to critical information and the know-how to conceal his tracks. God knows what he might have taken over the years."

"Taken? Why would he take anything? And who would he give it to?"

"There are a range of possibilities. He might been pressured. Someone threatening to expose his past. Or he may have been trading."

"Trading for what?"

"Information on Rab Harper."

She opened her mouth to protest. Then closed it again.

"It's no secret, Róisín," Kilpatrick said. "We all know he's had lines in the water since day one. What if he hooked a source? Someone in the Republican community, maybe, who worked with the Russians or the Arabs in the old days. Someone who wanted quid pro quo."

"I don't believe it. He'd never sell us out. Not even for Harper. There's no way."

"Maybe. But this is about more than us. Lawlor was a Grade One systems coordinator. That means he had high-level access to government databases, including GCHQ. His clearances there were higher than the Chief Constable's."

"So you think he's gone Wiki Leaks? Jesus!" She could feel the heat in her face. She knew she'd have two red spots high on her cheekbones. "That's bollocks, sir. You know it as well as I do."

"I don't know anything of the kind, Detective Chief Inspector. I have no idea where Lawlor is, or what he's up to." The marble eyes stared. "Do you?"

The question hung between them. The urge to spit out what she knew was overwhelming. She felt hot and cold at the same time. She looked down at her mug. It was half empty. But the tea was cool enough to drink now. She took a good swallow.

"No sir," she said. "I don't."

She stood up and put the wet mug on his desk. Hopefully it would leave a ring.

28

It was a long walk from Kilpatrick's office to the back of the building where her unit was located, but Róisín still took her time walking down the passageway between the cubicle farms.

The idea that Lawlor was trading secrets was rubbish. She wondered whether all the panic had something to do with Kincora. The boys' home had come up in an investigation into sexual abuses by several prominent people. Maybe Lawlor had seen something back then, or someone. A policeman or a politician, perhaps. Someone junior then, who would be very senior now.

Her team occupied a seven-cubicle module at the far end of the second floor of the headquarters building. She was proud of the fact that hers was the only operational team in the building with more women on staff than men. She was also proud of the fact that her team had the lowest turnover and highest attendance record in the headquarters.

Sean Grady was her star. He was also the only civilian on the team. So she cut him a degree of slack in certain areas. Like his dress. And his working hours. And his workspace. He had built a wall of six monitors on one side of his cube, like a City stock trader. The other side was covered in ostentatious pictures of drag queens and boy bands. A green and white Celtic FC scarf hung down one corner and there was a large plastic statue of the Madonna in the other. Róisín knew Sean was a classic soul fan and hated football, and only went to Mass with his mother at Christmas and Easter. But he took great delight in trolling some of his colleagues.

"I'm here, I'm here." Grady was hurrying towards her. He wore a tight blue turtleneck sweater that covered up his tattoos, and a pleather bomber jacket. And a frown.

"What?" She softened her tone. "Sorry. It was a weird weekend."

"I've something weird for you. Check this out." He held up two sheets of paper. The top one was a printout of a Sudoku super grid, six boxes, with numbers scattered across the squares. Some of the numbers were printed, others written in Grady's scrawl.

"I don't have time for games, Sean."

"That's why you need to see these. Look, these puzzles are bullshit." He separated the sheets. "Second, it's a fax. When was the last time anyone sent a fax? I mean, it's fax to email, but still. Talk about the dark ages."

She rolled her eyes. "I've no time for this, Sean."

"Seriously." He thrust it at her. "Look at it."

She scanned the page. She saw immediately what Grady meant. Someone who didn't play Sudoku might think they were perfectly normal, but the grids all had duplicate numbers, making them impossible to complete.

"Who sent this?"

Grady pointed to a line on the top sheet. Róisín Mackey. And a number she didn't recognize.

She felt a hollow sensation. She pointed Grady to an empty

conference room. Something told her to check the phone had been hung up properly.

Grady slid into a chair. "I figured it was bollocks. Fax to email? You?"

"So why the hell did you even open it?"

He waved his hand. "Ach yes, normally I'd just trash it. But it was sent to my gamer address, which made it a wee bit special."

"Like, a Steam account or something?"

"No, it's an old MSN address that I use for all the games I sign up for. And because I know you weren't even aware of that address, and yet had apparently somehow contacted it, I thought it was worth a wee look."

"Please tell me you didn't do that at home."

"Do I look like I came up the Lagan in a bubble? I went down the Youth Center and opened it there."

"Sean!"

"Ah, no bother. The fella who runs the place sicks an industrial-strength antivirus on their machines every night. He doesn't want some inspector from the council coming in and seeing what the lads are looking at during the day, if you know what I mean. The AV scrubs 'em clean as a whistle."

"And how did he lay his hands on a program like that, I wonder."

Grady grinned. "Friends in the lowest places."

She separated the sheets of paper and studied them. The first page was a fax cover sheet. It was a generic form, with the word FAX in capitals and an address box that took up the top quarter of the page. All the fields in the box were blank. The second page was the puzzles.

She frowned. "I've never done fax to email. What format

does it come in? Is there an attachment?"

"PDF. No text in the body of the email."

"Anything in the subject line?"

"Let's play, with an exclamation point."

"And the email was clean otherwise?"

"As my Auntie Grainne's diaphragm." He waggled an eyebrow. "She's a nun."

"For God's sake, Sean."

"Aye." He chuckled. "Exactly."

She stared at the grid. She clicked her fingers. "Give me a pen."

He produced a Bic biro with a ragged end. She used the empty space on the cover sheet to write down the numbers 1 to 26, then wrote the letters of the alphabet under them."

"Don't bother." Grady leaned back and stretched in his chair. "I ran A1Z26 on it myself. Nothing."

Along the bottom of the cover sheet was a tiny line of numbers and letters. 07/11/2015 0010110000011 MOTT OSDG SFGL GNTT FPSD BGBF GPKH 900011000.

Róisín pointed. "Seven groups of four letters."

Grady slid forward onto the edge of his seat. "Transposition cipher? You need a seven letter key."

She nodded. "You see any words in this combination?"

"Just the one." He pointed at the string of letters. "Motto."

"Right. And then this." She drew a circle around the next six letters.

"SDGSFG?" Grady rubbed his upper lip. "I don't know..."

"St Dominic's Grammar School for Girls."

"If you say so. But that's still only six letters."

She wrote in capitals on the cover sheet.

"Veritas?" he asked. "How do you get that?"

"It means truth." She was writing numbers under the letters now.

"Yeah, I'm not completely uneducated. But why veritas?"

"Veritas is the school motto for St Dominic's."

He was staring at her. "It's a Catholic school."

"What?" She raised an eyebrow. "Did the name Róisín Mackey not give it away?"

He shrugged. "You never know, these days."

"Well, now you do."

She turned back to the paper, hiding her smile. She had made a grid of the seven groups of letters. Now she wrote them out again, in a long string, and in a different order. JOHNGROGAN NEWPORTGOQUIETLYAL.

"John Grogan. Newport. Go quietly. Al." Grady was on his feet now, his awkwardness forgotten. "Who's Al? Or is it A.L.?"

She glanced out into the office. But there were just the lines of cubicle walls, the tops of heads bent over keyboards. Nothing out of the ordinary.

She turned to him. "Can I trust you, Sean?"

"Well sure you can, Inspector Mackey." He was smirking. "Now I know which side you play for."

She stared at him until the grin slid off his face.

"What?" he said.

"I need you to do some digging." She held out the paper. "But I need you to do it through back channels."

He looked uncertain. "Okay."

"And I need you to do it from home."

29

The two SUVs pulled up to the side of the empty street. There were four men in each vehicle. They wore dark clothes and carried short-barreled automatic weapons. One of them handed Lawlor a black ski mask, and he pulled it over his head, smiling to himself at the irony.

It took nearly half an hour to climb the hill. The ground was tussocked and uneven, dotted with shrubs and small trees. Lawlor was breathing hard and sweating by the time he reached the hedgerow at the top.

The hedge had already been prepared, the branches cut and the ground around the roots loosened some time before. The team leader, a gym-sculpted giant named Darius, pulled the foliage to the side, and his men moved through the gap and spread out. A groomed stretch of lawn ran thirty yards from the back of a wide, two-story house. Upstairs, all the lights were out. Downstairs, there was a wide picture window that looked into a kitchen, where Lawlor could see the heads of two men sitting at a table.

The house belonged to Fermin's mistress, and had been under surveillance by Ovian's men for months. Fermin was a careful man. He varied his routine constantly. The only exception was a bi-weekly visit here. Every second Monday, the mistress got a two-day break from her job as a shift supervisor at a shipping center. Fermin took a roundabout route, traveled with four men and varied his time of arrival and departure, but he always stayed the night.

Two men ran across the lawn. One ran a knife up the join between the two sliding doors and slipped inside. Lawlor found himself counting seconds, holding his breath. Just over three minutes passed, and one of the men reappeared in the doorway. He signaled, and Darius wrapped an arm around Lawlor's shoulder and pulled him close.

"Okay, Irishman." He smelled of fried onions. "Let's see what you can do."

The thick carpeting on the floor of the living room and the hallway deadened the sound of the men moving through the house. Passing the kitchen, Lawlor smelled cigarettes and stale coffee. The two sentries had been gagged and tied to their chairs with tape. One of them was unconscious, his chin on his chest. The other was mesmerized by the silenced machine pistol pointing at his face, and the masked gunman behind it.

Darius walked carefully up the stairs. He carried a Glock 19 with a tactical flashlight mounted below the barrel. He had been in the house several times over the months since they had discovered the vulnerability. He had slipped in during the day, posing as a cable technician while Fermin's mistress was at work. He had prepared the route in, cutting the hedge and breaking the catch on the sliding door. And he had walked up the stairs, over and over, to see which ones creaked.

Lawlor followed him, pouring with sweat, the blood loud in his ears. He had forgotten the intense strain, mental and physical that came with moving soundlessly through a house.

He moved carefully, placing his feet in the depressions in the carpet pile left by the leader's boots. A third man moved behind.

They reached the landing and stopped for a moment. Moonlight spilled through the open door of an empty room on their right, illuminating the closed door of the master bedroom.

Darius held up three fingers, then pointed at the closed door. The man behind Lawlor took hold of the handle. He turned it slowly and eased the door open.

The door made no sound, but Fermin came awake as soon as it opened. He was fumbling for the phone on the bedside table when the Darius reached him. He shoved his gun into Fermin's cheek, forcing his head back on the pillow.

There was no need for torchlight. The curtains were open, and the full moon made it as light as day. The other gunman had moved fast around the bed to cover Fermin's mistress. She was still asleep, on her side, covered by a sheet, a duvet pushed into a heap at the end of the bed.

Darius used his free hand to unplug the bedside light and take Fermin's phone. He pushed the muzzle of the gun into Fermin's cheek and ran his hand under the pillow.

"Wake up your whore."

Lawlor felt a stab of irritation. The front door to the house was double-locked and reinforced with a sheet of steel. The windows were all triple-glazed. But that wasn't the problem. The problem was that they weren't supposed to make any noise, at all. They were supposed to be like wraiths, coming and going without a sound.

Darius tapped the muzzle of his gun on Fermin's forehead. "Wake her. Quietly."

Fermin sneered. He nudged the woman. "Gabriela. Despiér-

168

tate."

She woke up slowly at first, and then all at once, eyes open wide and the start of a scream in her throat when she registered the man in the mask and the gun in his hand. She tried to sit up, but the gunman lunged forward and she shrank back, moaning. Fermin was gripping her arm, murmuring to calm her.

She lay quiet, blinking rapidly, her breath coming fast. Fermin put his arm over her chest and held her there.

Darius called out an order. Two men hurried up the stairs and into the empty bedroom. There was a crumpling sound, and then something tearing. Fermin turned his head.

Darius said, "They are getting your room ready." There was a grin in his voice. "We have some questions for you."

Lawlor's irritation bloomed into anger. He had explained the need to have Fermin off-balance and disoriented, and have him placed in an environment that had been carefully prepared to deliver maximum shock. There was no other way that Lawlor knew of making an interrogation both short and bloodless.

Silence was key. Fermin and his mistress were to be separated. The mistress sedated; Fermin stripped, hooded and gagged. Meanwhile, half the team would work to prepare the spare room. Windows blacked out. Plastic sheeting on the walls and the floor. A chair. A table. A tray of surgical instruments. The air conditioning turned up high.

Fermin was to be brought into the room. Tied naked and shivering to the chair. Then Lawlor would enter, wearing white protective overalls, a hood, mask and gloves. He would show Fermin the instruments, one by one. An inquisitor in a scene-of-crime suit. Then he would remove Fermin's gag. And Fermin would tell him everything.

But Darius was blowing it. The shouted order, the taunts, it was all working in Fermin's favor, giving him information, letting him know he was dealing with human beings, and not faceless, emotionless machines who could not be negotiated with.

Fermin seemed to shrink back slightly from the gun pointed at him. Then he spat in Darius' face. Darius recoiled and Fermin reared up, jabbing at Darius' throat with one hand, batting the gun away with the other. Darius punched Fermin in the face, driving his head back onto the pillow.

The other gunman glanced across, and Fermin's mistress saw her chance. She jackknifed under the sheet and drove both of her heels into the gunman's chest. The Glock went spinning across the room, but the gunman ignored it, and pulled a knife from his belt. It was a six-inch blade, painted black. Fermin's mistress wasn't impressed. She stood up on the bed and kicked the sheet away. Her naked body looked luminous in the moonlight. The man with the knife laughed and said something in Armenian.

"Don't," Lawlor said. The gunman ignored him and climbed up onto the bed, the knife held in front of him. Fermin's mistress shifted her feet so that she was side-on to the man, her weight on her back leg. The gunman took a step towards her and she kicked her front leg at his face. He wobbled on the uneven surface of the mattress, lifting his knife hand to parry, and her foot hit his forearm.

The knife spun in the air, the heavy blade pulling it downwards. Point down. Directly between Fermin's thighs.

Fermin sucked in breath. The sheet below his groin bloomed scarlet. Darius grabbed the knife and stepped back, keeping his gun pointed at Fermin's face. Lawlor shoved him out of the way and pulled back the sheet. Fermin was naked. The cut on the inside of his right thigh didn't look like much, except that blood was pumping out of it like water from a punctured fire hose. The bed was already soaked.

Lawlor jammed his fist into the fold of Fermin's groin, leaning all his weight on what he hoped was the point where the femoral artery passed over Fermin's hip bone. Behind him, Fermin's mistress was screaming. And then she was silent.

"Secure him," Lawlor ordered, and Darius took two zip ties from his belt, trussing Fermin's arms to the bedstead.

Fermin was breathing hard, staring at the cut in his leg. The blood flow had dropped to a trickle. His breath was stale. "Is it bad?"

"Yes, it's bad. I think it cut your femoral artery. But we can deal with it, if we get you to a hospital."

His eyes narrowed. "You're the Irishman."

"Am I?"

A half smile. "I had a lot of guys looking for you."

"It wasn't the welcome I expected. Who gave the order?"

The smile widened. "I can't tell you that."

"You're really saying that the guy who's literally got your life in his hands. If I take my hand away, that'll be that."

"So do it, Irishman."

Lawlor was right on top of him, all his weight on his fist, his free hand supporting him on the bed. In the moonlight, Fermin's eyes shone, as though they had been chromed. Lawlor held his gaze for a moment. Then he took his hand away.

Blood spurted across the bed. Fermin's eyes were wide.

"Like I say. Your life in my hands." Lawlor leaned as close as a lover, his fingers warm with Fermin's blood, poised over the cut on his thigh. "Now, please. Tell me what I want to know."

30

Ovian paced the floor. His face was white, the skin stretched tight across his nose and cheekbones, as though his skull had swollen. He wore a white shirt and the same suit, as though he had not been to sleep.

Darius stood beside the door. He had given his report, and eased backwards until his back was pressed against the wall and he was as far away from Ovian as it was possible to be, while remaining in the same room.

"My orders were that if anything went wrong, everyone in that house was to be killed," Ovian said.

Lawlor examined his hands. There was blood in the cuticles of his fingers.

"But now Darius tells me that everything went wrong, and no one was killed. Can you explain this to me?"

"You wanted Fermin alive. I kept him breathing." Lawlor tried not to let his eyes drop to the gun under Ovian's arm. "The price was letting everyone else live."

"I wanted Fermin talking, you fool. I wanted him tied to a chair and crying for his mother. I wanted him to cough up his secret and then go back to his life without anyone in his organization knowing what happened to him."

"What about the guards? And the woman?"

"He would have dealt with them. Paid them or killed them. Either way they would have been silenced. By him, and not by us. Now the worst has happened. The woman is alive. His men are alive. Fermin is alive. And he knows who you are." He slumped back in his chair. "It would have been better if we had killed everyone."

"I could take a team back," Darius said. "We closed the house up tight. Tied them all up and stuck them with GHB. We still might be able to clean things up."

Ovian dismissed him with a wave of his hand. "Too late. It will be dawn soon. You're going to shoot two men in a car in broad daylight?"

He turned his attention back to Lawlor. "I should kill you for this."

"No, you should give me a parade and a medal. This whole thing was a disaster in the making. Break into a guy's house, knock out his people and his mistress, interrogate him, sedate him and then get out again without anyone noticing? How likely was that to happen? Especially with a bunch of monkeys like your lot."

Darius was fuming. Lawlor could see it was taking every-thing the man had not to take out his weapon and shoot Lawlor in the head. Ovian could see it, too. He flicked his hand, and Darius hurried out of the room.

Ovian paced. To the door. To his desk. And back again.

"How likely is it that Fermin will survive?"

"He lost a lot of blood. He might make it, if they diagnosed him correctly. If they treated him correctly. If he's not a rare blood type. If there are no complications."

"So, maybe."

"Maybe."

Ovian's cheek twitched. "You should have brought him here. I could have got him a doctor. Perhaps even more quickly than the hospital."

"Your guy said the same thing. But the way he was bleeding, he needed a whole emergency room, not just a doctor. If we'd brought him back here, he would have died for sure."

Ovian was staring at him. Or, more precisely, through him. Lawlor could almost hear the gears turning in his head as he weighed all of his options, and arrived at his next decision.

"Perhaps you are right. Fermin alive is better than Fermin dead. Perhaps. But you are no use to me."

"We made a deal."

"On which you failed to deliver. Fermin was supposed to wake up a broken man. A puppet. Instead, if he wakes up at all, he will be enraged. He will want his revenge."

"He might want it, but he won't take it. Just like you won't kill me."

"And why is that?"

"Because, in the end, he told me. He told me what, and he told me when, and he told me who."

Ovian's eyes glittered. "And did he tell you where?"

"Yes," Lawlor nodded. "He did."

31

The SUV inched along the 101 freeway. Lawlor sat alone in the back, watching the traffic, half an eye on the head of the driver as he thought back to what had happened in Fermin's mistress' house.

Ovian knew that Fermin had been feeding information about the Armenians' business dealings into the federal system. What he didn't know was the identity of Fermin's contact in the federal headquarters in Westwood. There was a code name, Pullman. But Ovian wanted the real name, to make his own deal. Lawlor's job was to find out who Pullman really was.

It had all gone wrong, until it had gone right. Watching Fermin's expression change, Lawlor had known what he was feeling. The unnerving calm that comes with rapid blood loss, the cooling sensation, the fogginess rolling over him, like a mist over hills in the evening as his blood pressure dropped. He had seen Fermin's eyes flicker and his lips move, and he had leaned forward.

"Federales." Fermin's voice was barely a whisper. "They paid me a hundred grand to put a bullet in you, man."

"FBI?"

"FBI. DEA. I don't know." He gave a slight shrug.

"Who gave you the order? Pullman?"

"Yeah. Pullman."

"Who's Pullman?"

Fermin closed his eyes. Lawlor had eased off, watching the blood seep over Fermin's thigh, slower this time, like water over a slab of stone.

"I can stop the bleeding any time I like. But I need a name."

Fermin shuddered, panic in his eyes. "Kawasaki. Billy Kawasaki."

"That's good." Lawlor bore back down, squeezing the artery shut again. "Where can I find him?"

Fermin blinked, his eyes unfocused. "Valeria."

Lawlor had glanced at Fermin's mistress. She was unconscious, but breathing.

"She's fine." He leaned on the wound. "Where can I find Kawasaki?"

Fermin's eyes fluttered. "Mulholland."

"And he's the one you've been passing information to? About Ovian?"

"Asi es, ese." Fermin's voice had sounded like leaves rustling. "Pullman's the man."

Ovian's government contact had run the names Billy, Kawasaki and Pullman through the federal database and come up with nothing. Google spat out a restaurant called Kawasaki on Mulholland Drive in the Hollywood hills. Ovian gave Lawlor instructions: confirm Kawasaki was Pullman. Pass on the terms of a deal. And leave.

"We still have eyes on Miss Tran," he said. "In case you decide not to return."

The driver took a road that wound up like a long, dark tunnel through the trees. Izakaya Kawasaki was nestled in a sharp bend in a road that wound along the hill crest. A long line of cars parked on the side of the road gave the place away. The driver slowed as they passed a doorway surrounded by ivy and lit by a single bulb. There was no sign, but there was a cluster of well-dressed people standing in line, checking their phones and ignoring each other.

"Fucking L.A. Always a line to eat," the driver muttered. "You want me to turn around? I'll have to find a place to park."

"Drop me. Then find a somewhere you can watch the door."

It was cool, and the air was clear. The restaurant was perched on the crest of the hills, the cities of the San Fernando valley laid out below like a technicolor blanket. The man in the front of the restaurant queue glanced up from his phone and frowned at Lawlor as he opened the door.

It was like stepping across the ocean and into a bar in Osaka. The room was divided by a long counter that ran from the door to a terrace that seemed to hang over the valley. On the left was a small kitchen and bar. Two men in blue and white chefs' tunics shuttled in a smooth rhythm between a work surface and a stove. A third man wearing a black Hanshin Tigers baseball cap was drying glasses at the bar. Stools lined the counter, and on the right several booths lined the wall. Every table was full, and all but one of the stools was taken.

The barman lifted his chin as Lawlor approached. "Drinks only at the bar, man. You wanna eat, you gotta get in line."

"Just a Sapporo, please." Lawlor sat down. When the man set a glass in front of him, he asked, "Is Billy here?"

"Who wants to know?"

"Tell him Lawlor's here to see him."

The barman put his towel down and stepped into a niche

behind the bar. When he came back he was followed by a fourth man, short and wiry, dressed in khaki shorts and a faded red-and-orange Hawaiian-style shirt.

"Lawlor." His blue eyes were a startling contrast to the walnut color of his skin. "Why would that name mean anything to me?"

"You asked Fermin to find me. Here I am."

Kawasaki was silent for a moment. "I heard something about a hit on his girlfriend's place. Is he gone?"

"Depends on who was on duty at the knife and gun club."

"USC?" A hint of a smile. "You did him a favor."

"He might not see it that way, if he makes it."

"So what do you want?"

"I want to know why you asked him to arrange a reception for me, Pullman."

If Kawasaki was surprised, he didn't show it.

"And what if I don't feel like telling you?" he said.

There was a commotion behind him, as a large party got up to leave. The five people at the bar went to take their seats in the restaurant, and Lawlor found himself alone at the counter. Kawasaki hadn't moved.

"You don't look like FBI," Lawlor said.

"No?"

No. Something a shade or two darker. Lawlor could see it in his eyes. The wary, patient stare. The calm. Kawasaki stood loose and steady, unmoved by the noise of the restaurant swirling around him.

"You're a fixer," Lawlor said.

"That's one word for it."

"Who pays you?"

Kawasaki shook his head.

"How much?" Lawlor asked.

"More than you could ever afford."

"And how would you know that?"

A grin. "I have an eminent source."

"What if I could offer you something else?"

"Like my life, I suppose."

"Why not?"

"You're gonna shoot me down in my own place? Maybe have one of Ovian's guys put an RPG through the window? Kill us all?"

"Ovian?"

"Don't play, Lawlor. You didn't get to Fermin on your own. Ovian's his biggest competitor. Or partner, depending on what day it is. He's the only one with the resources to get you here this quick. And with the muscle to back you up. Assuming you do have backup and didn't come here with just your dick in your hand."

"I'm not that stupid."

"Maybe." Kawasaki gave him a searching look. "But you are that crazy. I've seen your file. You did some wild shit back in the day."

"Another life, entirely."

"Oh yeah? And just how did you manage to get my name out of Fermin?"

Lawlor said nothing.

Kawasaki nodded. "Guys like us don't lose our edge, not really. Rub off the rust and there's still a blade underneath."

An image flashed in Lawlor's mind. Jerry Fyffe at the bar at Aldergrove, elbow to elbow with the rest of the team after a snatch op. All pumped with adrenaline, wide grins and wide eyes, the bar cluttered with bottles and glasses and nine-millimeter Brownings.

"Ovian wants to make a deal," he said.

"And why would I want to do business with him?"

"Because if you don't, he'll cut you off. He'll tell everyone who you are and what you do. You'll be out of business in a heartbeat. And dead in a ditch a week after that."

Kawasaki chewed that one over for a few seconds. "So what do you suggest?"

"Ovian wants the same deal Fermin got. He feeds you intelligence on his competitors. You push it up the chain. He takes advantage of any ensuing chaos."

"I don't have any leverage against Ovian. And I don't do business with anyone I can't squeeze, if I need to."

"Sounds like you're in a pinch, then."

Kawasaki grinned. "I can always just disappear. It wouldn't be the first time."

Lawlor nodded. His mind was racing. He didn't care about Ovian's deal. As for the threat against Tilly, Lawlor was confident she could look after herself. But he wasn't going to leave Kawasaki's restaurant without the name of the man who had pulled all the strings on this operation, who had recruited Jerry Fyffe and lured Lawlor across an ocean and a continent to be killed.

"What if I could give you some leverage."

"Like what?"

"Ovian told me he has a guy in the FBI. I bet he has people in the local cops."

"I'm sure he does. But I don't know who they are."

"What about Harper?"

Kawasaki's face didn't change. "Who?"

"Robert Harper. He's a bomb-maker. Former IRA. Very

much a wanted man back in the UK. He's working for Ovian. Not bombs anymore: he's a computer guy now, but like you say, rub the rust off him..."

"I don't know him."

"He's got an Armenian name now. He married into Ovian's family in Armenia while he was on the run. If his name got to the right federal agencies, they'd be crawling all over Ovian in a minute."

"So he'll kill him."

"I don't think so. Ovian does his best to make it look like there's just a business and family connection, but I'm pretty sure Harper has something on him."

Kawasaki looked thoughtful. "There was some talk about an Armenian hacker a couple of years ago. They said he was the guy who stole an NSA backdoor into a Microsoft program."

"Wheelspin. I remember."

"Whoever it was made a lot of money holding a lot of people for ransom. You think it could be your guy?"

"Maybe."

Kawasaki grunted. "If it is him, every federal agency in the country will want a piece. And Ovian would definitely not want to attract that kind of attention."

They watched each other for a while.

"Now I know about this Harper dude, I could just pick up the phone and make this deal without you," Kawasaki said.

"You don't know his new name."

"You've given me enough to go on. I could find out who he is in less than a day."

"Maybe, maybe not. Somehow he's managed to live here in plain sight for more than ten years. He's had some help. He might not be as easy to identify as you think." He shrugged.

"But if you give me a name, I'll give you a name in return."

Kawasaki thought about it for a moment. Then he shook his head. "You seem like a good guy. But it's my reputation we're talking about here."

"You'd rather preserve your reputation than your life?"

Kawasaki laughed. "You're not gonna kill me."

"No? What about that edge you were talking about earlier?"

Kawasaki was halfway into a smile when his face froze, his eyes flicking over Lawlor's shoulder as the door swung open behind him. The smile disappeared, and someone brushed against Lawlor's arm and slipped onto the stool beside him.

He didn't need to look to know who it was. The perfume gave it away. But he looked anyway.

She winked at him, and turned her attention to Kawasaki.

"Hello Pullman," Tilly said.

Kawasaki's face was as blank as a steel door. "Do I know you?"

"Aww, after all the sweet messages you've been sending me this past week?" She leaned over towards Lawlor. "Actually, they weren't sweet at all. They were actually kind of threatening."

"That's why you flew to Santa Monica," Lawlor said.

"Well, I drove, but yeah. I needed to get out of Vegas without this asshole finding out. Don't be fooled by the aloha shirt. He is not a nice guy."

"Not when I don't get paid," Kawasaki said. "And you owe me a hundred grand."

"And I was going to pay you. Until you started shaking me down for more."

"You were late."

"And when have I not paid you before? I just needed a few

more days. It's the least you could do for me after the Iran thing."

Neither of them had raised their voices, but Lawlor could see the tension between them was attracting attention.

"Let's slow down a second," he said. "How did you even get here?"

She grinned. "Easy. I got away from those goons at the hotel. In the front door and out the back. Real basic. You remember Long, who picked you up? He followed them back to Ovian's place, and we watched until we saw you come out. Then we tailed you up here."

"And him?" Lawlor pointed at Kawasaki.

"Oh, I've known about Billy since we started doing business together. He gets stuff for me; I get stuff for him. We've never actually met, though, would you believe." She narrowed her eyes at Kawasaki. "We got along fine until he decided to sell me out to Homeland Security."

"You didn't pay me, Tran. What did you expect?"

"A little professional courtesy."

She pointed at Lawlor's beer. "You gonna drink that?"

Without waiting for an answer, she took the glass and sucked down a third of it.

"So." She took her phone out of her purse and placed it on the counter. "A hundred k plus a 20 percent late fee. Bitcoin or Tether?"

Kawasaki narrowed his eyes. "What's the catch?"

"Smart boy Billy. The catch is you call off the Homeland dogs. And you give my pal here what he wants."

"Fuck you, Tran."

"You know." Tilly looked around the crowded restaurant. "It would be a shame to watch this place burn to the ground.

I've heard Ovian kind of specializes in burning buildings. And reputations. And you're next on the list."

There was a buzzing sound. Kawasaki pulled a phone from his back pocket. Checked the screen. Gave Lawlor a blank look.

"Bad news?" Lawlor asked.

"For you." Kawasaki held up the phone. "Fermin is dead."

It was like being punched in the stomach.

Kawasaki turned about and filled a glass with water. He placed it carefully in front of Lawlor. "Shit happens, man."

Lawlor stared at the glass. He thought about the slick feeling of Fermin's blood under his fingertips. He picked up the glass and drank. His hand was steady.

"You think there's still a deal to be made with Ovian?" Kawasaki asked.

"I don't see why not."

"Tell him to come here." Kawasaki jerked his head back towards the cooks and the barman. "We'll take real good care of him."

As though on cue, one of the cooks looked up from the grill he was working. He was the opposite of Kawasaki, large, heavyset and muscled, with the wide, high cheekbones of a Pacific Islander. The sleeves of his short chef's coat were rolled up above his biceps, showing a pair of faded tattoos. His coat bulged slightly at the small of his back, giving away the gun tucked into the waistband of his shorts. The two other men were variations on the same theme. And now Lawlor was looking around the restaurant in a different way, at lines of fire and escape routes, and concealment points for heavier weapons, under the counter and behind the shelves. Even if Ovian got his men in before a meeting, sitting at tables around the restaurant, they would still be at a disadvantage.

Kawasaki's crew would be able to lay down fire into any corner of the place, and protect a withdrawal through some kind of exit out of the back.

Kawasaki smiled, watching Lawlor's quick appraisal of the ground. "Tell him we open at five, every day but Monday. Get busy around six. And no reservations." He smirked. "So if he gets here late, he'll have to stand in line with everyone else."

"I'll tell him." Lawlor waited. "And the name?"

"When I get my deal with Ovian, we trade names."

Lawlor shook his head. "I need a name now."

"Sorry buddy. No deal, no names. That's it."

"Give him the name," Tilly said. She was sitting back on her stool, her arms folded, a tight expression on her face. "Do it. Or you can forget your money, and I'll put the word out. Your name. Your address. Your everything. You won't find it so easy to run and hide after that."

"What if I shoot you in the face first?"

She smiled. "Then my file on you gets sent to a dozen addresses. And you'll never get paid again, my friend."

Her phone buzzed. She looked at the screen and her smile disappeared.

"What?"

"Ovian's coming. My guys are parked past the bottom turn on Mulholland. He just drove past. Two SUVs"

"How long?"

"Three minutes. Five, tops."

Lawlor looked at Kawasaki. "Last chance. I can get out to his guy outside and call him now. Or he and his lads storm in here spraying bullets and it all comes crashing down."

"And if that happens, you'll never get what you want." Kawasaki was calm. "So I suggest you get yourself out on the street there and stop the man. Cell coverage is for shit until you get up here, so you'll have to do it in person. Tell him he has a deal, just like we discussed. Tell him he can even come in, alone, and we can shake on it. But if even one of his crew steps in here without an invitation, it's over."

He leaned back on the counter behind him. The two men in the small kitchen had stopped work and stepped up to the bar. One was staring at Lawlor and Tilly, the other at the door. Lawlor knew if he could see through the wooden counter, he'd see a pair of automatic weapons slung under the bar, loaded and ready to go.

"And our trade?"

"You get me this deal first." Kawasaki smiled. "Then you'll get your name."

32

It was cool outside, and quiet. They stood for a moment under the eaves of the restaurant, listening. There was a light wind blowing and the pine trees that lined the road were rustling. There was no sound from the traffic in the valley below.

"You need to get out of here, Tilly," Lawlor said.

"Oh yeah?" She seemed very cool.

"I've got something to offer Ovian. You don't. He doesn't know who you really are, but by now he'll have a good idea of who you might be. There's no good reason for him to keep you alive if he catches you again."

She thought about that for a few seconds. "Are you going to be okay?"

He shrugged. "We'll see."

"How can I reach you? Counter-strike?"

Lawlor grinned. "So you did catch that. I wasn't sure, filled up with horse tranquilizer the way you were."

"Oh I heard you. I just don't know your player handle."

"What? Garylawlor, all one word?"

She sputtered. "You're kidding."

"Hiding in plain sight."

They walked out to the road and he stopped, one ear tuned

for the sound of the heavy engines of Ovian's SUVs. He turned to her, to say goodbye, but as he did so he heard a crack-thump sound, and saw Tilly's head snap back.

He dropped to the ground, not thinking, just reacting, moving back into cover on elbows and knees. A second round thumped over his head, and he rolled, driving hard off his hips into the shadow of a parked car.

Tilly was on her back, not moving, her mouth half open, what was left of her face glistening in the light from the small lamp above the restaurant door. It was an effort to look away.

Someone was screaming inside the restaurant. Lawlor lay flat on his stomach. His body was in overdrive, heart pumping, pouring sweat, but the cool, distant part of his mind was putting the brakes on his system, forcing him to think. He scanned under the car, looking for movement across the road. The bullet had hit Tilly on a downward trajectory, which put the shooter in an elevated position across the road. In one of the houses, or on a garage. He or she might know where Lawlor was, but couldn't hit him: the car body provided cover from view, and its engine block cover from fire, even from the rifle the shooter was using. But Lawlor knew he couldn't stay where he was much longer, and he knew the shooter wouldn't, either.

The ground under Lawlor's cheek began to rumble, and a moment later, two SUVs swung in front of the restaurant. At the same time, the door to the restaurant cracked open, and the brim of a Hanjin Tigers hat poked out. Lawlor got into a crouch behind the car, and when the first of Ovian's men stepped out of their vehicles, he sprinted for the door, crashing through it and sending the barman sprawling, his hat spinning across the floor.

Lawlor slammed the door closed and locked it. Inside, the restaurant felt weirdly calm. There was a man lying on the floor, his shirt drenched with blood. A woman knelt beside him, crying, while one of the chefs administered first aid. The rest of the customers were packed onto the back balcony of the restaurant, a waiter ushering them down a rickety wooden staircase onto the hillside below.

Kawasaki was standing in the doorway to the terrace, his arms wide, palms down, like he was calming a small herd of cattle.

"I guess I should have put steel plates in the wall," he said. "What do we have?"

"Two cars, boss." The barman picked up his hat and put it on backwards. "Ten guys."

Kawasaki was still for a second. Then he slid the terrace door closed, walked behind the bar and took out a pair of Heckler-Koch machine pistols from a cabinet. He handed one to the barman. He nodded to Lawlor.

"Cops and ambulance are on their way." He slapped his hand on the bar. "If Ovian's coming in here, you'll be better off on my side of this."

"I'm not sure I want to be anywhere near you at all."

"Your funeral."

A rattling sound came from the door.

"Three, two, one," Kawasaki counted, and the door burst open, parts of the lock skittering across the floor like shrapnel.

"Surimasen!" Kawasaki called out, and fired a three round burst into the wall beside the door. He had a huge grin on his face. At the other end of the counter, the barman was on one knee, covering the door from the side. Lawlor stepped back into the corner of the room, where the bar met the outer wall.

190

There was a pause. A fast conversation outside in a language Lawlor didn't understand.

"Don't shoot," someone called out.

Kawasaki smirked. "I won't if you won't."

"Okay, okay." A pause. "One man coming in. No weapons."

"No problem, then." Kawasaki pulled his weapon tighter into his shoulder and took the pressure up on the trigger. Lawlor pushed himself as far back into the corner as he could.

A man appeared. His hands came first, fingertips together as he swept the noren curtain open in an almost delicate motion. He stepped inside, head bowed, his hands high and wide, palms out. He was dressed all in black, shaved head, jump boots. One of the men who had guarded the door back at Fermin's house.

"Cops are ten minutes out, buddy," Kawasaki said. "Better make this quick."

"Two minutes." The man said. He held his hand out towards the door, like an introduction. "Just to talk."

"Come on, then."

The man stepped back and nodded, and Ovian came into the room. White shirt, gray suit, a slight bow of his head, as though he was just coming for dinner. He glanced around the room, his gaze resting briefly on the wounded man, who was sitting up now, his back against the wall of the terrace. "What happened here?"

"Like you don't know."

Ovian shook his head. "This has nothing to do with me."

"Whatever." Kawasaki jerked the machine pistol for emphasis. "Say what you've come to say and fuck off."

Ovian looked pained. "We can at least be civil, can we not?"

"There's nothing civil about putting a bullet through my

wall."

"As I said. Not me. I just came to do business."

Kawasaki jerked his head at Lawlor. "I thought that's what he was here for."

"I'm glad to hear I can trust him to represent my interests." Ovian glanced out of the door as the sirens grew louder. "But I suggest we discuss the details later."

"That's probably a good idea."

A movement on the balcony caught Lawlor's eye. And then a muzzle flash. The floor-to-ceiling glass shattered, and the restaurant exploded with the staccato tattoo of automatic weapons, and the fast, heavy barking of handguns.

And then, nothing.

Lawlor leaned to the side to look into the room. Ovian was flat on his face, his bodyguard on top of him, gun out and pointing at the terrace.

"How many?" Lawlor shouted.

"One man. I think I got him."

"Is he still there?"

"Gone, I think."

Lawlor moved in a crouch along the front of the counter. The barman was lying on his back at the end of the bar, clutching his neck, his breath coming fast and shallow. Lawlor took his weapon, checked the load and inched towards the broken window of the terrace. He dropped onto his belly and wriggled to the top of the stairs. There was an M4 carbine on the landing, and a scattering of empty cartridges on the stairs. He glanced into the darkness, just long enough to convince himself the shooter was gone, and then scrambled back into the room.

The sound of sirens was deafening now. Ovian and his man were gone. Kawasaki was nowhere to be seen.

Lawlor forced himself to think. He couldn't go out the front door, and into the arms of the police. They would arrest him and lock him up and it would take a long time to get free. He couldn't go down the stairs at the back, in case the shooter - or shooters - were waiting for him.

He crawled backwards into the niche behind the bar.

"LAPD! Coming in!"

It was a tiny office, a shelf desk with a laptop on it. A chair pushed to the side, and a carpet pulled back. A trap door wide open under the desk. A thick smear of blood on the edge.

Lawlor smiled despite himself. He knew there would be an exit of some kind. Kawasaki was the type to keep an ace up his sleeve.

He looked cautiously into the hole, half-expecting Kawasaki to be waiting for him, gun up and ready to shoot. But there was nothing but blackness. He had a fair idea of what waited for him. The restaurant was cantilevered over a steep hillside. There would be a long, nervy drop into a prepared pit. Gravel, maybe. The kind of thing an ex-paratrooper might be comfortable with. Not for the first time, Lawlor wished he'd taken the jump course and got his wings when he still had the knees for it.

"LAPD!"

The cops were inside the restaurant. Lawlor wiped down his gun with the edge of his shirt and tossed it under the desk. If the cops were down there, he didn't want them catching him armed. He eased himself into the hole. His feet found a ladder and he followed it, down and down, until he could see under the platform to the lights of the valley below.

The ladder ended. He eased himself lower, reaching for the ground, but there was nothing but space. A shout came from

above him, and he let himself hang.
And then he let himself go.

33

There was a landing pit, but it was filled with sand, not gravel, and it hadn't been used or maintained in a while. Greenery had spread over its edges, and Lawlor's left foot skidded on the overgrowth as he landed. Pain stabbed his knee as he rolled onto his side. He lay in the weeds for a moment, assessing the damage, and straining his eyes in the dark.

There was no moon, and a screen of trees shut out the lights from the city below, but he could see a scar in the hillside, the path that led from the bottom of the restaurant's fire escape down to the road below. He went to stand up, and put his hand on something soft.

Kawasaki was face down in the weeds, his legs bent jump school-style, and his knees and ankles pressed tight together. But his shirt was shredded, and there was an exit wound the size of a saucer in his upper back. His body was still.

Lawlor reached into the back pocket of Kawasaki's shorts and took out his phone. He waved it in front of Kawasaki's face, and it opened to show a picture of a beach and a palm tree. He navigated to auto-lock and reset the phone to the maximum.

He got up into a crouch, ignoring the pain in his knee, and

backed up the hill until he reached one of the iron supports of the cantilevered restaurant. He scanned the terrain in front of him, the spread of open ground and the screen of trees that could hide a platoon, let alone a pair of snipers.

Except maybe there wasn't a pair. A pair would have split up, one out front, the other in the back, to make sure that Lawlor couldn't get away. But it had taken several minutes for the shooting to start on the restaurant terrace. So maybe just one sniper, two shots out front, and then displace. Round to the back of the restaurant to finish the job...

Two shots. The first dead center on Tilly. The second... He closed his eyes, playing the event back in his head. Saw again, Tilly's head snapping back. He felt his throat close and tears start in his eyes, and he thrust the images away, and forced himself to focus.

He had reacted to the instantaneous crack and thump of the shot, rather than the sight of Tilly being hit. He had fallen as she fell, and reached the ground just a fraction of a second behind her. The second round had thumped over his head while he was crawling backwards. One, maybe two seconds later.

A long time, for a professional.

Which meant there was no longer a reason to be crouched in the dark, waiting for the cops to come hustling down the hillside. He checked the phone was still unlocked, then walked left, nursing his ankle and knee, until he came to a wall of scrub, as dry as a bone, and as loud as a marching band, if he tried to push through it. He eased his way downhill beside the trees until a gap appeared and he was able to slide into the tree line and out of sight.

There was the barest trace of a path, a vague parting of

vegetation and forest debris. He followed it, ducking under tree branches and pulling brambles loose when they tugged at his shirt. When he was far enough into the trees, he took the phone out of his pocket, crouching over to minimize the light. He had closed all the apps except for a map, which showed him he was on the edge of a forested ravine that led down to the valley. He studied the map for a moment, memorizing it. Then he pushed the phone into the back pocket of his trousers.

It took his eyes a few minutes to adjust to the dark, and then he moved. After ten minutes, he reached a small clearing. He squatted at its edge, waiting for the shapes and the shadows around him to separate.

The sounds of the night filled his ears: a slight breeze stirring the trees above him. A car passing, far below, the noise of its supercharged engine filtering up the slope. A faint smell of burned wood made sense of a black smudge in the center of the clearing, and a rough ring of stones. There were dark patches of material scattered around the space. Clothes. Shopping bags. A homeless encampment, although one that didn't appear to have been occupied for a while. There were none of the usual smells: no urine, no spilled beer or liquor. It was deserted.

And then the darkness beyond the clearing seemed to shift, and a voice filtered across. "You gunna squat there all night like a frog on a lily leaf, big man?"

Lawlor felt a wave of sadness.

"Jerry Fyffe. You're not sounding too well."

A grunt. "That big bastard with the nine clipped me. I've never been shot before, can you believe it?" He shifted, and let out a wheezing sound. "It's like being buggered by Satan himself."

"How bad, would you say?"

"Dunno, mate. There's no exit wound, but my back hurts like a bastard. I think the round tumbled. Might have been a ricochet. I can feel a leak in there. Hopefully it's not my aorta."

"You can walk, though."

"Just about."

"So let me get you out of here and down to a hospital." Lawlor rocked forward, but froze when the shadow made a fast move. He knew there was a gun pointing at him, and even half dead from blood loss his old comrade would be able to put a bullet in him at that short distance.

"Easy now," he said.

The shadow moved again, and for a moment Lawlor saw his old team-mate's face in the gloom.

"It'd be easier if you kept coming at me."

Lawlor held up his hands. "Then I'm staying right here."

"Suit yourself. It's the same either way."

"How's that?"

"The job, mate. It's the job." A pause. "You're the job."

"So why didn't you slot me earlier? Don't tell me I moved too quickly."

"Moment of weakness." His cough sounded like a wet rag being slapped on a stone. "Won't happen again."

"I'm sure."

"You moved pretty quick for an old dog, I'll say that for you," Fyffe said. "They told me you were half in your grave."

"I was for a while, there. But all this running about's given me a new lease on life." He reached into his back pocket and slid out the phone, keeping it pressed to his hip, hoping the light from the screen wouldn't show. "You want to tell me who hired you, Jerry?"

"I can't."

"Why not? It's not like I'm going to tell anyone."

"No, mate. I can't tell you because I don't know. The freelance life. You know."

"I can't say I do."

"Everything's done online. Assignments over email or Signal or whatever, payments in crypto. Dead drops for the kit. No names."

"Except my name."

"Aye. Sorry about that, mate. But it's either you or my wee girl. So not much of a choice, really."

"Christ, Jerry." Lawlor thought about the photo in his email, the awkward smile on the girl's face. "When did they take her?"

"Couple of days ago. Just after I sent you that photo. They told me where Harper would be, and paid me fifty grand to take the snap and send you the email and the card. I thought that was that, but then they lifted Annabel. They told me I'd not get her back until you went down. Then they added Tran and Kawasaki to the list." He sighed. "Sorry, old son."

The image of Tilly, laughing at his gamer handle, flashed in Lawlor's mind. He squeezed his hand around the phone, letting the edges gouge his skin. He pushed the memory away.

"Don't worry about it." It was an effort to say the words. "I'd more than likely have done the same."

"Good of you to say."

They were both silent. Fyffe's breathing had a damp, labored sound to it, like someone mopping a floor.

"I'd still like to know who's behind it, Jerry."

A sigh. "Government, for sure. The emails had that

pompous air about them, you know. And the kit's a giveaway. Brand new M4. Still had the packing grease on it."

"Not stolen from an armory, then."

"Right from the factory, mate. And the rounds were in unmarked boxes. So not commercial. Whoever sent it, they aren't the kind of people you say no to."

"The same people that told you to send me a postcard, you think?"

"Oh aye. The instructions came from a different email address, but it was the same bullshit Opsec attitude, right enough."

Lawlor thought for a minute. "When you sent me those messages, Jerry. Did it cross your mind you were helping them set a trap for me?"

Silence. Then, "It was fifty grand, mate. I was strapped. What can I say?"

Lawlor twisted to the left and threw the phone. He had it clamped between thumb and forefinger, and he threw it like he was skimming a large flat stone, jerking his arm forward and snapping his wrist, aiming for the center of the shadow, hoping to hit Fyffe's face or his hand or the gun. Hoping that Fyffe's reflexes had been slowed by injury and trauma and blood loss. Hoping that a quarter-pound missile of glass and metal and electronics in the face might distract him.

He used the momentum to launch himself off his good foot, pushing him both forward and slightly to the side, to shift out of Fyffe's line of fire, and get inside his reach.

There was a bang, like having a door slammed on his ear, and then another, and another. He was moving as fast as he could, but it still felt as though he was in water, chest-deep, pushing against a current. He had a rock in his hand, somehow, and he threw it at the pale oval shape that materialized out of the trees, and then hurled himself after.

He slammed into Fyffe, shoulder first. He punched him hard in the throat with the knuckles of one hand, and scrabbled for his eyes with the other. His fingers came away wet. Fyffe was choking, sliding sideways, but somehow still on his feet and Lawlor leaned on him and turned on his side and saw Fyffe's hand was trapped in a fork in a branch, where he had wedged his gun hand to steady his aim.

He picked the gun up off the ground and squatted beside the limp body. Fyffe's breathing was shallow, a low rasp through his ruined airway. His face was a dark mess. The rock had split his nose. There was a cut above his left eye, which looked as though it might have been inflicted by a thin, hard electronic device.

Lawlor searched through his pockets. There was nothing. No ammunition, no keys, no wallet, no ID. As clean as Lawlor had expected he would be. Nothing to tell him where he should even start looking for a trail.

And that clinched it. He sat his old friend upright, his back against the tree. Something slid to the ground, and Lawlor saw the smartphone, the beach scene now pixelated and redacted behind the shattered screen

He slipped the phone into his pocket. He put the gun into Fyffe's hand.

"You take care of yourself, mate," he said, and started down the hill.

34

Róisín felt a tightness in her calves and eased off as she turned up onto the Belmont Road. She hadn't warmed up enough, but the need to get out of the office had been so intense, she hadn't given herself the time. She shouldn't be running. She should be at her desk, leading her team, but she knew after the morning she'd had, she'd more than likely be in the toilets, finding another way to let off steam.

She had run middle distance at school. She was fast. But she never competed. She sat out team trials, called in sick, or injured. And when there was no getting out of it, she always made sure she finished in the middle of the field.

The nun who coached the team had never mentioned it. She was a middle aged woman, who doubtless had seen a thing or two. Perhaps she had seen the signs on Róisín.

Her legs were warm now, and she leaned into the rise, pumping her arms as she picked up speed.

She had lied to Kilpatrick about Lawlor. Over and over. The realization shook her. She didn't think of herself as the kind of person who lied. Avoided, sure. Deflected and dissimulated, yeah, sometimes. Manipulated, okay, maybe. But outright lied? Lies and truth were black and white. You were safer with shades of gray. She had learned that early, found out what happened when you got caught in a lie. She remembered her father putting her over his knee. Squeezing her arm. The musty smell of his trousers.

Her cheeks burned.

There was a flash of red brick on her left. The hill steepened, and she squared her shoulders, straightened her back and picked up her pace. Powered over the crest of the hill.

And then down, into a narrow lane screened by trees, a dark green tunnel. Down past farmhouses and outhouses, down to the city spread out in regiments of gray slate and red brick and whitewashed pebble dash. Down to the golf club. Recovered now, strong again. She hopped the fence and ran through the club, around the greens, hoping that someone would challenge her so that she could get into his face a wee bit.

Do her career even more damage.

Jesus, God. What had she done?

She had protected a friend. A good friend. The only one who had stood with her after her divorce. The only one who never looked sidelong at her or gossiped, or had to shut up when she came into a room. The only one who listened without asking questions, and without trying to fix things.

There were tears in her eyes. She brushed them away and ran down the golf club driveway, across the road and then onto the Comber Greenway, a smooth strip of tarmac and a clear run back to HQ.

She badged her way in. Feeling good. And suddenly not so good. Parked in the front rank of the car park, in the senior officer's row, was her ex-husband's BMW. And sitting in the passenger seat, head bent over her phone, Andrea.

She was halfway to the car when Dennis emerged from the building.

"What's going on?" She was suddenly breathless. "Why's Andrea here?"

"I've been calling you." His mouth was twisted. He was chewing on the skin on the inside of his cheek.

She checked her phone. Fourteen missed calls. She groaned inside. "I turned off notifications for my run. Sorry."

"I needed you."

"Well, I needed some bloody time to myself, Dennis." Her voice snapped across the car park. One of the sentries looked up, then looked away.

"Something's come up. I need to leave Andrea with you for a couple of days."

She rocked back on her heels. "A couple of days? What's so important?"

"I have to go to London. To see a specialist."

"What for?"

He frowned. Looked at the car. "Prostate. They found something."

She felt as though someone had stuck a pin into her. "Jesus, Dennis. Cancer?"

"Not sure. That's what the specialist is for." He took out his phone and glanced at the screen.

"My God." She looked at the car. Andrea was still head down, oblivious, her thumbs moving over her own phone at lightning speed. "Why London?"

"Because that's where the best oncologists are, Róisín, for heaven's sake."

"Sorry. Yes. I'm sorry." She could feel herself winding up, like a spring under tension. "What about school?"

"I talked to her teachers. They're all revising for exams just now. She can check in by email."

"And you have to go straight away?"

"It's a really good doctor. Usually you have to wait months to see him. But he has an opening tomorrow, so I'm going to fly over tonight. I'll be back by the weekend. Friday, probably. Maybe even Thursday. I'll come and pick her up."

"Right." She was hot and sweaty, and not just because of the run. "So you mean you're going to leave her now?"

"Yes, Róisín." His voice was sharp. "She has a bag packed."

"Well you can't just leave her here, Dennis. I have work."

"Where then?" He had his hands on his hips, looming over her.

She fought down the urge to shove him back a few feet. She dug in the back pocket of her running tights, pulled out her keys. "Take her to the flat. I'll be back at five tonight."

"You want me to just drop her off?"

"She's fourteen years old, Dennis. She can be left for the day. You're going to have to trust her to be on her own sometime. You can start now."

He took the keys.

"Andrea." Róisín beckoned, and Andrea got out of the car and slouched the few feet to where Róisín stood. "Your dad's going to take you to my flat. I'll be back at five. Will you be alright?"

She brightened. "I don't have to stay here?"

"No. Best if you don't."

"Good." She scowled at the guard on the gate. "This place gives me the creeps."

Róisín hid her smile. "When Dad drops you, you go straight into the flat and lock the door. Stay there. Help yourself to whatever's in the fridge. Do not leave. I'll be calling to check in on you. Did you bring your laptop?"

"Aye."

"Yes, Mum."

She rolled her eyes. "Yes, Mum."

"Good. WiFi password is on the fridge, if you need a reminder. I'll be calling your teacher to find out what work you have to do, and I'll expect to see the fruits of your labor when I get back, okay?"

"Okay."

"Right then." She leaned forward and kissed her daughter on the forehead. "On you go. See you later."

She slouched back to the car. Róisín turned to Dennis. "Does she still have that tracking app on the phone?"

"Yes."

"Good." She turned her phone on, checked the app, flipped the notification switch on the side of the device. "I'll keep an eye on her. What time's your plane leave?"

"Two."

"Well, have a good flight. And Dennis?"

His face was tight. "What?"

"No matter what else you are, you're her dad. So I hope you're okay."

35

She watched them drive out of the front gate, then checked her own phone. She scrolled down the notifications, looking for a text or an email from Grady.

There was nothing. Which was not entirely surprising. She was used to him disappearing. But it seemed to Róisín that running down a single name, even via back channels, shouldn't take this long.

She sent a flurry of texts, then showered and dressed, and made the long trek to the back of the building. Shona Curry was sitting on her desk, legs crossed, earbuds in. She yanked them out when she saw Róisín. "Nothing from Sean, guv."

"John?"

A head shot up from behind the cubicle partition. Sergeant John McDonagh, a young, pale man, with a wedge of red hair and permanently flushed cheeks. "Ma'am."

"Anything?"

"Not a sausage. I emailed and texted him, but he's not responding."

She looked into Grady's cubicle. A screensaver of the Starship Enterprise cruised slowly across the wall of monitors. The clock on the wall said it was ten minutes to eleven.

"Give him until midday, John."

"Then what?"

"Then call his mum and send a car around to his house."

He scowled. "Yes ma'am."

As an Inspector, she was entitled to an office, but she preferred to be on the floor, like the rest of the team. Her cubicle looked a lot like Lawlor's office, she realized. It was black and gray and chrome and uncluttered. There was a pad of gray stick-it notes and a wall planner. A monitor and a keyboard. And a desk phone, with a red message warning light that was blinking at her.

Two messages, the first from a police sergeant at the station on the Stewartstown Road, asking her to call him back. The second from a Doctor Michael Rees at the Royal Victoria Hospital, making the same request.

Róisín stabbed out the doctor's number. He picked up immediately. "This is Rees."

"Detective Inspector Róisín Mackey. Returning your call."

"Ah yes. Hold on." There were hospital sounds in the background, a tannoy announcement, and then the sounds disappeared. "Sorry. Just going somewhere quiet. Are you still there?"

"Yes, I can hear you."

A rustling sound as he sat down. "Have you heard from Stewartstown Road, Detective Inspector?"

"They left a message. I called you back first. What's this about?"

"I see. Well, I'm sorry to be the one to give you this news, but an employee at Blackmountain Quarries found a man this morning on their worksite. I was called to the scene and pronounced him dead. The only identification he was carrying was a PSNI pass card."

It was like being plunged into ice water.

"Sean Andrew Grady is the name on the card, but the photograph is a bit indistinct. Your colleagues at Stewartstown ran his name and you came up as his supervisor. We'll need you to come and make a preliminary identification."

The cold feeling was gone. Now she was hot. Burning up. Her heart racing. She could imagine the blood surging through her, the arteries flooded, her veins bulging. The pressure, building and building. Pressure that had to be released, or part of her might burst. Her head. Her heart. A hand reached out to the pen holder on her desk. Her fingertips buzzed as she touched the points of pencils, the cool metal of the scissors.

"Detective Inspector?"

"Sorry, yes." She pulled her hand back. Clutched it to her chest. "I'm sorry. I'll be right there."

She put down the phone. Put her palms flat on the desk. Sat for a while, wondering when the shaking might stop.

The sergeant was a thirty-year veteran of the old school, with the raw face and battered ears of a rugby prop forward. He had pulled up a map of the area around the quarry on his phone.

"There's a wee path along the top here." His finger was so large it nearly obscured the screen.

"Looks like he fell from there." The sergeant's voice was matter of fact, but his tone was soft. "It's about a seventy foot drop, at the highest point."

They were sitting in the hospital cafeteria, drinking orange-colored tea out of flimsy plastic cups. They were waiting for Sean Grady's mother to finish making a formal ID. Róisín felt dull inside, as though she wanted to cry, but had forgotten how. "Is that the usual path walkers take up there?"

"Well, the main walking path is a loop. You go from The Barn coffee shop, down the hill and then back up left to the TV masts. This wee track takes a bit of finding, if you don't know your way. I had a wander along it and there's a lot of litter. Empty cans, cigarette butts. A couple of condoms. It's very muddy, too. I nearly went arse over tip a couple of times myself."

"So, not exactly a hill walker's paradise."

"Not in the dark, anyway." He shifted in his chair.

"Spit it out, Sergeant."

"Well, the mountain's a popular place for courting couples." His neck was crimson, the blood filtering up into his face. "Gay couples, mostly, I'm told."

Róisín felt a sting of annoyance. "Sean wasn't gay."

"Right, ma'am." The sergeant nodded. But Róisín could sense his skepticism. Would Sean tell his boss if he was gay? This was Northern Ireland, after all. The old prejudices ran deep.

She shook her irritation off. The man was just doing his job. He'd find out whether that was a reasonable line of inquiry in due course.

She focused on the facts. Sean had hit his head in the fall, either on the uneven walls on the way down, or at the bottom. Granite crystals in the contusion above his left ear matched the stone in the quarry, and the blood spatter was consistent with a fall. The doctor said death would have been almost instantaneous.

"How did he get up there?"

"Ma'am?"

"He took the bus to work. I don't know if he had a car. Did

you find one?"

"He doesn't have a car registered. There is a bus service goes up the Springfield Road, the 106 to Crumlin. He might have taken that and walked up. A lot of people do that."

The door to the cafeteria swung open. A uniformed female constable helped a weeping Mrs Grady to a table.

Róisín said, "So he took the bus, went for a walk or whatever, slipped and fell?"

"That's what it looks like at first glance, ma'am." The sergeant watched the constable settle the older woman, and go to fetch her a cup of tea. "Unless you can think of a reason someone wanted to do him harm."

A skin had formed on the surface of her tea. The sight of it turned her stomach.

"Ma'am?" The sergeant was half out of his seat. She waved him away.

"I need to get back to the office."

A lie. What she needed to do was to get to Sean Grady's place. Before anyone else did.

36

Lawlor had no idea where he was, or where he needed to go. He'd been lost before, for periods of time: in the jungle, in the mountains; but he'd always had a map or a compass, or a destination at least.

Now he had nothing. The phone had power, but its shattered screen made it unreadable. The obvious thing to do was to keep going downhill until he reached the city, but he knew that would be obvious to the police, too. His vague memory of maps of Los Angeles told him that the spread of lights far below the restaurant was the San Fernando Valley, and that the Valley was north of the Hollywood Hills. Downhill, then, was north.

He followed the faint trail down through the trees to a sandy hiking path. There was still no moon, but the trail was as wide as a high street and easy to see. Lawlor shuffled along, his right knee stiff, his ears and eyes scanning for anything that didn't belong in the woods.

As he walked, he began piecing together the story Fyffe had told him, putting it together with what he already knew about Rab Harper, and about Bobby McEwan, now returned from the grave. Someone had hired Fyffe to get Lawlor to Los Angeles.

Then the same person, if Fyffe's instincts were right, had ordered hits on Tilly and Kawasaki. And on Lawlor. But why had the order to kill Lawlor come so late?

Except that the order had not come late. Fermin told him he'd been paid a quarter of a million dollars to put a bullet in Lawlor's head. And he'd been hunting Lawlor almost from the moment he arrived in L.A. Which meant Lawlor had been lured all the way to L.A. to be killed. Which made no sense at all. If someone wanted him dead, why not kill him in Belfast? And why now?

Something nagged at him then, something he'd seen or read that had caught in his mind. He shook his head. Whatever it was, it would come to him.

He refocused, put himself in the place of the people who had given Fyffe his orders. Their plan to lure Lawlor had worked initially, and then gone awry. Fermin was dead. But they had Fyffe as a backstop. They had his daughter. Kill Lawlor or she dies. And tie off the loose ends, too: Kawasaki and Tilly.

But how did they know about Tilly? They hadn't tracked Lawlor through Las Vegas. They couldn't have known she was in Santa Monica. Only Ovian's people knew. Which meant someone in his organization was leaking. Perhaps even Ovian himself.

Lawlor's knee was throbbing. He sat on a fallen tree beside the trail.

Whoever was behind this had both resources and influence. They knew who Harper was, and where he was. They had the pull to take him off a most-wanted list. They had money and access to equipment. Fyffe was right: it smacked of government.

But the big question was, why? Why go to all this trouble?

He was just a computer security guy at a regional police headquarters. But somehow he had run into something that involved some powerful people. And recently, too. Again, Lawlor had the feeling of something snagging in his mind, like a tiny bump on the surface of his brain. He went back over it, focused. But got nothing.

He shook the feeling of frustration away. He would remember, in time.

He stretched his leg again. It was beginning to stiffen. His mouth was sticky, and he realized it had been hours since he had drunk anything. He was in danger of dehydrating, which would make him dizzy and weak and would impair his judgment. He felt the unbearable urge to roll over the side of the log, settle into a bed of pine needles and go to sleep. He put his face in his hands and rubbed his cheeks, feeling the bristle of a day old beard rasp on his palms. And then he hauled himself to his feet and carried on.

The trail ended at a main road. There was no sidewalk, just a soft shoulder of splintered tarmac, strewn with litter. Not the place a normal person would go for a stroll. Not even with a dog. But there was no other option. He needed to eat and drink and rest. He put his hands in his pockets and did his best to walk down the hill without limping.

The supermarket was a monster, looming over a wide boulevard at the foot of the hill. It was good in some ways, bad in others. Good because it was open when most other shops would still be closed. Bad because it had cameras and a guard, and he looked as though he'd spent the night in the alley behind the store.

But the guard didn't even glance at him as he walked in, and the sole clerk at the checkout looked glassy-eyed.

Lawlor took a basket and filled it. Sandwiches, water, a disposable razor. The checkout counter was crowded with boxes of chocolate and chewing gum. Gift cards were stacked in a custom-made holder. Apple, Google Play, Visa. He took a Snickers bar and dropped it into the basket.

He had no cash and no ID. But he had Kawasaki's phone. The shattered screen made it unusable. But he had kept it powered on and activated, with no apps running, and the screen at the lowest light setting. Now it was time to gamble.

"Can I use Google Pay?"

The clerk looked at him, blankly, then pointed to a receptor beside the credit swipe.

"I hope this works." Lawlor held up the phone. "I dropped it. And I don't have any cash."

The kid shrugged.

Lawlor waved the phone over the receptor. There was a pause, and then the till chattered and spat out a receipt. The kid handed the slip to him. Lawlor caught a waft of skunk.

"Thank you for shopping at Timothy's."

Lawlor hesitated. He didn't think the phone was compromised yet. If it was, they would have been on him long ago. But they would almost certainly be watching Kawasaki's accounts, and the transaction he had just made would be flagged.

He pointed at the Visa cards. "How much is on these?"

"Hundred bucks."

"I'll take five."

The clerk nodded sleepily. He unhooked the cards, slid them one by one over the reader, tore off the activation strips at the back, and tapped his keyboard. Lawlor crossed his fingers and waved the phone like a magic wand. He felt a surge of something between relief and glee when the till chattered out another receipt.

The young man handed him the stack of cards, with the slip on top. His eyes were as distant as the clouds. "Thank you for shopping at Timothy's"

Holding onto the phone was a risk. It was the only lead he had, but it was also a beacon that, once the people behind Kawasaki and Fyffe worked out they needed to turn it on, would lead them right to him. It hung like a burning coal in his pocket as he hurried down the street. After a block, he turned up into a neighborhood.

The house he was looking for was at the end of a long block. A For Sale sign on a post hammered into the front lawn. Three garbage bins on the curb. Lawlor dropped the phone on the ground, and stamped on it, hoping that no one was watching from a neighboring house. Then he picked up the pieces and tossed them into what he hoped was the correct receptacle. And quickly moved on. He was a long way from safe. He had money, food and water, but he needed a place to clean up. And he needed access to a computer.

He came to a small park. There were swings and a sand pit. A couple walking their dog. He sat on a bench and ate a sandwich. He could feel the eyes of the dog walkers on him. An over-sized, scruffy middle-aged man, sitting alone beside a kids' playground. The fact there were no kids around made no difference. He had to move.

He stuffed the sandwich into his mouth and threw the wrapper into a bin. Washed the bread down with water. Kept walking. Down towards the main road.

He felt an itch in the center of his back, like the red dot from a range finder. A helicopter chattered overhead, and he ducked his head and turned down an alleyway overhung with trees.

He crossed another side street and came to the parking lot of a coffee shop. He went inside, ordered at the counter, paid with a gift card and went to the bathroom. The water on his face was like a blessing. He took his shirt off and worked quickly, washing and shaving and combing his hair as quickly as he could, ignoring the periodic rattle of the door handle behind him.

He slouched out of the bathroom, head down, and picked up his coffee to go.

He eased along the street, hands in his pockets, looking for somewhere he could get online. Libraries wouldn't be open for another hour, maybe two. If he could even find a library. Internet cafes were a thing of the past, killed by the smartphone. What he needed was an electronics store, somewhere he could do a few quick searches on a computer. But this was a residential area, full of cafes and clothes shops.

He drained his coffee cup. Dropped it into a bin. The sun told him he was heading west. A street sign told him he was on Ventura Boulevard. A name he knew from a song he had heard once. He eased along, finding the balance between keeping up his momentum while suffering as little pain from his knee as possible.

A police car raced past, siren wailing. He stilled himself, kept his pace, just a guy on the street, walking to the bus stop, to a cafe, to work.

He passed a strip mall with a cafe, a nail salon, a taekwondo studio. And a phone store. The employees were all college kids, happy to let the old man play with the latest devices.

Hiding in plain sight, Harper had said.

Lawlor logged in to a data scrape site he had used many times in the past and tapped in Harper's Armenian name. There was nothing for Rehan Markosian, but there were Seda Markosians listed to five addresses, and he used a maps app to verify their locations. Street view told him the first three were in apartment buildings in the center of a city called Glendale. The next was a two-story townhouse on a nondescript residential street in Beverly Hills. The third was a rose-colored, crenelated folly in a gated community far up the coast.

Harper's pink palace.

37

The house was in a development at the end of a private driveway at the top of a hill. The community was secured by a gate and guardhouse and what looked on the maps app like a long, high, possibly electrified fence.

Lawlor had his taxi driver drop him at the bottom of the hill. It was nearly noon, and the sun was a white-hot orb in a cloudless sky. There was no sidewalk and no shade. On his right was a short, sheer mud cliff; on his left was a steep, rocky drop to the coast road below.

The fence was as high as it looked on the app. It had signs warning about electric shock. But Lawlor could tell that if it was ever wired, the wires weren't connected now. Probably because of the risk to pets. Security had been further compromised by the homeowners, who had screened the fence with trees and hedges on the inside.

Harper's place was located at the far end of the development, looking out over the ocean, but Lawlor resisted the temptation to try working his way around to it on the down slope side. It was the obvious route, but there was no cover. On the right, on the steep up slope, there was a small wooded area. Lawlor walked into the trees, his shoes scrabbling on the dry dirt, his knee screeching at him as he lurched from tree to tree, as quietly as he could.

Every property he passed seemed to have a dog. He couldn't see them, but they mapped his progress, dashing out across their lawns, barking madly from windows. But there were no sirens, and no challenges. Dogs in the hills must bark all the time, he supposed. At coyotes, or raccoons, or skunks, or snakes, or deer.

The fence and the treeline made a kind of tunnel that led all the way to a wall of rock that marked the end of the development. A final fence post was hammered into the ground, and the builders had strung lines of barbed wire between the post and bolts drilled into the rock face. But someone, kids perhaps, had cut the wire long ago.

Lawlor waited until it was dark and it looked as though everyone was in for dinner. Then he swung himself around the post and through the gap, and found himself on a scrubby path that led around the outside of a hedge border of a garden. Beyond was a wide turning circle. The road was illuminated, barely, by a line of dim street lamps, spaced at wide intervals along the pavements. Harper's house was the last on the block, on the other side of the street, just before the circle. It looked even more like a Victorian folly in the shadows. Its driveway was occupied by a single black SUV.

Lawlor walked directly through the least illuminated part of the circle, directly through its center, hoping he looked like a man just out for a stroll. He cringed inwardly, bracing for a shriek of a security guard's siren. But there was nothing but the sound of his feet on the road.

He assessed his route as he walked. The driveway led to a three-car garage the size of a missile silo, built adjacent to the house. There was no access around the near side, but on the far side, abutting the next property, there was a tiny gap, an access point for the construction crew, or maintenance workers. Lawlor passed under one of the wan streetlights and then turned towards the gap, and pushed his way in.

There was a smell of damp earth and cat urine. Cobwebs clung to his face and hands as he scraped along the narrow passage, and it was a relief when he found himself in the open again. He stood in the darkness for a moment, getting his bearings, and then stepped onto a thick lawn of grass and looked at the back of the house.

Silhouetted by a low-hanging moon, the place looked like a miniature movie castle, with a turret at each end and a crenelated wall joining them. There were three large bedroom windows on the first floor, all dark. The ground floor windows were all lit. On the left, a kitchen, on the right, a dining room, and in the middle, a living room with a patio door.

Harper was in the living room. He was zip-tied to a chair. He had masking tape wrapped around his mouth. His face was wet with tears and red with rage. There were three men in the room with him. Lawlor recognized one of them from Ovian's entourage. They were laughing at something that was happening on a long couch, the back of which faced the window.

Lawlor knew he couldn't be seen, but his instincts made him step back into the shadows. He made his way around the lawn to the garage. There was a side door, unlocked. A light switch on the wall. There was a silver Lexus sedan in the bay, and an assortment of gardening and maintenance tools stored in a rack on one wall. There was a row of drawers below, full of bolts and nails and nuts and washers, all sorted into neat compartments. And tools. A box cutter went into one pocket. A long-shanked flat-head screwdriver into another.

He sat back on his haunches and thought for a moment. There was no barbecue grill. No propane tanks or lighter fluid. No matches. Nothing to create a diversion with.

He thought some more, and then he took a box of wire wool out of one drawer. Popped the back of a stud finder and removed the nine-volt battery. Fitted what looked like a titanium bit to a battery-powered drill.

He turned out the light to the garage and sprinted across the lawn. He shoved his way along the path by the side of the house and ran to the black SUV in the driveway. He lay on his back and wriggled underneath and got to work with the drill.

The titanium bit went through the metal like a hot skewer through cheese. He drilled two holes, and wriggled out from under the car, twisting away from the petrol pouring out of the tank. He tore the wire wool into wads, and rubbed the contacts of the battery over one of them. A pop of flame appeared, and he tossed it under the car. Nothing. He did the same with the second wad, and then the third. Was it diesel fuel? He lit a fourth wad, tossed it onto the wet ground and the gasoline vapor caught, a sheet of flame blooming under the car. He jumped back, and hurled the drill through the car's rear passenger window. The car alarm went off, and he sprinted for the front door of the house.

He crouched in the shadow at the side of the door, watching the vehicle as the flames tore around it. The car alarm was squealing. He could hear a faint commotion inside the house. Someone shouting. Lights went on in the house across the street.

Harper's front door burst open, and three men ran out,

then stopped on the pathway. They were all twisted up, not sure if they should run for the car, get back and find a fire extinguisher, or just stand and watch as it burned. Lawlor ran behind them, into the house. He slammed the door and locked the deadbolt.

A kid's trick. Simple, but effective.

He ran into the living room. Harper's wife lay face down on the couch, naked and apparently unconscious. A fourth man was fumbling with his trousers. Lawlor cannoned into him, driving him off balance and onto the couch. He pulled the screwdriver out of his pocket. It was thin and new, and with Lawlor's weight and momentum behind it, the chisel tip sliced easily through the cartilage between the man's second and third ribs. Lawlor angled the tool upwards and drove it home, until the shaft stopped him.

The man heaved under him, and Lawlor twisted the chisel and pulled it loose. He dragged the man onto the floor. The men outside were beating at the door. But Harper had not skimped when he built his palace. The door was a heavyweight block of solid teak. Full-length hinges on one side, and a double deadlock on the other. And the windows were triple glazed. There was a sledgehammer in the garage, but by the sound of this crew, it might be a few minutes before they figured that out.

Harper's wife was unconscious but breathing. It was hard to tell how much abuse she'd taken, but there were welts and bruises on her upper arms and shoulders, as well as her buttocks and thighs. Her face was bright red and puffy, and there was a deep scratch across her forehead that was oozing blood. He covered her with a throw blanket that was on the back of the couch.

Harper's eyes were bloodshot, and his face was wet with tears. It made it hard to get the masking tape off from around his mouth.

Lawlor's fingernails managed to work a tab loose. "This is going to hurt."

Harper braced, and Lawlor hauled on the tab. Harper's face went red as the tape tore out the hair at the nape of his neck, but he didn't utter a sound. Lawlor wrapped the loose tape around his fist and, with a single, massive jerk, ripped the rest of it away.

"There's a gun safe under the stairs." Harper's voice was a croak. "2741."

Lawlor used the box cutter on the zip ties securing Harper's hands and feet to the chair. He ran into the hallway. There was a small, innocuous-looking cubby under the stairs, the kind people used to stow cleaning supplies or winter gear. Inside was a small safe with an over-sized keypad. Lawlor punched in the numbers and the spring door swung open. Fastened to the back wall with pull-release brackets was a his-and-hers pair of revolvers, Smith and Wesson 686s, one with a two-and-a-half inch barrel and the other like something Dirty Harry would use. Underneath were stacks of boxes of ammunition.

Lawlor grabbed the guns. Both were loaded. His estimation of Harper notched higher. Revolvers were a good choice for home defense. A lower load than an automatic, but a simpler mechanism. They could be stored fully chambered and left for months at a time, if they were well maintained. And six or seven shots were normally all you needed.

But this was more than a home invasion. Lawlor shoved a box of ammunition into his pocket.

He was halfway back to the living room when he heard the

crash of glass. In some ways the men had been sharper than he thought; in other ways even more dumb. Sharper, because they hadn't even bothered going to the garage for tools, just thrown a piece of heavy lawn furniture through one of the floor-to-ceiling sliding glass doors. Dumb, because they were all clustered together on the lawn, one in front, two behind, in a nice, tight triangle.

They all held automatics, and the one in front raised his as Lawlor came through the door. But Lawlor's weapon was already up, and he fired twice, hitting the man in the chest and throwing him back onto the grass. He didn't see how the other men reacted, because he was on the ground, rolling right, towards the desk, away from the center of the room and the couch where Harper was tending to his wife.

Lawlor threw the hand cannon across the carpet to Harper, figuring he was more used to it than the shorter-barreled weapon. He put his hand in his pocket and came up empty. He looked behind him and saw the box of ammunition lying where he had dropped it, in the doorway. Right in the line of fire.

He glanced around the side of the desk. The two men in the garden had made up for their previous lack of tactical awareness and spread apart, weapons up and ready, covering the window.

He could see them, psyching themselves up. In their place, with two men down, their vehicle out of commission and cops and fire on the way, he might have been tempted to cut his losses. Make a run for it, over the fence and down the hill. He knew they were thinking about it. But he also knew the culture they were trained in, the fear and shame that inspired elite units to achieve remarkable things, but also could undermine them just as effectively: shame at not completing their mission, at letting their comrades die easily and unavenged, at not killing Harper, fear of being humiliated by one man with a drill and a battery and a handful of wire wool. Most of all, though, fear of what Artur would think of them, and, consequently, what he would do to them before they died.

Harper had picked up the gun.

"Two targets," Lawlor said. His heart was belting, but he kept his voice low and even. "You left, me right. On two." He waited a beat. "One. Two."

His estimation of Harper racked up another notch. Instead of popping up, he slid left, away from the couch, drawing fire away from his wife, snapping off the seven rounds in his chamber in three disciplined groups.

Lawlor was doing the same thing, but moving outwards, past the desk and towards the window. He had only five rounds to fire, and no time to get back to the door.

The two guys were better than he expected. They had more than twice the amount of ammunition that Harper and Lawlor had, and they were using it well. He was the initial target, and they zeroed in on him quickly, but the left hand guy switched fire to Harper as soon as he began firing. Lawlor fired two fast rounds at the man on the right, then his last two, and dived through the broken window to go after the first man's gun.

He landed hard on the man's back, and was immediately covered in blood. The man had spun around when the rounds had hit him and landed on his face, his arms splayed out like a man surrendering. The exit wounds from the .357 slugs were like two ragged sinkholes. Lawlor slid over his back, scrabbling for the automatic that was still in the man's right hand. There was a sound like a cat-o'nine-tails cracking over his head, and the hammering all around him as the last gunman fired, the sound ricocheting off the back wall of the house behind him.

He grabbed the automatic and rolled, over and over, into a line of shrubs. He checked the weapon, and then he rolled back once and popped up. The gunman was kneeling on the grass, leaning to one side, his weapon on the grass in front of him. He looked at Lawlor. He looked at the gun. He couldn't pick it up. His arm was twisted around, so that his elbow and his wrist pointed downwards. It looked like a branch that had been torn half way loose from a tree by a passing truck. His shoulder was a bloody canyon.

A gun fired behind Lawlor and the man dropped. Harper stepped out of the shattered doorway. He had an automatic in his hand. Lawlor cursed himself for a fool. If he had paused to think for a second, he would have realized what Harper had seen. That the man he had killed with the screwdriver was armed. So there was no need for him to go diving out the window like some kind of circus performer. The gun was probably stuck in the back of the man's trousers the whole time. Well within arm's reach.

The adrenaline crash hit him, and he began shaking. He licked his lips and tasted copper, and a surge of bile rolled out of his guts. He twisted around and vomited. He made it to his knees before the nausea punched him a second time.

He was clearing his mouth, spitting, wiping his hands, trying to shake off the dizziness when Harper walked slowly past, into the garden. He stopped, there was another flat report, and he walked back.

"We have to go. Now," Harper said.

Lawlor dragged himself to his feet. Behind the house was

an orange glow. He glanced at the couch. "Your wife needs a doctor."

"No doctors. No hospitals. It's not safe. We have to go." Harper paused in the doorway, leaning on the metal frame. "You'll have to carry Seda to the car."

Blood had soaked the left side of his shirt and trousers. Lawlor bent and pulled the shirt up. There was a hole in Harper's front, just below the curve of his lower left rib, and a matching hole in his back.

"Through and through," Lawlor said. "You can't go anywhere now. I'll wrap it, but you need a doctor, right now."

The shock of cold metal on his cheek stopped him.

"No. Fucking. Doctor." Harper twisted the gun and pressed it into Lawlor's ear. "Pick her up. Carry her to the car. And drive. You can play nursie when we're out of here."

"Okay." Lawlor stood up slowly. "But only if you leave the gun."

They stared at each other for a moment. Harper's face was tight with pain, but his eyes were clear. He let the automatic drop to the ground.

Lawlor stepped up into the living room. The revolver he had used was lying on the ground, beside the desk. He picked it up, tipped out the empty brass and reloaded from the box he had dropped in the doorway. He stuffed a handful of rounds into his pocket.

"Why do you get a gun and not me?" Harper asked.

"Because I'm a lot less likely to use it." Lawlor handed him the box. "Wipe this down. Put it in the safe. Then wipe that down too, and follow me."

He gathered up Harper's wife and carried her out to the garage. He put her on the back seat of the Lexus, and the gun

228

in the glove box. Harper struggled into the passenger seat, and when Lawlor started the car, he opened the garage door.

For a second, Lawlor had no idea what to do. The front of the house looked like the aftermath of a mortar strike. Fuel from the SUV had spread all the way across the road and down the hill, so that there was a pool of fire the size of a small lake in front of Harper's house. The car was a brightly-burning shell in the middle of the pool, and a burnt orange plume of smoke rose like a pillar into the sky.

And there were people everywhere. They had all come out of their houses, and were standing in the street, craning their necks. Pointing at the garage.

Lawlor floored the accelerator, and the Lexus surged out, lurching backwards over a row of shrubs as Lawlor steered clear of the flames. Then he pirouetted the car and shot forward towards the gate, catching a woman in his headlights, white-faced and frozen, before he swerved over the curb and into the street.

He saw the lights before he heard the fire engines coming up the hill. The security team had left the entry gate open, but not the exit, and Lawlor leaned hard on the accelerator, driving the Lexus hard in a race to be first to the gate.

The sirens were blaring now, as the firetrucks came up the hill, the noise competing with the straining engine of the car. Lawlor swerved into the left lane of the driveway, gripped the steering wheel and stood on the pedal as the lead firetruck crested the rise and its headlights beamed full into his face. The truck's horn sounded like a warship. Lawlor was muttering a prayer. And then they were past the kiosk, over the line, and Lawlor hauled the wheel to the right and the car was skidding past the fire truck, its horn like a hammer in his ear as they whipped down the hill, past an ambulance and a pair of police cruisers, and on down to the sea.

38

They passed the store at the bottom of the hill and reached a road junction. Beyond was a stretch of sand, and, after that, the ocean.

"Left or right?" Lawlor said.

"Right." Harper's voice was faint. "I'll show you."

They drove in silence for a few moments.

"Tell me about Seda," Lawlor said. "What did they give her?"

Harper shook his head. "She has epilepsy. They wouldn't let her take her meds. And when they started..." His voice trailed off.

Lawlor felt a coldness inside him. He thought about Harper giving the men the coup de grace on his lawn. He said nothing.

"There." Harper nodded towards a restaurant on the water. It was a low-slung building built on small promontory. There was a large parking lot, half full of cars. Lawlor pulled across the traffic and into the lot.

Harper's chin was on his chest.

"Stay awake, Rab." Lawlor slapped his face, and Harper blinked.

"I found Fyffe." His voice was slurred. His eyes drooped.

"Stay awake." Lawlor opened the car door and ran to the service entrance of the restaurant. The door opened onto a kitchen, full of steam and the smell of frying oil. Three men in chefs' jackets looked up, staring.

Lawlor looked down at his shirt and chinos, soaked with blood. "I need the manager. There's been an accident."

One of the men said something in Spanish and pushed through a swing door at the far end of the kitchen. The door swung again, and a tall man, dressed in jeans and a t-shirt came in. He was gray-haired and had sleeves of tattoos, like an aging surf punk. He took in Lawlor in a single glance. "You hurt?"

"No. But my friend is."

The man said nothing. Everyone in the room was watching Lawlor. "My friend's name is Rehan. He says he knows you. He told me to come here. He's outside. In the car. With his wife."

It was that last sentence that seemed to galvanize the man. He gave an order in rapid Spanish and the cooks went back to work. He walked easily down the kitchen towards Lawlor, like a man used to trouble. His eyes were a startling Adriatic blue.

"Okay," he said. "Let's see."

His name was Stewart Conway. After he had put Seda into bed in the recovery position and bandaged Harper as best he could, he told Lawlor his story: former paramedic turned drug dealer turned card sharp, he had won the tumbledown fish fry restaurant in a bet a decade before. It turned out he was the sucker, because the restaurant was little more than a shack, and was mired in debt, but Conway saw a chance. He had quit all his bad habits and channeled what savings he had into the fish fry, but it hadn't been enough, and he had asked one of his regular customers to take a chance. Harper had written a check for $250,000 on the spot. They called it a loan, but Harper never asked for interest, and every year when Conway made an installment payment, the check was never cashed. So Harper and Seda always ate for free.

"And you're Lawlor."

They were sitting in the bar of the restaurant, waiting. It was after midnight, the staff had all gone home, and Conway had called a guy he knew. Outside, the wind had picked up, and the waves were churning along the breakwater below the restaurant's windows, making a sound like a waterfall.

"What makes you say so?"

"He's described you often enough. Big bastard, black hair, green-gray eyes, hands like shovels, a look like a hangman's uncle."

"Is that verbatim?"

"Pretty much."

A big wave slapped into the rocks and sent spray skittering across the glass of the window. The moon was a thin crescent in an empty sky, bright enough to reflect on the water out at sea. Lawlor was lost for a moment.

The wall of the restaurant lit up as a car turned into the lot. Conway went to open the front door. A small man hurried inside. He carried a backpack with a UCLA Veterinary Sciences logo stitched onto it, and a sweatshirt with Animal Rescue written across the chest.

Lawlor said, "You've got two patients. Male, late 40s, gunshot wound in his left side. Nine-mil. Looks like a lucky shot, through and through. He's conscious and he can move around without too much pain. I patched him, but he's lost a lot of blood. The second is female. Early 40s. She had some kind of seizure and passed out."

"She has epilepsy," Conway broke in. "She must have been off her meds."

"When did the seizure occur?" the man asked.

"A few hours ago," Lawlor said. "She hasn't come to. But she hasn't seized again, either."

"Okay." The doctor looked around the room. "Where's the GSW?"

"They're both in my trailer."

"That thing out the back?'

"Yeah."

He shook his head. "Well, if he can walk, you'd better get him in here."

Conway left and the man unzipped the backpack. It was a fully equipped emergency medical kit, complete with drips and drugs and surgical equipment. The man glanced up and met Lawlor's eyes. "Problem?"

Lawlor shook his head. "No problem."

The door opened behind him. Conway stood there, his face blank. "Looks like he wasn't as lucky as you thought," he said. "He's dead."

Harper had died sitting beside his wife, holding her hand. The medic unwrapped the bandage work, prodded Harper's distended belly and said he had bled out internally.

"And her?" Conway asked.

Seda was sleeping like she had just run a marathon, breathing in a slow, deep, even rhythm. The doctor took her temperature, checked her blood pressure, examined her bruises and closed the cut on her head with a line of steri strips. Then he clapped his hands together, loud, beside her ear. She didn't move. He shrugged. "She'll wake up when she's ready."

"When will that be?" Conway asked. The doctor shrugged again. He packed his bag and they followed him back into the restaurant.

"When she does wake up, she'll be dehydrated." He produced a pill bottle, like a magician. "Give her one of these every six hours, and make sure she drinks plenty of water."

Conway took the bottle and the doctor walked out. They waited until his car had driven away.

Conway sighed and sat down heavily at the bar. "Now would be a good time to have a drink," he said wistfully, eyeing the shelves of bottles. "But I'll have twelve years at the end of this month."

"Sometimes a little time is all it takes."

"Amen, brother. One day at a time, right?"

"Right."

He poured sparkling water into a glass and pushed it at Lawlor. "I can take care of the car. Guy I know runs a chop shop in Van Nuys. But I don't know what to do with Rehan."

"Don't worry." Lawlor gave him a half-smile. "I know some people who'd love to take care of him."

39

Conway's car was a large white pickup truck. It looked to Lawlor as though it would stand out like a firework display at a funeral, but Conway assured him that there were more pickups sold in the city of Los Angeles than in all the farm towns of California put together.

Lawlor asked for three pieces of printer paper. On the first, he wrote a message in block capitals and tucked it into the chest pocket of Harper's bloody shirt. On the second, Conway sketched a rough map in pencil. The third Lawlor folded into three and put on the passenger seat. They rolled Harper's body in a tarp, pulled it into the back of the truck, wedging it tight against the tailgate. Then Lawlor set out on the road.

The speed limit was fifty miles an hour, and Lawlor stuck to it, precisely, the way a man might if he had no drink taken and wanted to go faster, but suspected the police might be waiting with a speed gun around any of the bends in the road.

He wore Conway's jeans and his hoodie and a black baseball cap with SF emblazoned on it in gold. He kept the window down, to stop himself from falling asleep. He was still wired with adrenaline and anticipation, but he knew that could wear off at any time, and then he would crash, hard.

He mulled his situation as he drove. There was no longer any reason for him to be in Los Angeles. Harper was dead. Tilly was dead. Fyffe was dead. There was a chance that he had managed to stay off the radar of the local police, but there was no doubt Ovian would be after him. And then there was whoever had hired Fyffe and Fermin and Kawasaki to contend with. It was time to disappear. But to do that, he needed a diversion. Something that was going to ring a few bells in Washington, D.C.

The highway merged with one freeway, and then another, heading north. He took the first exit and saw the great, twenty-story slab of the Federal Building on his right. He drove past and turned into a residential street. He found a space and pulled the truck into it, then turned off his lights and engine.

Conway had called security at the Federal Building a joke. And so it looked, to the casual observer. There was a post office on the ground floor, and mailboxes on the street outside. There were no barriers or guards. Nothing to stop the citizens sending or picking up their mail. Even at four in the morning.

But Lawlor knew there would be a lot more there than met the eye. Sensors. Cameras. He looked up and saw the winking red light of a drone doing a slow loop of the perimeter.

He slipped out of the truck and removed the license plates. Tucked them under the passenger seat and started up. His hands were sweaty on the grip of the steering wheel. He drove through the streets, first away from, and then towards the building. He knew there would be surveillance on him now, and plenty of it. He kept his speed even.

There were speed bumps in the road parallel to the building, and, in the middle of the road, as Conway had promised, two mailboxes. He stopped at the second box and leaned out of the window. He had his cap pulled low and his hoodie up. He took the folded piece of paper off the seat beside him and poked it at the mailbox slot. Then he dropped the paper on the ground.

He got out of the truck, faced away from the building, bent over and impatient, like a guy in a hurry. He picked the paper up and put it in the mail slot, then turned to get back into the truck. He glanced into the bed of the truck and stopped, as if he'd seen something wrong. He went to the tailgate, fiddled with the lock, gave it a shake, then climbed back into the truck and moved off.

The road was brightly lit. Lawlor could see there were two more speed bumps ahead of him. He sped up. Checked his seat belt. There was a loud bang as the truck bounced over the bump, and Lawlor looked in his rear view. There was nothing in the road.

He floored it, and the truck leapt forward, its front tires hitting the second bump at nearly thirty miles an hour. The shock was intense, like being thrown off a mechanical bull. The seat belt cut into his shoulder, but he kept his eye on the mirror. The truck was in the air when the back wheels hit the bump. Another bang, as though they had collided with something. And then all four tires were on the ground, skidding, then gaining traction, and then the truck was powering away, leaving what looked like a tattered roll of carpet in the road.

Lawlor hit the junction and turned sharply left. The road ran between a television studio and a baseball park. There was a traffic light, still green. Lawlor barreled towards it, imagining the havoc behind him. The crash teams going for their vehicles, the instructions being issued to overflight, the scramble call to the bomb squad. He had three minutes; five at the most.

He could feel the sweat trickling down his flanks now. His

heart was racing. He swung right at a traffic light, under the freeway and into another residential neighborhood. He flicked his headlights off and turned left again, trying to keep his breathing slow and level. He could hear sirens behind him, and the unmistakable sound of a high speed helicopter above.Both sides of the street were jammed with vehicles. He found himself counting pickups. Nine on a single block. Conway was right.

He passed another junction. Lights ahead of him told him he was moving closer to a main road. Which was where all the chase and cordon vehicles would be moving, and over which the helicopters would be flying. He was out of time.

He had to ditch the car in a driveway and take off on foot. He would have no time to put the plates back on, not that it would make any difference: the chase teams were looking for a white pickup. If they saw one parked in a driveway, they would check it for sure. He felt bad for Conway. He would have to report the vehicle stolen, which was not the clean solution Lawlor had promised.

There was a single family home halfway down the block, with a short driveway. Lawlor was about to pull in when he saw a gap between two hybrid vehicles across the street. But was it big enough?

He fought down the panic mounting in him as he made the assessment. If the space was too small, he would waste valuable seconds trying to get into it. If he nudged one of the cars, the alarm might go off. He wasn't familiar with the pickup. He had no idea how long it was. And he was used to driving on the other side of the road.

But the space looked big enough. Just. Maybe.

He did a fast K-turn, lined himself up and eased the truck

backwards, bestowing a blessing on the engineer who created power steering as the truck swung into the space in a smooth movement, the front bumper clearing the car in front of him by what felt like a hair.

He snapped off the engine and the lights, then flicked the switch on the overhead light to off. He paused for a beat, then grabbed the screwdriver and the plates and slid out of the passenger door, closing it as quietly as he could. He crept to the front and screwed the plate on, then did the same to the back. Then he used the key to lock the car from the passenger side, and walked away.

40

Seda was sitting out on the restaurant's narrow terrace, wrapped in a blanket, chain-smoking and looking out at the ocean. The tide was going out and there was a strong smell of rotting seaweed. Conway was making coffee in an old percolator, watching her. The restaurant was full of the smell of hazelnut roast.

"She woke up a couple of hours ago," he said.

"What did you tell her?"

Conway stared. "I said he was shot in the gut and died holding her hand. I don't know much more than that. You're going to have to tell her the rest."

Lawlor nodded. He watched her light a cigarette. It had taken him nearly five hours to get back. After he had walked away from Conway's truck, he had ditched his hat and sweat-shirt in a rubbish bin, then jumped the fence into the hospital. He had sat under a tree in the dark, watching the helicopters and listening to the sirens until it all died down. Then he had waited some more.

At first light, once people had begun leaving their houses, he walked down to the main road. His trousers were dirty and he had only a T-shirt on, but this was L.A., and he attracted no more attention than the homeless man he passed sleeping on a bus bench. He had bought a cup of coffee and a doughnut and consulted a bus map. Three buses and two hours later, he was back at the restaurant.

He handed Conway his car keys. "Avery Street. Just north of the junction with Santa Monica Boulevard."

Conway pocketed the keys. He handed Lawlor two cups of coffee and jerked his head towards the window. "You're on."

The sky and the sea were different shades of gray, like an army blanket dipped in water. There was a light onshore breeze, strong enough to make his eyes water. Harper's wife was sitting in an Adirondack chair, wrapped in a brightly colored blanket that looked like a souvenir from a trip to Mexico, her feet up on the rail of the deck.

Lawlor put one of the mugs of coffee on the armrest of her chair. "I'm Lawlor."

She flicked her ash onto the deck, her eyes on the sea. "I know who you are."

The anger was boiling off her, like steam from a hot spring. He had a sudden memory of her, sprawled face down on her couch, and behind her, the man he had killed, struggling with his belt buckle.

"I'm sorry."

She turned her head, slowly. She had the look of a body pulled out of the water. Lank hair, around a face devoid of color. But her eyes flashed like lightning in a dull sky. "Why are you sorry? My husband is dead. His child, abandoned. His wife, raped. Isn't that what you wanted?"

His face was suddenly hot. He opened his mouth, then closed it again. He shook his head.

The skin seemed to tighten on her face, making it even paler where it stretched over her cheekbones. "So what the fuck did you want, Lawlor?" She made his name sound like a curse. "Do you even know?"

His mouth tasted foul, as though his own sewage was filtering up from his guts. The coffee tasted like formaldehyde. The wind dropped and he stepped past her to the rail and emptied his cup into the sea.

"I thought I knew," he said. "Now I hardly know which way is up."

She took a long drag, then flicked the cigarette past him. The wind pushed it back, so that it bounced off the rail, showering his bare arm with sparks. He brushed them off and turned to grind out the butt under his shoe.

She was young, he realized. Maybe not even thirty.

"Your daughter..."

"What about her?"

"You said..." He stopped. There was no good way of asking. "Is she safe?"

"From you? Yes."

"And from Artur Ovian?"

Her eyes hooded for a fraction of a second, but there was no other sign that the name meant anything to her, or that she was afraid. "What makes you ask that?"

"You got her out."

For the first time, she seemed to notice the cup on the arm of her chair. She sipped the coffee and made a face, but wrapped her hands around the drink. "We had a plan in place. A contingency. When something goes wrong, she goes to a friend, that friend sends her on to another friend, and so on until she is safe."

"That's a lot for a kid of...how old?"

"Twelve." Her eyes hooded again. "But she is strong. And we practiced a few times, in the vacations."

"Have you spoken to her? To be sure she's okay?"

Narrow eyes. "Why the fuck do you care, Lawlor?"

"I had two kids myself, once."

She held his gaze and then, after a while, she nodded. "What were their names?"

"Thomas. Tommy. And Andrew." He was surprised at how easy it was to say the words out loud. In the past he had found it caused him physical pain. After a while he had stopped saying their names at all.

"I never knew before," she said. "I read the news archives from back then. They gave your name, but not your boys. I was surprised the news people were so respectful. Not like here."

"We came to an understanding."

The corner of her mouth rose a fraction. "Now you sound like an Armenian."

She took a packet of Marlboro from a fold in the blanket and tapped out a lighter and a cigarette. She held out the pack.

"It's been twenty years since I smoked," he said.

"And twenty years since you killed a man, too."

He tugged a cigarette loose and bent for a light. He took a quick drag, and felt the instant, warm familiarity of the smoke in his mouth and his lungs. He blew out in a long stream. "How do you know I killed anyone?"

"I can't imagine we got away from Lubya and his men without you killing them all."

"Your husband did his bit."

She looked out to sea. "He practiced a lot. But he never killed anyone before, he told me." She looked up. "Not even then."

"I know that now."

"What else do you know?"

The smoke was harsh on his tongue. He dropped the cigarette and ground it out. "Not much. He died before he could tell me."

"You're back where you started."

"Not even that."

The end of her cigarette sparked as she dragged on it, and she tilted her head back to exhale. She kept her eyes on him the whole time. "So. What did you do with my husband?"

"I left him at the Federal Building."

Her eyes narrowed. "Why?"

"It seemed like the best solution."

"Best for who?"

"For everyone. You're on the run now, right? So you can't take care of him. I put a note in his pocket telling the Feds who he really is. They'll run his prints, and then send him back to Belfast. His mother'll look after things."

"You've thought of everything."

"That's the problem, Seda. I'm not really thinking at all."

The tide was coming in, and the water slapped and gurgled under the deck. His skin bumped and he rubbed his forearms.

"You're cold," she said. "We should go inside."

41

It was almost lunchtime. A tough-looking Latin man with a wide mustache and a neck tattoo chopped vegetables in the kitchen while Conway wiped tables and set out cutlery. Lawlor and Seda sat at a table by the window and Conway brought them glasses of iced water. He stood for a moment, fidgety, but when she nodded at him, he walked away and left them alone.

There was some color in her face now, touching the edges of her cheekbones and filling out her lips. She drank half her water, the ice cubes clattering. "So what will you do now?"

The question made him feel like a fool. From the moment he had left his flat in Belfast, he had barely considered any kind of plan beyond what to do at that given moment. Get out of Ireland. Get to America. Stay alive. Find Harper. He had no exit route, no escape plan. He had some money, but no passport. He could go to the Irish consulate, he supposed, claim it had been stolen. But what would that trigger? And when he got home, what then?

"I'll figure something out," he said.

"They won't reopen the investigation into who killed your boys, will they? Now that he's dead."

"No."

She gave him a searching look. "What if I can tell you where McEwan is?"

"How?"

She leaned over the table. "Do you know why Rehan was so valuable to Artur?"

"He told me some of it. He said he helped him steal information."

"From their home computer systems." She began reordering the cutlery on the table. "He called it the Internet of Stings. A bad joke. But a good product. Kompromat on judges, policemen, politicians, everything. Very useful to Artur."

"And he taught you."

"Not me." She flicked the idea away with her fingertips. "I am bad with computers. But there was one area that I was very helpful to him. Can you guess?"

Lawlor looked down at the table, at the cutlery and condiments, precisely arranged. Seda smiled, a real smile that reached her eyes. "I am a very tidy person. Rehan was not. So I organized things for him. Everything, in fact. Including an archive of all the information he gathered. Every little secret. For Artur and for him."

"And you think you can find out what it was that he was going to tell me?"

"I'm the only one who knows how to search the archive."

"You can't go back to the house."

"It's not in the house." She pointed up at the ceiling.

"It's in the cloud."

She nodded. "And I can get it for you."

She sat back, picked up her glass and drank the rest of the water. She kept her eyes on Lawlor the whole time. gray-green, with flecks of gold. Warm to the touch, but with an iron core.

"You're not giving it to me for nothing," he said.

"No. I'm not."

"So what's the deal?"

She folded her arms. "I'm on the run now, like you said. My daughter is safe. For now. I can get to her. And then we'll move again, until we're a long way away. But we'll never be completely out of Artur's reach."

"You had a plan to get your daughter out, so I'm guessing you've thought about all the other stuff, too. Money. Identities. Everything you need to get away clean, right?"

She said nothing.

He shrugged. "I don't see what use I can be to you."

"It's not just about us." She was hugging herself now, and all the enthusiasm had left her face. "Have you ever been to Armenia?"

"No."

"It's mostly villages. Even the cities are villages, really. Everyone knows everyone. And every family in every village has someone out here, in America, sending money back, sponsoring people to come. They become like godfathers. Like the movie."

He nodded. He could see it now. "Artur is a godfather."

Her mouth twisted. "The godfather of godfathers. He knows my village, very well."

Lawlor said nothing. The bell on the restaurant door jangled and a couple came in and sat down. Conway went to take their order.

She was grinding her teeth, the muscles in her cheeks pulsing. When she looked up there were tears in her eyes. "I am the only one of my family in America. Everyone else is

248

there. My parents. My brothers and sister. Everyone."

"And if you run..."

She nodded, and batted away the tears that slipped down her cheeks.

He felt heavy in his chair, like someone had dropped a sack of cement into his lap.

"So what's the deal?" he asked, although he already knew.

She looked at him, iron eyes through a curtain of tears. "I tell you where McEwan is..." She stopped.

"And in return?" He needed to make her say it, to make it real for both of them.

"You kill him." She sat up straight. "You kill Artur."

42

"I can't do it."

They had sat there through the lunch hour as he thought through it. Conway brought them food. They ate in silence, and he took the plates away. The restaurant had emptied. Conway locked the door and put up a sign saying 'Closed'. He started wiping down the tables for the second time. Lawlor was aware of his eyes on them.

A bright red spot burned above each of her cheekbones. "Can't? Or won't?"

"Both. I'm not an assassin."

"You came here to assassinate my husband."

He said nothing.

"You've killed people before," she said. "In the army. I read your file."

"It's not the same."

"Because Artur has bodyguards?"

"That's part of it, sure. But also because back then I had a half a dozen guys with me and I was armed to the teeth."

Her lip curled. "You're afraid."

"Yes, I'm afraid. I'd be a fool not to be. I'm not from here. I don't know this area. I barely know which side of the road to drive on. I don't know where Ovian lives or works, or who guards him and how many of them there are. I don't know what weapons they carry, if there are dogs, if he has family, what car he drives. I don't know any of those things, and those are all things that I'd need to know. Add to that, I'm a fifty-year-old-man with a buggered knee, who until yesterday hadn't fired a shot in anger for more than twenty years, and you'll understand why the very notion of going up against a guy like Ovian scares the shit out of me."

Her eyes burned. "You waited twenty years and traveled thousands of miles to kill Rehan, and he was the wrong man. I'm giving you the chance to find out who really did murder your children. Do you want your revenge or not?"

"I do. But not at that price."

The agitation was boiling through her now. She hooked her hair behind her ears and folded her arms, then shoved her hands into the pockets of her sweatshirt.

"I can pay you."

He shook his head. "I know what I'm capable of, Seda, and I'm not capable of doing what you want. Money can't change that."

Her lip twisted. "Money can change everything."

"Not for me."

She sighed. "I don't understand this. You came here with the plan of killing a man. Now you won't kill another man, even though your aim is the same. It makes no sense."

He watched her. He wanted to tell her that he had never had a plan. Only a direction. He had moved across an ocean and a continent, with no aim other than to satisfy a blind urge to take revenge. No tactics, no strategy. Just kill and then... He didn't know what. He had thought countless times about what he would do in that moment, how the act of vengeance would be carried out, but beyond that, nothing. He knew that it wouldn't bring him relief, or erase his scars. Now that he thought about it, he assumed he would die, that someone would kill him, that somehow his life would end, because there would be nothing else to live for.

But how could he explain that to a young woman with everything to live for. A whole life ahead. A child who depended on her. A family, somewhere.

"You won't help me?" she asked.

"I can't. I'm sorry."

"In that case I'm going to have to help myself." She pushed her chair back and stood up and it was a second before he realized that the object in her hand was a gun.

He put his hands on the table, palms down, slowly and carefully. It was the Smith & Wesson that he'd taken from Harper's house. Conway must have searched the car and found it. It was a snug, serious weapon that would make a small hole going into his chest and tear a crater the size of his fist on the way out. The hand that held the gun was steady, and the eyes behind it steadier still.

He said, "You really think he wants me that badly?"

"I hope so. You're all I've got. You killed his guys."

"One of them. Your husband took care of the rest."

"I'll make sure you get the credit."

He said nothing. He wondered how long she'd had the gun on her. Probably long before he arrived, tucked into her jeans or in the pocket of the sweatshirt. Not a borrowed pair of jeans like his, he realized, too late. Not a borrowed sweatshirt. Her clothes, kept in Conway's trailer.

He glanced at the door. Conway was standing there, his hip

against the bar, his arms folded.

"Did Rab know?" Lawlor asked.

She laughed. "You have no idea what you're talking about, do you? You know nothing about my husband. You came here with your assumptions about him, all of which were wrong. And now you make more assumptions. You are a stupid man, Lawlor."

"I'll take that as a yes, then."

The gun was still pointed at his chest. It weighed just over a pound, but her extended arm showed no sign of strain. Which spoke of a lot of time on the range.

She said, "What do you know about human trafficking?"

"I know it happens. I know it's bad. I don't know about the details."

"Hundreds of girls are trafficked from my country every year. Thousands, maybe. Lured away, or sometimes just stolen."

Her voice was steady. She sounded like an academic giving a lecture. But the gold flecks in her eyes glowed like embers fanned by a breeze, and he could sense the rage in her.

"The men who took me came in the middle of the night. There were just two of them, but they put a gun to my brother's head and walked me out of the door. So easy. They put me in the back of a van with three others. We all fell asleep. When we woke up, we were in a kind of warehouse. It was very dark. The place was full of men, all drunk and shouting and laughing. Like it was a party. They threw us onto mattresses and the men all lined up and took their turn. I don't know how many. I don't know for how long."

There was the sound of a dishwasher starting up. Out of the corner of his eye, Lawlor saw Conway, still leaning on the bar, watching and listening.

"The next day, I was brought to a large room," she went on. "There were fifteen or twenty of us there, sitting on the floor, like we were in class. None of us was older than fifteen. Some were much, much younger. A woman came in. Very beautiful. She wore a leopard-print skirt and sunglasses in her hair. She smelled like roses. She looked at us, pointed at me, and two men carried me out. I say carried because I was so sick with fear, I couldn't even stand. They put me in a car, with leather seats and air conditioning. We drove for an hour, the men on either side of me, the woman in the front, looking out of the window. No-one spoke to me. We stopped at a big house. The men brought me in, and sat me down in a large room, on a couch covered in silk. I had never seen such things before: the car, the upholstery, the AC, the silk. It was like being in a dream. I sat on the edge of the chair because I was conscious of how filthy I was. I didn't want anyone to beat me for making a mess.

"After a while, Artur Ovian came in. He was very gentle. He apologized to me, and told me the men who raped me would be punished. He explained that he had spoken with my parents and come to an agreement. I was to be married to his cousin. In return my family would have more land and a gift of money, to buy livestock, repair their house, build a new barn, whatever they needed. Of course, none of this would happen unless I agreed. He had a satellite phone with him. He dialed it, then handed it to me. My father was on the other end of the line. He told me that he had consented to the marriage. He said I could refuse, of course, but by now everyone in the valley knew what had happened to me. I knew what that meant. So what could I do? I married the man I knew as Rehan. The man who used to be Robert Harper."

Lawlor's face was hot. He could hear his own breathing in his ears. "You were Harper's cover story."

Her mouth twisted. "The other part of the agreement I learned only later. The head man of Dasli, my village, was paid a lot of money to sign papers saying that Rehan was his son, that he went to school in Lacin and then at the National Polytechnic University in Yerevan. The match with me created a complete legend for him. Birth, childhood, education, marriage."

"At the age of fifteen."

She shrugged. "Not so unusual in the mountains. But Rehan was appalled. The woman with the leopard print dressed me like a whore for my first meeting with him. Short dress. Makeup. High heels. I could barely walk. I thought Rehan was going to faint when he saw me. He went as white as a sheet. They left us alone, to get to know each other. He wouldn't even look at me. I had to beg him to agree to the marriage. On my knees. I told him Artur would put me back in the brothel. He had been in Yerevan long enough to know what that meant."

"So he agreed."

She smiled. "He was a good man. Really. He didn't lay a finger on me. He gave me my own room, let me live as independently as it was possible for me to do so there. He asked me to help him learn the language; in return he taught me computers. After a few years, we became friends."

"Friends?"

"Yes." She glanced at Conway. "Just friends."

43

It wasn't much of an opening, but Lawlor took it. He jerked forward out of his chair, batting Seda's right arm away with his left wrist and then wrapping his right hand around the top of the gun, pulling it forward and out of her grasp, all in one smooth movement, exactly as the unarmed combat specialists had taught him more than thirty years before.

Her mouth made a perfect O. A match for the barrel of the gun that pointed at her now. He took a quick step around the table, seeing a blur of movement out of the corner of his eye, Conway moving fast behind the counter. Lawlor stepped close, held Seda's right arm with his left hand, pulling her to him as he heard the definitive crunch-crunch of a cartridge being racked into the breech of a shotgun.

She was cool enough. She tilted her head back and refused to look at him. The red spots on her cheekbones were the only sign that she might be scared.

She said, "You don't strike me as the kind of man who'd shoot a woman."

"I hope the same goes for your boyfriend."

Lawlor recognized the weapon. A Mossberg 500. A wicked piece of ironwork, painted black, with a pump action and the stock removed. A great weapon, in certain situations, but not a precision instrument at a distance. There was a big risk that if Conway used it, he would cut both Lawlor and Seda in two.

It took a second for Seda to see it. Her eyes narrowed and she tried to pull away, but Lawlor held her tight.

"If you stay right here, no one gets hurt. Not you, not me, not him." He kept his voice low, felt her relax a little. He let the pistol point at the floor and kept half an eye on the kitchen as he turned towards Conway.

"Why don't you put the gun down and we'll talk."

Conway didn't move, but the way he was grinding his teeth told Lawlor all he needed to know.

"Is your man in the back, still?" Lawlor asked.

"No."

"Right then. At the count of three, we're going to put all the hardware down on the floor. Under the table. Sound good?"

Conway didn't answer.

"Look, you're not going to shoot me. And I'm not going to shoot you. I'm certainly not going to shoot her. Which means all these guns are only raising the level of anxiety in here. And that's no way to go about making any kind of important decision. Wouldn't you agree?"

Conway looked at Seda. She nodded.

He squatted down carefully, holding tight to Seda's arm, watching as Conway bent. He placed the Smith on the floor, and nudged it under the table with his toe. When he stood up, there was no weapon in Conway's hand. They crabbed across the room, to a table by the window. Lawlor eased Seda into one chair and sat beside her. He pointed at the chair opposite him and Conway sat down.

Lawlor slid his foot forward and slipped the hook of his heel gently around the leg of Conway's chair. He turned to Seda. "I'm sorry I'm no good to you. I can't kill a man who's done nothing to me personally, no matter how evil a bastard he might be. It's just not who I am anymore. Do you understand that?"

She gave him a look of contempt. He ignored it. "I'm not going to let you trade me, either. I don't think he'd want me anyway, and even if he did, I don't think it'd be enough. As potatoes go, I'm far too small. So the question is, what would be enough? What do you have that he wants?"

"What do you mean?"

"I mean if Harper knew there might be day he'd have to run, he wouldn't have shared everything with his boss. He'd have kept something back."

Her eyes flickered for a moment. And then her mouth set. "I would have known. I told you. I organized everything. He was a mess."

Lawlor thought about Harper in his house in L.A., squaring the file off against the edge of the glass table. "Maybe he fooled you."

Her face set. "I don't think so."

"You said yourself you weren't that close. Married, sure. But I know dozens of men who live secret lives from wives they've lived with for years and had kids with. You weren't even sleeping together."

"We were intimate. Maybe more than most couples."

"I'm not saying you weren't close. I'm just saying he maybe didn't tell you everything about himself. Kept stuff back. To protect you. Can you think of anything like that?"

"You're wrong. He hid nothing from me. Sure, we didn't have sex, but otherwise I knew everything about him. And he knew everything about me."

Conway moved. He shoved the table forward and pushed his chair back hard at the same time. Lawlor was ready for it, but Conway was younger and stronger and he felt himself stretched, the edge of the table in his chest, pushing him one way, the leg of Conway's chair pulling his leg the other. He grabbed the table to steady himself, jerked his foot backwards, dragging the chair out from under Conway, who went sprawling onto his back. Then he put his hands on the edge of the table by his chest and shoved hard, driving it into the fallen chair.

He stood up and stepped around the table. Conway was on his knees, scrambling, going for the Mossberg. Lawlor kicked him hard in the belly, aiming the toe of his shoe at the solar plexus. Conway dropped like a punctured football, and rolled onto his side, knees up, groaning, clutching his belly. Lawlor stepped around him, went to the center of the room and picked up the gun.

"Don't move!"

He was still bent over, the Mossberg in his right hand. He stayed in a crouch and peered over his shoulder. Seda was aiming the Smith at him, two-handed this time, arms extended, feet shoulder width. She looked right at home.

"Drop it," she said.

He began straightening up. "Really? It might go off."

"Don't be cute. Just put it back on the floor."

Lawlor was standing straight, facing her, the Mossberg on his right side, barrel pointed down. Slowly, he reached for the pump action, his eyes locked on hers. Then he worked the action back and forth, once, twice, all the way to eight, hearing the shells rattling tock, tock, tock on the wooden floor. Then he flipped the gun over his shoulder, sending it cartwheeling over the counter where it smashed into the line of bottles behind the bar.

"Safe now," he said.

"That was a dumb thing to do." She steadied herself.

He gave her a long look.

"I'm finished with this," he said. "I'm going home."

"The fuck you are." Her eyes were dark behind the black hole in her hand.

He said, "You ever shot anyone before?"

She didn't answer.

"Didn't think so." He put his hands in his pockets, turned and went for the door.

"Lawlor!"

He stopped. Took his hands out of his pockets again and stood there, looking through the smudged glass in the door. Green water and white sky. Lead weights at the end of his arms.

"I'll fucking shoot you!"

"No, love. You won't." He turned around and held out his hands. In his right hand, three cartridges; in his left hand, four. The brass gleamed dully in the dim light of the room. He let them drop to the floor.

"Fuck." She spat out the word and threw the gun at him. He stepped left and it went over his shoulder and hit the wall. Somewhere, a phone began to ring.

Lawlor bent to pick up the rounds he'd dropped on the floor. Then he went to pick up the Smith. His hand was trembling slightly and he had to dry his palm on the leg of his trousers. Behind him, the phone stopped ringing.

He pushed on the catch on the left of the revolver and the

cylinder swung open. He tipped the seven cartridges into his hand.

Seda was staring at him, the two red spots high on her cheekbones. "It was loaded?"

"All the time."

"So what about those bullets?"

"From the gun safe in your house. I grabbed an extra handful, just in case."

For the first time, she laughed. "I could have killed you."

"You wouldn't have."

There was a muffled ping. Conway was sitting up, clutching his stomach. He dug into the back pocket of his jeans and held out a phone to Seda. "It's yours."

Seda took it, and began tapping at the screen.

Lawlor put the gun on the counter. He poured the bullets into a glass. He looked at Conway. "I told you not to try anything stupid."

'Fuck you, man." Conway's voice was a wheeze.

Seda made a sharp, high sound, like a hurt animal. Her right hand held her phone to her ear. Her left hand was clamped over her mouth. Her eyes were huge.

Conway pulled himself up. "Seda?"

She took her hand away from her face. She was as white as the tips of the waves breaking outside the window. "It's Emilia."

"What about her?" Conway went to her but she put her hand up, and held him at bay.

She turned to Lawlor. "Emilia. My daughter."

She held her breath for a moment.

"He has her."

44

Brenda Grady hadn't let Róisín in after she'd identified her son's body in the hospital. She'd been too upset. This time, when she answered Róisín's knock, she didn't say a word, just stepped back to allow her to walk into the narrow hallway and down to the kitchen.

She hadn't needed to point the way. Róisín had been brought up in a house just like this, in a similar cinder block, not too far away. Perhaps Brenda Grady could see it in her face.

The hallway was dark and cramped, no more than three feet wide, so the kitchen was a surprise. It had an airy, modern look that belied the fact that the house had been built before the First World War. The table was seasoned wood, the counter tops some kind of patterned stone. The appliances and the sink were all made of stainless steel.

Róisín sat at the table and looked into the postage stamp-sized garden. The mug that Brenda Grady placed in front of her was made of fine china, decorated with peonies. The tea was the color of rust.

"I've no biscuits, I'm afraid." Her face was drawn and there were dark circles under her eyes.

"I'm so sorry, Mrs Grady."

"Brenda, please. Sean talked a lot about you. Said you were one of the good ones."

"Sean was one of the good ones, Brenda. And I'm not just saying so."

She nodded, and looked out of the window, the tea on the table, forgotten. "You'll be wanting a look at his room, I suppose. It's up the stairs, on the left. You won't mind if I don't go up with you."

The room was small and neat and spare, about what Róisín had expected. There was a narrow bed and a small work desk, and a framed print of Albert Einstein sticking out his tongue. The desk was empty, except for a laptop PC and a pair of bright-red cushioned headphones. The machine was turned on, but the screen was locked. Róisín didn't bother trying the password.

She found a notebook in a drawer. Sandwiched inside it was the paper copy of the sudoku fax, with Róisín's notes scribbled on it. Another drawer was full of correspondence. Official mail from PSNI; bills, including several from providers of Internet-related services that showed Grady spent a lot of money on enhanced access to the Web. Nothing personal.

"May I take these?" She showed Brenda Grady the notebook and the laptop.

"Go ahead."

"Officers will bring them back later."

"I don't need them." Her voice was dull. "I don't know anything about computers."

Róisín sat down again. "Brenda, I know you went over this with Sergeant Murray, but I wondered if you'd remembered anything else."

She shook her head.

"Only, we've had a look at his mobile, and there were no calls or texts that evening. I know Sean left the office before lunch, because I sent him home. And he got back at two, is that right?"

"He stopped for a sandwich at Sparta in the city."

"Aye, you said. And then you went out? At five? "

"I went to St Theresa's. I teach a cooking class from six to nine. I stay and chat after with some of the other ladies, while we tidy up. I got back just after ten."

"And you saw Sean?"

"No. I just said goodnight to him through the door."

"Did he reply?"

"No. But the light was on. I supposed he had the computer on, and his headphones."

"Did that happen often?"

She shrugged. "More and more these days. He likes his privacy. I don't know what he's up to, playing games or whatever. But I leave him to it."

"And then you went to bed. And you didn't hear anything?"

"I'm a good sleeper."

"Would you have heard someone ring the bell or knock on the door?"

"I'd have heard that, sure. But I didn't."

"Okay." Róisín clutched the laptop tighter. "You don't know if he had a girlfriend or anything, do you? Someone he might have made an arrangement to meet later?"

Another shake of the head. "He never had a girlfriend. He preferred his computer. He said that's where he met people and made friends. He said it was way more healthy than going down the pub and drinking ten pints. And after the way his father was, I can't say he was wrong about that."

Róisín said nothing. Brenda Grady looked at her, intelligent dark brown eyes in her sunken face. "You too, eh love?"

Róisín squeezed her hand. "Thanks Mrs Grady. I'll be in touch."

Sean had encrypted all the data on his laptop, so although the tech unit was able to access it, they couldn't read anything. Breaking the encryption would take a lot longer, they told her. She suspected, knowing Sean, that 'a lot longer' might turn out to be never.

That left the notebook. But a quick glance though its pages suggested it would be a dead end. It was full of lists, all of which appeared to be related to work.

A phone was ringing in one of the cubicles behind her. She pushed the pickup button on her display. "Computer Crimes. DI Mackey."

"I'm looking for Sean." A male voice, deep and ragged. A West Belfast accent.

"May I ask who's calling?"

A pause. "Mark Summers."

She waited. The seconds passed. "May I ask what this is regarding, Mister Summers?"

"Is Sean there?"

"No, he's not. Can I help you?"

She could almost hear the man on the other end of the line weighing his decision. Finally, he said, "I run the Youth Center. Sean stops in sometimes, helps me out with the computers."

"Oh yes?"

"Well, he got some stuff faxed to him here, a couple of days back. He told me he'd be by to pick it up, but he's not been by."

"Which Youth Center is that you work at, Mister Summers?"

"Gleneagle. On the Ormeau Road."

"I know it. Look, will you be there for the next hour or so?"

"I'm going nowhere."

"I'll see you in a few."

Mark Summers was about fifty years old, graying around the temples, but with the lean, whippet look of a fell runner. His face crumpled when she told him about Sean.

"I can't believe it." He sat down on his desk. It was a Formica-covered refugee from the 1970s, like the blackboard, the leather medicine balls, the wood-handled skipping ropes and almost everything else in the room.

"What would he have been doing up on the Black Mountain anyway?" Summers said.

"I was about to ask if you might know the same thing."

He shook his head. "I go running up there with a cross-country club sometimes. And I know that path. You have to know that it's there to get on it. Hard enough during the day. Bloody impossible at night."

"Had he ever been up there with you?"

"Sean?" he half-laughed. "No way. And how would he get up there at that time of night, anyway? The buses don't run after ten thirty, and he had no car."

She glanced at the pile of papers on his desk. "You said he had a fax sent here?"

Summers riffled through the papers and removed two sheets.

"When did you last speak to him?" Róisín asked.

"Tuesday afternoon. He called me." He pushed the fax over the table. "This came in the next morning."

She scanned the pages. A cover sheet, and a printout of a request for information response from the Driver and Vehicle Licensing Agency in Swansea. A name, John Grogan. An address in Newport, and a photo of a driver's license.

"Everything alright?"

"Oh." She realized she'd been staring at the photo. "Yes, yes. Everything's fine."

"Who's your man? Some villain?"

"I'll be honest with you, Mister Summers. I've no idea." Not a lie. But not quite the truth. There was something about the photo. She had definitely seen the man before. "But I'll check it out."

She folded the pages and tucked them into her bag. Summers got to his feet, and together they walked through the center. The hall was full of teenage boys, playing seven-a-side, and they hollered and whistled at Summers as they passed.

"Sorry about that," he said.

"No problem. Some of them look pretty good."

"There's a few good players. Not that I know one end of a football from the other, mind."

"You don't coach them?"

"Naw. There's a fella comes over from Belmont. Shug Williams. Used to play winger for Linfield."

He laughed at the expression on her face. "Aye, a lot's changed, hasn't it?"

"And just as well."

They walked on in silence until they reached the end of the hall.

"Will there be a service, do you know?" he asked.

"I'd say there would be. Will his mother not tell you?"

"I don't know her."

"I could give you a call when I find out."

"If you wouldn't mind."

He was about to open the door for her, but stopped. There was a frown on his face. "Why do you think Sean asked that stuff to be sent here? You must have a fax in your office, no?"

"We do, of course." She had the sudden urge to get away from there, as quickly as possible. "But it's on one of those photocopier hybrid jobs, and you know those things. They're always breaking down."

He grunted. "Still, I thought everything was on computers and email these days."

"You'd be surprised how many government departments seem to be living in the last century."

He snorted. "I would not indeed. You should try requesting grant money from Stormont. The other day, I had to ..." He stopped, red in the face. "Sorry. I was about to go off there."

"No problem. Sometimes up at Knock I feel like I'm working in the Dark Ages myself." She pushed the door open. Smiled at him. "Thanks for calling, Mister Summers. I'll be in touch."

45

The cafe was Seda's idea. Lawlor wanted a public place where Ovian would feel at ease, but not so comfortable that he could hope to put a hole in him without anyone paying undue attention. Zahrad was a small, narrow place off Central Boulevard in Glendale. There was a service counter with a pastry display on the left, a row of tables on the right. A single two-top table in the window. To the left, a hairdresser; to the right, a bank. And the Glendale police headquarters across the street.

There were two cops at the counter, ordering coffee and baklava. Ovian was already sitting in the window, dressed in his dove-gray suit, a tiny cup of coffee on the table.

Lawlor sat down in the empty chair. Ovian tilted his head at the man behind the counter. The two cops had taken the table closest to the door. They were both heavyset men in their twenties, made bulkier by the stab-proof vests under their uniforms.

"Your guys?" Lawlor asked.

Ovian made a half shrug. "Affiliated."

"Maybe this place wasn't such a good choice after all."

"No. This was a very good choice. The coffee is excellent

here. And the *nazook*. I ordered you some. I hope you're not allergic to nuts."

The counterman placed a cup of espresso on the table, and a small plate containing four square cookies. Ovian took one and bit into it. There was a small explosion of phyllo pastry.

"Please, have one. They are the best outside of Yerevan."

"Thank you, but I'm not hungry."

Ovian brushed pastry flakes off his jacket. He looked disappointed. Lawlor sipped his coffee. It was strong and smooth, like drinking a square of raw chocolate.

"Very good, am I right?" Ovian was smiling.

Lawlor nodded. "Very good."

"Seda knows I like this place because I order all my pastry from here for family events. Family being very important to me. You understand." The smile was still on Ovian's face, but his eyes were like two polished stones. "And when I tell you I would do anything to protect my family, I think you understand this better than anyone."

"Even destroying someone else's family?"

"Of course. That's what war is. Country against country, tribe against tribe, family against family."

"So this is a war."

"The moment my family is threatened, I go to war." The smile was gone. "So, yes. This is a war. And war to me means total war. No rules, no half measures."

"Scorched earth."

"Exactly." He drank the remains of his coffee.

"Not much room for error."

"The error is on the part of he who starts the war."

The door to the cafe swung open, and two more men came in, dressed in lightweight suits. They were at last a decade older than the patrolmen, and their hair was a little longer, but they still looked like cops.

Lawlor said, "Where's the girl?"

"Safe."

"Her mother will want something more specific."

"Tell her Emilia is with her cousins."

One of the detectives was leaning on the counter, chatting to the patrolmen. He made a show of checking his watch, and the uniformed cops stood up. One of them glanced apologetically at Ovian as they hustled out of the cafe. The two detectives followed. The door swung shut and the cafe was empty.

"What will it take for you to let her go?" Lawlor asked.

"You don't know? Surely Seda told you about his archive."

"She mentioned it."

Ovian chuckled. "I bet she did. Did she tell you how it is secured?"

Lawlor shook his head. Ovian signaled for another coffee.

"I received an email from Rehan at noon yesterday. Yes, I know. He was dead by then. How did he die, incidentally?"

"A stomach wound. Courtesy of one of the men you sent to gang-rape his wife."

Ovian gave him a blank look, then leaned back to let the cafe owner clear the table and put a second espresso down.

"The email explained that Rehan had set up what he called a burn vault. Every day at nine, it texts him. If he doesn't respond by noon, control passes to Seda for twenty-four hours."

"And if she doesn't respond?"

"Forty-eight hour lock down. Then everything in the vault gets sent to a list of email addresses. Journalists, I assume. Police. FBI." Ovian shrugged. "He was quite thorough."

"What triggered it?"

"His heart. He had a pacemaker put in a few years ago. Specifically for this reason. He tried to conceal it from me, but I found out, of course."

"Why didn't you stop him?" Lawlor asked.

"How? He was the only one with access. Confront him in the wrong way and he panics. I needed to be careful. I needed to convince him to destroy the records, which meant I needed him safe, and I needed an incentive." He smiled.

"I was the incentive."

"Indeed you were, Mister Lawlor. It was very hard to get Rehan to go out to dinner in Santa Monica the evening he was photographed. He is - was - a very cautious man. He knew his photograph was on all the police databases, and as a result, he was very careful. But I convinced him that he would be surrounded by people, that he needed to show willing, and meet our Latin partners to cement a lucrative deal, and that we would be inside the entire time. All lies, of course."

Lawlor was very still. Ovian's smile widened. "You are beginning to see it now."

"I think I am."

"Someone wants you dead, very badly." He picked up his coffee cup and drained it. "I do not."

He placed the empty cup carefully on its saucer. "Or I did not, at least. I wanted you alive. For years I have been asking certain people for this, asking if they might find a way to send you to me, to allow me to make a trade with Rehan. I had almost given up, until one day I got a call. Bring Harper into the light where we can see him. Where we can photograph him. Where we can bait a hook for Gary Lawlor and reel him across the ocean and the continental United States. And kill him."

"Why would Harper agree to burn the records if someone was just going to kill me? What use would I be to him dead?"

"He didn't know you were to be killed. All he knew was that I was going to deliver him to you, so that you could go back to Ireland and help clear his name. In return he would destroy the records."

"So what went wrong?"

"Whoever it was that wanted you dead wasn't willing to wait. When you disappeared from your home in Belfast, they panicked. They knew you'd be coming to Los Angeles, and so they decided to hedge, and contracted with my Latin friends. Their coverage of the street is admittedly far superior to ours, so the decision made tactical sense. But it ruined my plans. When Harper heard men were out to kill you, he naturally amended our deal to say that he would not burn the vault until you were safely back in Ireland again and able to clear him."

"The call you got," Lawlor said. "Who was it?"

Ovian smiled. "So now it appears we all have something at stake in these negotiations. Seda wants her daughter. I want those records destroyed. You want a name."

"Seda wants more than her daughter back. She wants something to guarantee that you won't go after her family."

"My word is not enough?"

"What do you think?"

A shrug. "If she wants Emilia, she needs to provide proof that the entire archive has been destroyed. Or she lets me destroy it. Then I let them both go, to wherever they wish, and pledge to leave them and their family alone. In return for brokering this deal, you get a name. And then we are all happy."

"You seem remarkably cool about giving this person up."

"My deal with them was to get you here. They reneged when they contracted with the Hondurans. I owe them nothing."

"But how can I be sure that you're giving me a real name?"

Another shrug. "You can't. Just as Seda can't be sure I won't burn her village to the ground. And just as I can't be sure that Rehan didn't lie to me and that there is a back door into the vault that Seda can use to extract a few choice pieces of information to hold over me."

"And if she did?"

"And I found out about it?" He took a long pause. "She knows what I would do."

Lawlor sat for a while, the sun warm on his shoulder.

"She won't like the terms," he said.

"I don't much like them myself. But there is no other offer."

Lawlor nodded. "What I don't see is why you're including me in the deal. I've done nothing but give you a headache from the moment I landed. But you're willing to hand over what I'm assuming is a valuable piece of information like it's a piece of..." he jabbed a finger at the pastry on the edge of Ovian's saucer. "Whatever that's called."

"*Nazook.*"

"I can see why you might be suspicious, but this is more than a tip for a messenger."

"How's that?"

"I need someone that Seda will trust. And, if not trust, exactly, someone she will believe."

"Why would she believe me? Especially now I have an incentive."

"Because you have a much greater incentive to tell her not to take this deal. Once the 48 hours have passed and the archive is unlocked, Seda will be able to gain entry, which means you, too will be able to gain entry, and acquire the information that Rehan was going to provide you. The name of the person he believed ordered you killed. The person he believes was responsible for the death of your children."

It was a moment before Lawlor realized he was holding his breath. He exhaled slowly, his head swimming slightly, his eyes focusing on the motes of dust turning in the sunlight between them. He was acutely aware of the gun digging into his pelvic bone.

"Seda knows this, of course," Ovian went on. "And she knows what it means to you. So when you tell her you have rejected the opportunity to ever acquire this information, in favor of the deal I have offered, she will believe it."

"Why?"

"Because you are a good man, of course."

"A good man? I came here to kill someone."

"But you didn't, did you? And you had plenty of opportunity. I gave you a loaded gun myself. But you didn't pull the trigger."

The sound of a siren made them both turn towards the window. A patrol car powered out of the driveway of the police station across the street.

Ovian asked, "Did Seda offer you a deal? To kill me in return for the name?"

Lawlor didn't reply.

"I thought so. But you didn't take the deal. Not because it would be next to impossible, but because that is not who you are, Mister Lawlor. You have killed men, and you will kill if you have to. But you are not, at heart, a killer. I know this. Seda knows this. Which is why when you go back to her and tell her that we must trust each other, and that this is the best deal we can possibly make, all of us, she will agree."

46

Lawlor had been at the Observatory for hours. He had walked slowly around the building, watching faces and cars and selfie snappers and looking out for anything that looked unusual. Which, in Los Angeles meant almost everything. When the sun set, he watched to see who wasn't looking up at the Hollywood sign or down at the city, and when the sky faded from turquoise to navy blue to black, he watched the cars flow out of the lot in a one-way stream, to see who stayed behind.

He made one last pass around the walkway, counting the couples left gazing down at the blazing grid of red and white and yellow. No one gave him a second glance, and he didn't see any face twice, and he watched from the shadows as two by two they sauntered to their cars and away.

Seda arrived at half-past eleven. Her headlights washed the sky as she made the turn into the lot. He watched her walk uncertainly across the grass and past the plinth opposite the Observatory's front doors. She was wearing jeans and dark sneakers, a dark shirt and jacket. She had a small bag slung across her body. She walked with a slight stoop, one hand clutching the strap, the other clamped over the bag.

"Over here," he said. He was standing beside a low wall

under the trees. She didn't acknowledge him, just made a half turn and walked towards the sound of his voice. Her face was as white as the half moon that hung low over the hills behind her.

"There are still people here," she said.

"Just a few couples looking at the view."

She looked around. "Will he come alone, like we said? Just him and her?"

"I think he will. He doesn't want you to send those files. He'll do what he needs to do to keep that from happening."

"And once he has what he wants, what if he just decides to kill us? There's nothing to stop him doing that, is there?"

Lawlor felt the weight of the gun in the small of his back. "Not really. But I don't think it'll happen."

"Why not?"

Lawlor sighed. "Because, like I said before, he can't take the risk that you've held something back. If you have, and he kills you, and whatever it is gets into the world, he's done for."

She sat on the wall beside him. "I haven't held anything back."

"So you said."

"You don't believe me?"

"It doesn't matter what I believe. It only matters what you do. Holding something back is one thing. Using it is another. You can only use it in retaliation, if he breaks his word. If he gets even a hint that you've broken yours, he'll do everything he said he'd do. To you and your family. That I do believe."

"Mad," she said.

"What?"

"M.A.D. Mutually assured destruction. That's what this is."

"That's right. That's exactly what it is."

278

She smoothed her hair back and tugged on the strap of her bag, like it was a lifeline. "I'm nervous."

"Me too." He thought about sitting down, but he was too wired. He shifted his belt, felt the cylinder of the small revolver grind against his spine.

A second wash of light swept across the sky. "Here he is."

The car parked directly opposite the plinth, its headlights saturating the lawn and casting a long shadow that reached almost to the Observatory doors. The engine hummed.

Seda twitched, like a nervous horse. "What's he doing?"

"He's talking to Emilia. Telling her what to do and when. Warning her what not to do. Keeping her calm."

The engine snapped off. Then the headlights. High above the parking lot, the Hollywood sign seemed to leap off the hill, glittering under the half moon. A small flock of birds leapt up from the trees on the other side of the car park and swept over the lawn, so low that Lawlor could hear the hum of the air around their wings.

The car doors opened, the interior lit up, and Lawlor saw Ovian and, in the passenger seat, someone with a head of blonde hair. He heard Seda's breathing pick up, and put his hand on her back.

"I'm okay," she said.

"Wait here." Lawlor stepped out of the shadows. Ovian said something to the girl. The moonlight glinted on her hair as she nodded, and Ovian began walking, alone.

He and Lawlor met in the center of the lawn.

"Not so many people around this time," Ovian said.

"I counted six. Three couples. Enjoying the moonlight around the back. Are any of them yours?"

Ovian's skin looked like molten steel under the moonlight. "I may be many things, Mister Lawlor. But above all, I am a man of my word."

"I'm counting on it."

Ovian made a show of checking his watch. "Six minutes."

"Okay. I'm going to tell Seda to come over here now. She'll stand on my left. You call Emilia over. She stands on your right. So they're facing each other. Clear?

"I understand."

"When Seda gets the text from the archive, she'll hand you the phone. At the same time, Emilia will walk across and stand beside Seda. You delete the archive. You'll get a verification message. Choose yes. Then you'll receive a confirmation message that the archive has been destroyed."

"That's all?"

"Did you want someone to email you a receipt?"

Ovian half-smiled. "Very well. Shall we?"

He turned and gestured.

Emilia was tall for a twelve-year old, with a head of straight, blonde hair that reached to her shoulders and was cut straight across her forehead. It was immediately obvious whose child she was. She had Conway's snub nose, and Seda's wide mouth. Her chin wobbled as she watched her mother walk across the lawn.

"Mom?"

"Hush now, Emilia." Ovian turned to look her in the face. "Not a word, remember?"

She shrank away from him, wrapping her arms around herself. She nodded.

Seda had her phone in her hand. Her face was set, her jaw clenched, the light from the moon hollowing her cheeks. She stepped behind Lawlor, and came up on his left. She had her eyes on the phone. There was no sound. No birds, not traffic. Not even the wind. Lawlor found himself counting. Five. Ten. Fifteen.

The phone buzzed. Seda swiped the screen with a finger and held out the phone. Ovian reached for it.

"Wait," Lawlor said. He motioned to Emilia. "Stand beside your mother."

Emilia stepped forward and Ovian took the phone. The light from the screen cast deep shadows from the ridges and scars on his skin. He took a moment to read, then tapped the screen. It flickered, and he tapped again. He handed it back.

Seda tried to stuff the phone into her purse, but it fell to the ground. She took a step back, using her left arm to push Emilia behind her, her right hand dipping down into her purse and coming out with a small, ugly automatic.

The gun was a tiny thing, all raw edges and unpolished metal. It was less than five inches long, but Ovian was less than five feet away.

"Don't do it, Seda." Lawlor reached behind him. "He'll have planned for this. Even if he doesn't have people here, watching us right now, he'll have left instructions. If he doesn't come back alive, it's over for you. You'll be running forever. And your family..."

She hissed like a cat. She was shaking all over, like someone pulled out of an ice bath, the muzzle of the gun making arcs and whirls and figures of eight.

And then she steadied herself.

The gunshot sounded like a whip cracking. It bounced off the white walls of the Observatory and the cliff side of the Hollywood Hills. Back and forth, over and over.

Emilia screamed. Seda was face down on the ground, the automatic on the grass beside her.

Lawlor thrust the Smith & Wesson back into his belt. He picked up Seda's gun. It felt like a toy.

Emilia was kneeling on the grass beside her mother, her face in her hands, crying in heaves. Lawlor knelt. He turned Seda onto her back. She stared up at the sky, blinking fast, her mouth working, but no sound coming out. Her left shoulder was wet with blood.

"I'm sorry about that, girl." He tore her coat open, and then the shirt underneath. "I had to do it. I'm sorry about this, too." He felt for an exit wound. He could feel splinters of bone grinding under the skin. A real mess, but by the look of the bleeding, nothing that would kill her.

Her eyes closed, and he slapped her face lightly until she opened them again. "That's good. You stay with us, now. Your daughter needs you. Okay?" He tore the sleeves of her coat and shirt loose, pulled them gently off her arm, then used them to plug and bind the wound.

"Emilia."

She sat up. Her face was streaming with tears.

"Can you help me?"

She stared at him.

"I need your help. We need to help your mother. Can you help me?"

She nodded.

He pointed. "Put your hands here and here. Put as much pressure as you can. There may be some blood, but keep everything tight. Do that and she'll be right. And whatever you do, don't let her go to sleep."

"You're not leaving?" Her voice was ragged.

"I'll be right over here. Be sure to keep her awake."

He got to his feet. Ovian had gone back to his car. He was leaning on the hood, his arms folded.

"I've been told so many times that a highly-trained man never really loses his edge," Ovian said. "I suppose I never really understood what that meant before now. You were very fast."

"I only needed to be faster than the sniper you have in the trees back there."

"I came alone."

"You did?" Lawlor was ejecting the rounds from Seda's tiny pistol into his hand. "Well, something disturbed the birds earlier."

He made a quarter turn and threw the bullets into the bushes. The empty magazine followed, and then the gun.

Ovian was staring at Seda, lying in the grass, her daughter kneeling over her.

"She was upset," Lawlor said. "She wasn't thinking clearly. She won't make the same mistake again."

Ovian shook his head. "She wants revenge, Lawlor. Just as I did. Just as you still do. A bullet in the shoulder will not stop her. I saw it in her eyes. She has become a wolf now. And I have to put her down."

"Kill her and you kill yourself."

"Because she made a copy of Rehan's archive?" Ovian laughed. "There is very little in there that can hurt me now. You said it yourself."

"I'm not talking about the archive." Lawlor reached into his back pocket and took out a folded envelope. "I'm talking about your medical records."

Ovian smirked. "So you hacked into a clinic. Bravo."

"Harper talked a lot about you," Lawlor said. "He told me that when you were burned, in that house fire, you refused to have any surgery done on your face. Not even basic first aid. He said it was because you wanted to scare the shit out of people. You wanted them to think you were impervious to pain. You wanted to look like a nightmare. Which makes a kind of sense to someone like Harper, I suppose."

He opened the envelope. "But your old pal Fermin didn't buy it. I didn't spend much time with him, but he struck me as a real know-your-enemy kind of guy. He told me he spread money all over Armenia, for years, trying to buy information about Artur Ovian. And he found out one very important piece of information."

The envelope contained several sheets of A4 paper. Lawlor held them up. "A friend of mine got this from a hospital in Baku last night. Fermin told me where to look."

Ovian was very still.

"From the Republic of Azerbaijan national records office. Ovian, Artur Cohar." Lawlor read. "Place of birth, Stepanakert, AzSSR. Date of birth 17 August 1972. Blood group A positive. So far so good."

He turned the page. "But then there's this from your clinic. Sorry to hear about your colon, by the way." He held up the page. "It's a bit confusing, you see, because it says here that your blood group isn't A pos. It's AB."

Ovian said nothing. The scars on his head and face looked as though they were made of molten steel in the light of the moon.

Lawlor folded the pages. "Stepanakert was almost destroyed during the war, wasn't it? But I wonder if you helped things along a wee bit. With the hospital and the City Hall. When the Azeris cleared everyone out, you must have thought that was that. But Fermin found out that when they started to rebuild the city, they found all the old records. Buried deep underground. And they relocated them all to Baku. For us to find."

It was a moment before the man who called himself Ovian replied.

"I don't see that this makes any difference," he said.

"No? How are the people in your organization going to take the news that you're not who you say you are? The real Artur Ovian was your boss, wasn't he? You were a flunky. Middle manager at best. Maybe one of the guys who came to paint his new house. But that story you told, about your wife. That sounded real to me. So what did you do? Wait until your boss got drunk and fell asleep, then take his wife to bed? You went out of the window, didn't you? Artur's bedroom window. There would have been people in the street. They would have seen. That's why they thought you were him. And you went with it. You were so badly burned and your voice was such a wreck, they couldn't recognize you. And all the rest of the team died in the fire. The real Artur Ovian with them. It must have been like an instant promotion for you." Lawlor shook his head. "Well, you've got balls, I'll say that. Balls like brass."

Ovian sighed. "So what do you want?"

"I want our deal." He jerked his head towards the girl and her mother, on the grass. "I'll make sure Seda doesn't try anything. I'll advise her to go somewhere, a long way from here. You let them go. You don't touch them. Ever. And you get me what I want."

Ovian touched the nub of flesh that used to be his ear. "Artur had a very distinctive face. High cheekbones. A strong jaw.

Nothing like mine. If you look closely, you can see we were nothing alike. But no one looks closely. No one looks past this mask. If they look at it at all."

Lawlor nodded. "Well, your secret's safe with me. If you agree to my terms. And give me what I asked for."

"You have given me very little choice, Mister Lawlor. I congratulate you." He folded the paper and tucked it into his jacket. And then he dipped his fingers into the breast pocket of his suit, and pulled out a business card.

Lawlor took it, and read it, and had an instant feeling of deja vu. Followed by the breathless, heady sensation of everything falling into place, like the tumblers of an open lock.

"This must never come back to me," Ovian said. "If it does, I will find you, wherever you are."

"Don't worry." Lawlor had kept one of the bullets from Seda's gun. He held it up between his finger and his thumb. Then he leaned forward and dropped it into the breast pocket of Ovian's suit. "I know how to find you, too."

47

Róisín shifted on the plastic seat in the ACC's outer office. Sean Grady's memorial had been a small affair, close family and friends in St Mary's Church. Shona had sobbed through the service, then drunk most of a half-bottle of vodka that she'd brought with her to the reception in the church hall. Róisín had spent most of the time talking to Sean's mother, and learned more in two hours than she had in all the time they'd spent working together, which didn't make her feel any better about things. Over stewed tea and curled-edged egg and cress sandwiches, she'd learned that Sean had wanted to be a psychologist, but excelled with computers; he had a shelf full of psychology and philosophy texts; he collected sea glass; he liked to go walking, on the beach and in the hills, sometimes with groups from the Boys & Girls Club, sometimes alone. He had never had a serious relationship.

Would he have been the type to go up to the Black Mountain on his own of an evening? His mother didn't rule it out. Sean was a solitary type. He would go out for hours at a time, but he never came back smelling of smoke or booze, and his eyes never had the glazed or fractured look that came with drugs. Mrs Grady had been a nurse in the eighties, which meant she'd

PRIMED

seen plenty of heroin addicts in her time. She knew what a druggie looked like, and her son was not one, she was sure of that.

Which left Róisín with the simplest explanation: Sean had gone for a walk, alone. He had slipped and fallen. He had cracked his head and died.

Kilpatrick was standing behind his desk, which struck her as unusual.

"Rab Harper's dead." His voice was flat.

"How? Where?"

"Gunshot wound to the torso. In Los Angeles, of all bloody places." He glared. "What do you know about this?"

"Nothing, sir." A pause. "Does this have to do with Lawlor?"

"Don't come all naive with me. Who else would it have to do with?"

"I..." She shut her mouth.

"Harper's body was dumped in the street outside a government office in Los Angeles. Fingerprints linked to one Rehan Markosian, but there was a note in his pocket saying who he really was. The FBI confirmed through Interpol."

He turned the page on a file on his desk. "I'm only going to ask you this once, Róisín, and I want a straight answer. Do you know anything about this?"

For the briefest moment, she considered telling the truth.

"No, sir," she said.

"If I find you're holding back on me, I'll have your hide."

"Yes, sir."

"And Lawlor hasn't contacted you?"

Safer ground now. "No, sir. Not a word."

"Well at least we know where he is. Perhaps the Americans will pick him up for us."

"Are you sure it's him, sir?"

"Don't be ridiculous. One minute he goes AWOL from here, the next the man who murdered his kids turns up dead. Of course it's him. If there's one conclusion we can draw from his inexplicable absence, it's that he's gone completely off the rails."

"Sir." She had the feeling she was opening a very creaky door to a very dark cellar. "What is it we want the Americans to pick him up for?"

It took a moment for Kilpatrick to answer.

"Haven't you been listening to a word I've said these last few days? Lawlor is a serious security risk."

"Just because he knows about our opsec systems, sir? Sure, his deputy knows all of that stuff too, doesn't he?" She caught Kilpatrick's look. "I mean, I just feel like I'm missing something. Like I don't have the full picture."

"Well, that's because you don't. None of us do. That's the nature of this kind of work. You're a police officer. That means carrying out the orders that your superior officers have decided are necessary to keep the peace."

The scar on the inside of her knee was suddenly itchy.

"So I should just follow orders, sir?"

"Yes, Detective Chief Inspector. You follow orders." Kilpatrick was red in the face now. "And you do it without question."

48

The card was plain white, of average thickness, with a name and a phone number laser printed on it in a plain font. The only thing making the card in any way remarkable was a small crest of the Department of State embossed in the bottom right-hand corner.

Lawlor studied the card for a while, running his thumb over the crest, and looked up at the Harry Truman Building. He had taken the bus, and then walked up 23rd Street to the entrance to Navy Hill. He had asked the guard what the building was being used for these days, and reminisced with him for a few minutes about the days when it was the headquarters of the Bureau of Navy Medicine and Surgery. Then he walked back. Then he did it again. Now he was standing directly opposite the Department of State building. He could see security people moving back and forth behind green-tinted bulletproof glass.

The State Department's main address was on C Street, but access to that side of the building was blocked. So he didn't know whether he was looking at the front door or the back. But he was pretty sure it didn't matter. He was paying what a security manual would term unusual and undue attention.

It took longer than he thought it would. Maybe their ancient computers were running slow, or their outdated, patched-up software was glitchy. Or maybe it was the beard he had grown on his long, dog-legged way across the country, riding trains and buses and staying in cheap motels.

A security guy pushed through a door. Then another. They wore the regulation white short-sleeved shirts and black pants and heavy belts weighted down with torches, sidearms, two-way radios and various other things. The Kevlar vests they wore under their shirts made them look wider and squatter than a regular human, as though they had been squashed in the lobby before they were sent out. One of them stopped by the twelve-foot concrete planter that doubled as a traffic barrier. The other stepped quickly through a break in the traffic. Halfway across, Lawlor saw it was a woman, her hair pulled back tight and wrapped in a neat bun.

"Sir?" She stopped in the street between two parked cars far enough from him to give her room to maneuver if he made an aggressive move. "Can I help you?"

She stood square on, shoulders back, like a woman standing at ease on a parade ground. Her left hand rested on her belt at her hip; her right rested on the butt of her sidearm. She had skin the color of a seasoned chestnut and her eyes were a shade darker. Clear and wary behind long lashes.

Lawlor held the card out. "Please tell this man I'd like to speak with him. I'll be at the wee coffee kiosk opposite the Vietnam Veterans Memorial."

The woman didn't so much as glance down. "I'm sorry, sir. If you need to make an appointment with someone in the Department, please either call or use the website. Do you need that information?"

Lawlor let go of the card. It fluttered to the ground and

landed on the toe of the woman's boot.

"I'll be there until five," he said.

49

Lawlor chose a bench under the trees. It was a warm day, but there was a fresh breeze coming off the river. People passed back and forth, on their way to and from the memorials. They were of all ages and nationalities and ethnicities. Some chattered loudly, and some were quiet and sober. Birds twittered in the trees around him, and a drone buzzed overhead like an angry bumblebee.

It was a half-hour before he arrived. He looked exactly the same the last time Lawlor had seen him, with his boss, Michael Foley, in the police headquarters conference room in Belfast. The same rumpled raincoat. The same wreck of a face, like a crumpled white paper bag, spotted with grease. The same strands of iron-colored hair slicked over his mottled skull. The name on the business card that Ovian had given him said Brian Coyle, but Lawlor had no idea if that was his real name. He did know that the State Department wasn't the man's address anymore. Foley had resigned as Secretary of State more than a week ago. Now he was running for President. With Coyle right by his side.

Coyle walked down the road to the cafe, made a turn around the building for appearance's sake, and then stood in front of it, hands in his pockets, looking around.

It didn't take him long to spot Lawlor. He crossed the road and stepped over the chain that bordered the path. He had the mournful look of a man who'd just found an insect in his salad.

Lawlor stood up and walked across the grass to the Vietnam Memorial. There were perhaps a hundred people there, some walking slowly the length of the black marble scar, some tracing the names with fingertips, some placing bunches of flowers at the foot of the memorial, or pushing folded messages into the cracks between the carved slabs. There was a large tour group from Taiwan, being lectured by an earnest young woman who was leading them slowly down the path, walking backwards in a bright yellow raincoat.

Lawlor tagged onto the end of the group. Coyle joined him, and they walked in step for a few moments.

Coyle sniffed and wiped his nose with the sleeve of his coat. "I did my first tour with the Agency in Vietnam. Saigon. Just before the place went to hell. You've seen that old news footage of guys pushing a Huey off the back of the Midway? That was my bird."

Lawlor said nothing. Coyle gave him a sidelong look. "You don't believe me?"

"No."

He chuckled. It sounded like a drunk hiccuping. "You're right. I'm full of it. The closest I've been to Saigon is the Westin in Honolulu. But that doesn't mean I haven't done all sorts of bad things in the service of my country."

"Is that what this is about? Serving your country?"

"Of course. It's sure as hell not personal. Fact is, I couldn't give a flying fuck about you, Lawlor."

"And yet you've gone to a lot of trouble. Flying to Belfast with that bogus file on Harper. Persuading the Israelis to doctor the forensics and the photos. And then paying off Fermin and Ovian and Fyffe. That's a lot of time and a lot of money."

Coyle didn't respond. He was looking over Lawlor's shoulder. Lawlor turned and saw a black SUV beside the bench where he'd been sitting. Three white men and a black woman were walking away from the vehicle towards the memorial. They wore jeans and puffy jackets and sunglasses, like a Secret Service field uniform.

"Of course you don't care about the cost, because it's not your money, is it?" Lawlor said. "It's Foley's money. This is all to do with the election. This is all to do with me not digging into the past."

Coyle was smiling, his eyes on the approaching team.

"I had a lot of time to think on the way over here," Lawlor said. "I took the train. Well, more like a dozen trains. And trains are great for thinking on. No real distractions. Just lots of time to let the mind run and remember things. Like coincidences."

The tourist group shuffled forward, and Lawlor walked with them.

"Like the name Paolo Moretti. It was a big coincidence, me seeing Moretti's name in a file about a porn ring, the same day you and Foley showed up in Belfast. But I missed it. Maybe because Jerry Fyffe's postcard showed up the same day. Did you plan that, or was it just luck?"

Coyle's hands were thrust deep into the pockets of his coat, his face blank.

"I might have forgotten about Moretti, except for Harper,"

Lawlor went on. "He got Moretti's name from a loyalist hood who was part of a crew that managed to hijack an IRA gun shipment. The same hood who planted the bomb under my car, less than a week after I ran across Moretti's name and put it through the system. A nice piece of symmetry there, don't you think? Which got me thinking about Foley."

The security crew were at the top of the rise at the end of the memorial pathway. They paused and regrouped, the black woman making hand signals.

"I remembered Foley from back then," Lawlor said. "He was the CIA liaison with MI5 in London. So I called a fella I know, who used to be in Five. He said your lot were a bit freaked out by the fact that most of the money buying IRA weapons came from the US. And that one of Foley's jobs was writing reports estimating arms traffic into the North. Not easy, as there were so many potential suppliers. But Foley somehow managed to land a source who gave him top grade intelligence on weapons flows into the province. He never named the source. But I think we know who he was. Paolo Moretti."

"How the fuck should I know?"

"Well, you were with the Agency back then, weren't you?"

"Not in Ireland."

"No, but you know how it works. Moretti's a pedophile. Foley finds out, and he turns him. The question is, how does Foley find out? It's not like they run in the same circles. Unless they do."

Coyle didn't respond. He had tucked his chin into his coat, so that he looked like an angry turtle.

"Conclusion: Foley's got the dirt on Moretti. But Moretti's also got some dirt on Foley. Photos. Or film, maybe. Something Foley absolutely did not want Moretti using as a bargaining chip in the event he got lifted for anything. So, to ensure that Moretti never even crosses paths with the police, Foley does a deal with a pal in the police to put a flag on Moretti's file. An alert, so that the moment anyone runs his name, Foley's mate gets a call, and can make sure that Moretti is squeaky clean before the peelers even arrive on the scene."

The tour group stopped. The guide was gesticulating as she came to the climax of her lecture. Maybe telling them the designer was of Chinese descent.

"That's a great story." Coyle's eyes were blank. "A real full-on fantasy."

"You won't mind me passing on my fantasy, then. Send a wee email to someone in the National Crime Agency, maybe. Or Five. Maybe even Europol. They won't send up a flag in PSNI headquarters. They'll fly in from the mainland. Foley's friend in Belfast won't know until they've got Moretti in a box."

Ahead of them, the team had split into two. One pair static at the top of the path, the other moving over the grass to flank them.

"Good luck sending your email, Lawlor." Coyle smirked. "You won't even be making a phone call."

"You're going to shoot me here? In the middle of this crowd?"

"We'll find a way to spin it. We'll use AI to make some videos showing you pulling a gun. Whatever."

They were at the halfway point in the Memorial. The goons were waiting at the top of the path, less than a hundred yards away. Lawlor made another half turn and saw three more watchers in their tell-tale gear, at the end of the path behind him. A neat trap.

He said, "What if I just disappear?"

Coyle grinned. "In a puff of smoke. Like a genie."

"I was thinking of something more subtle. Something less troublesome for you."

"I don't think you'll be too much trouble."

"Is that what Fermin said?"

Coyle didn't respond.

The tour guide appeared to have finished her lecture, and the group began pulling apart into knots, couples and friends chatting to each other. A couple dressed in matching purple and green warm-up suits had taken out their phones and were snapping photos. Lawlor stepped behind them as they took a selfie.

Coyle pressed close. "I have a lot of guys here."

"So do I." Lawlor nodded at the tour group, almost all of whom were brandishing smartphones and filming each other. "That's a lot of cameras. You can confiscate them all?"

Coyle gave him a sour look. "You've got it all figured out, huh?"

Lawlor said nothing.

"Even if you get loose, we'll track you," Coyle said. "We'll hunt you down."

"No you won't. I got into the country without you tracking me, and I've now crossed the continent twice without you getting as much as a sniff. So if I want to walk away from here and disappear, believe me, I will."

"We'll put you on the wanted list. Your face'll be on the wall of every police station from here to Hong Kong. The long way round."

"I'm quaking in my boots," Lawlor said. "Harper was on that list. And he was living here, free as a bird, in your back

298

garden."

The tour guide barked something, and led the way up the path, up the slope from the center of the memorial. The tour group followed, in dribs and drabs this time, as they stopped to snap more photos and record video.

"So what's your plan? Some kind of diversion?" Coyle's voice was tight.

"You're running out of time, Coyle. By the time this lot reaches the end of the path, I'll be gone. But you can stop me blabbing about Moretti and his filthy habits and his powerful pedophile friends. All you have to do is tell me who Foley has running interference in Belfast for him."

"I'm not giving you squat," Coyle said.

The blob of the tour group had lengthened into a line, two abreast, as they moved quickly towards the end of the monument. The four Secret Service people were waiting either side of the path. The black woman spoke into her sleeve. Lawlor could feel the other three behind him, like an itch in the small of his back. They were getting ready to move.

"You're right," Lawlor said. "There is a diversion."

Coyle smirked. "It won't stop my people. They're Secret Service Counter Assault."

"Yes. But they're not actually your people, are they?" Slowly, easily, aware of the eyes on him, Lawlor took his phone out of his pocket. "They're secret service. You're not. You're not even a government employee any more. So when there's an emergency, it's not you they take orders from."

He held up the phone. Tapped the screen.

Coyle was frowning. The four men at the end of the path were backing up, turning around, talking into their sleeves, making for the road. There was a slight buzzing sound, and the front of Coyle's coat seemed to shiver slightly. Then shivered again.

"You should get that," Lawlor said.

Coyle clawed the phone out of his coat. He jabbed the screen. "What?"

The volume on the phone must have been all the way up. Lawlor heard a tinny voice, not the words, but the tone of a staff sergeant or some such, giving a situation report. Clipped, objective, per procedure.

Coyle's face seemed to blotch, as though only half the capillaries that allowed blood to flow to his skin had survived a lifetime of alcohol abuse. "Don't give me that bullshit," he snapped. "Where is he now?.....Well, where did you last see him?.....When?.....I don't give a damn about procedure, this is an overreaction....... I'm telling you, it's a hoax....."

The tinny voice jabbered, slower and calmer now, like a patient teacher being firm with an entitled toddler. Coyle hung up. "Where is he?"

"Who?"

"Foley, you asshole. Where?"

"Oh, him." Lawlor smiled. "He's right where his schedule says he is. Fishing."

"What about his detail?"

"They're with him. But there's only one cell tower up there. And right now, it appears to be malfunctioning. No signal in or out. Which triggers an immediate emergency alert, right?" He nodded at the four Secret Service men hurrying back to their car. "These lads'll be off to lock down the office, I suppose. Leaving you all alone."

Coyle glared at him. He stabbed the phone again. "It's me." Pause. "Coyle." His knuckles were white. "Yes. Spindrift is still on the water. I have it on good authority.... Well, put a goddamn drone up and verify. And then put everyone back on station."

He hung up. "Idiot."

Lawlor said, "Spindrift?"

"That's the dumb-ass name the Secret Service gave him."

Lawlor smiled. "Goodbye, Coyle. And good luck."

The goons were gone. Lawlor started towards the end of the path.

"Wait."

Coyle was slouched over, his hands in his pockets. "You know I've never heard of this guy Moretti, right? You know I have no idea what you're talking about."

"I'm not recording you."

Coyle exhaled, heavily. "You'll disappear?"

"I don't want you coming after me. Especially if Foley gets elected. You're going to have to do something about Moretti then, and I don't want to be anywhere near you. Give me the name I want, and I'm gone forever."

"It was twenty years ago, Lawlor. How would I know?"

"Because you're Foley's bag carrier, Coyle. You know every dirty detail. Now give me the name."

Coyle chewed the inside of his mouth for a moment. He was still holding his phone. He swiped, and tapped on the screen.

"For the tape, I refuse to tell you a goddamn thing, about anything at all." He held up the device.

Lawlor had braced himself, but when he read the name, he was slapped by a tidal wave of feelings. Anger, outrage and surprise. And then a backwash of bitterness, and a sense of relief at finally having his answer.

He nodded, and Coyle pushed past him, through the tourists

and turned left at the end of the memorial. He hurried up the hill, past a bench where a woman sat, a wide sun hat on her head, and a laptop open on her knees.

Lawlor took his time, walking slowly, his eyes skittering over the rows of names etched into the marble, using the highly-polished surface as a mirror to check his surroundings. The tourists straggled ahead of him, chattering away amongst each other, now they no longer had to listen to their guide.

The woman on the bench looked up as he passed. She wore huge, round sunglasses that made her look like an insect. Along with the hat, they almost hid the bandage that covered the left side of her face.

"That's a nice hat," he said.

She looked up. "Thanks."

It was hard for her to speak, and only the right half of her face could smile. "It's a Tilly."

50

It was low tide, and a light onshore breeze carried the stink of rotten seaweed and spilled diesel up to the ruined castle. Lawlor stood in the shadows of the old keep, looking out over the causeway that linked the island to the mainland. He watched the lights of a car as they eased slowly along the coast road, then swung towards him across the narrow strip of road that straddled the water.

The car turned left, into the small lay-by beside the ruin. The engine stopped. There was the muffled sound of pop music blaring, and then silence. A door opened, then slammed shut. Shoes on gravel, then a shadow in the archway of the ruined castle keep.

"Smells like piss and spilled cider in here," Róisín said.

"The scent of your misspent youth."

She laughed, and sat on a low stone wall, hands in the pockets of a long coat, legs extended, crossed at the heel. "How long you been back?"

"Couple of weeks."

She was quiet for a minute, as she digested this.

She said, "Kilpatrick told me about Harper. Was that you?"

Lawlor didn't answer.

"They ID'd him from his fingerprints and dental records," she said. "But he's on file in America with another identity. So his ma's having a hell of a time getting the body back."

The wind had picked up slightly. The sound of tiny waves scraping up and down the stones on the shores of the lough filtered up to them.

"How's your case doing?" he asked.

"Which one?"

"The one that doesn't exist."

"Oh, that." She shoved her hands deeper into her coat pockets, like she was digging for spare change. "They warned me off, remember."

"And you did what they told you?"

"I gave you the file."

"You did. And you didn't make a copy, I suppose. You didn't hide it away in a drawer somewhere."

"Why would I do that?"

"You put a lot of time into it. You and what's his name, the one with the neck tattoos."

She paused. "Sean. Sean Grady."

"Is that the same Sean Grady I read about in the paper last month? Took a header off a cliff in the Mournes?"

"It was an accident."

"Was he still working on your case?"

"Sean? No." She thought for a moment. "Not in the office, anyway. We got into his computer and had a good look around, so I'm sure about that."

"What about at home? Was he the type who might do a little research on his own time?"

The silence filled in the space between them, pursued by the small sounds of night. The water on the shore; an animal

304

rooting about in the bushes.

He said, "You remember that name I recognized in your file? Paolo Moretti?"

"I remember you saying it rang a bell."

"I saw it twenty years ago. That bank holiday weekend, before..." He took a breath. "You took the Friday off, to go see your Dad in Cushendun. He got sick on his holidays."

"Right, yeah." Róisín chewed the inside of her cheek.

"I got a tip. Moretti's name came up. I ran him through the system, to get his address. I was going to drive up with you on the Tuesday to interview him."

"Except that Tuesday ..." Her voice trailed off. The wind gusted, carrying the distant sound of halyards rattling on masts in the yacht club on the other side of the bay.

"Look at the timing, Róisín. Twenty years ago, I ping Moretti on the system. Three days later, a bomb blows up my car. A couple of months ago, your trawl pings a computer owned by Paolo Moretti. A week later, I get a message luring me to the West Coast of America. Barely a week after that, your computer guy falls to his death. How does that sound to you?"

"It sounds like I might be next."

Lawlor smiled.

She shook her head. "But if it was so important to stop you chasing Moretti down back then, why didn't they finish the job?"

"Because the bomb did what it was supposed to do. It shut me up. I stopped being a copper the day Tommy and Andrew died. First I was on compassionate leave. Then the peace process shut Special Branch down. I was out of work. Paolo Moretti fell off the radar. Until you pinged him, and showed me his name in that file of yours."

"Okay. But why not slot you right here? It not as if we don't have enough local talent."

"That's not the question. The question is, how would someone who wanted to protect Paolo Moretti know when his name came up in a police database search?"

"They'd get with GCHQ, I suppose. Program the system to send up a flag." She shook her head. "You're seriously saying there's someone that high up who'd be involved in something like this?"

"Who says he needed to be high up? He just needs access."

"Okay, but if someone like that did exist, you're saying he was in cahoots with Rab Harper. A police working with an IRA bomber to kill another police? No way."

"You're right about that. It wasn't an IRA man at all."

"What do you mean?"

"I mean it wasn't Harper."

"And you know that how?"

"I found him. I spoke to him. He told me he was set up."

She scoffed. "Aye well he would say that, wouldn't he? Anything to save his skin."

"His skin didn't need saving at the time. He had the gun on me."

"So why tell you anything at all? Why not just shoot you and be done with it?"

"He wanted his name cleared, Róisín. He wanted to come home."

"Same thing, then. He needed you to believe whatever load of shite he'd made up."

"He made a lot of sense. We connected the bomb to him because of the chemical residue left by the detonators he used. But there was a flaw in the forensic reporting. I've read the records. We went after him because he consistently used those dets, but they weren't his only consistency. He always chose commercial targets, never human. Not even military or police. He always used active triggers, radio or wire line. Nothing passive; nothing initiated by the target. No tilt switches. No ignition triggers. Which means he didn't have just one signature, he had three at least. But once we had the residue from the detonator, that was it. We didn't ignore the others: we didn't even consider them."

"That's it?"

"What more do you need? The residue was the only physical evidence connecting Harper to the bomb."

"Apart from him being a bomber."

"There was a lot more than one bomb-maker still knocking about back then."

She sat silent, shoulders rounded. "Right," she said after a moment. "I can see we left a few stones unturned there."

"A whole wall of them."

She dipped her head, conceding the point, and her hair fell forward like a blackbird's wing. She tucked it back behind her ear.

"Okay. So the investigation was fucked. Fair enough. But listen to yourself a minute. You're saying there was some guy at headquarters who was well enough connected with GCHQ that he could maintain a flag on this fella Moretti. And who was willing and able to plant a bomb in a fellow officer's car to make sure Moretti wasn't exposed. That's..." She shook her head. "That's crazy."

"Is it? It depends on who Paolo Moretti is. Or how valuable he is to certain people."

"Like who?"

He didn't answer.

She stood up, her shoes scraping on the gravel. She was silhouetted in the archway by the moonlight, her face shadowed.

"So who's the guy? Did Harper give you a name?"

"No. He didn't get that far."

"So if Harper's dead, and he wasn't the doer, and he died before he could tell you who was, it sounds like you went on a long trip for nothing."

"Not at all. There were two names, you see. There was the one who planted the bomb in my car, and then there was the one who gave the order. Harper gave me the bomber's name straight off."

"So who was it?"

"A name you'll remember. Bobby McEwan."

"Oh, fuck." She was staring at him, her eyes two black hollows in the pale of her face.

"What?"

"John Grogan." She put her hands together and pressed the tips of her fingers to her mouth. "John Grogan is Bobby McEwan. I knew I'd seen him before. Fuck."

"What are you talking about, Róisín?"

"The fax. Sean had DVLA send it to the youth center. After we decoded the message in your email."

"Back up." Lawlor held up his hand. "What email? I never sent you an email."

"Not to me. To Sean. Using a sock puppet email address that looked like me." She stared. "That wasn't you?"

"No. What was it, exactly?"

"It was a sudoku puzzle. Except that it wasn't. The puzzles were all impossible. It was a coded message. It said John Grogan, Newport, Go carefully. Signed A.L." She shook her head. "I was sure it was you. There was the signature, and there was the code key. My old school motto."

"Believe it or not, I have no idea where you went to school, Róisín."

"So who the fuck was it?" Her voice was loud in the narrow space.

It was a moment before Lawlor replied. "Rab Harper. He knew a lot about you. He mentioned you were a sudoku fan. I told him to stay away from you."

"So why did he send it to me?"

Lawlor shrugged. "I had to do something dangerous over there. There was an even chance I might not have made it back. He was punting. Maybe he thought if you found out McEwan was still alive, you'd bring him in."

"If I'd put two and two together, I would have done my level best. Jesus." She pushed her hair back with both hands. "I can't believe I didn't recognize him. I can't believe he's still alive."

She thought for a moment. "And you know what? I can't actually believe Rab Harper thought he was your doer. How did he work that out?"

"McEwan told him. He likes to get drunk, go online and mouth off of an evening, apparently."

"But the lardy bastard could barely wind his watch, let alone make a bomb. Plus he was UVF, not IRA."

"Bobby wasn't a bad electrician in his day. And he knew his way around a car engine. He wouldn't have had to make the bomb, either. The man giving the orders would have got someone else to put it together, maybe even done it himself. Then get someone reliable to deliver it." He looked into the shadow of Róisín's face. "Do you remember how McEwan supposedly died?"

She paused. "Aye. House fire."

"You remember the address?"

She shook her head. "I was on the mainland then. Doing that admin course in Manchester. It didn't make the papers over there."

"It was Sandy Row," Lawlor said. "St George's Gardens. Number 28."

He stood in the archway, watching the headlights of Róisín's car sweep over the causeway, then rise and fall, as she bumped over the ruts in the road.

Gravel crunched behind him, but he didn't turn around.

"I underestimated Rab Harper," he said. "He was full of surprises, right to the end."

"He was a real belt and braces guy, I guess." Tilly was still speaking through the side of her mouth, to prevent the stitches in her cheek from pulling.

"Any problems with the car?" Lawlor asked.

"Not a one. I put the tracker on the side of the muffler. She'd have to get under with a flashlight to see it."

"What about the phone?"

"Easy. She doesn't organize her apps, so it was like hiding a tree in a forest. She'll never see it."

He shook his head. "I kept telling her to change her bloody code. But she never listened."

They watched as Róisín's car made the turn onto the coast road.

"This doesn't feel good," Lawlor said.

"I know."

"I've known her nearly thirty years."

"All the more reason to check her out." Tilly leaned into him. "So what now?"

"We follow, we watch and we listen." He put his arm around her and pulled her close. "And we find out who Róisín Mackey really is."

51

Lawlor watched from the tree line as Róisín's car made its way up the driveway to Johnson's house. He had been in the grounds all night, walking the perimeter, watching for dogs, looking for the ways in. He doubted he would have found it so easy a decade ago, but the IRA and the INLA had stopped killing policemen in their homes long since, and Dennis Johnson clearly felt able to let his guard down a little. The front gate to the property was wide open, and the wire fence that surrounded it had not been maintained. Johnson used to have an Alsatian, Lawlor remembered, but the dog must have died and not been replaced.

The place was a couple of acres in size. A river down one side, a single-lane road down the other, a new-ish housing estate at the back. A row of old stables where Johnson's parents had kept horses. One was used as a garage, another a storage room. A third was a workshop, well equipped and maintained, tools hung up in rows on a pegboard. Drawers neatly labeled: screws and nails, wires and fuses. A soldering iron. A vice.

That was as far as he got. The doors were all locked, the ground floor windows shut tight. It was a disappointment. Lawlor had stood beside the back door, fingering the disks in his pocket, the three bugs that he had brought along, in the hope of concealing them about the house. At least he still had the app that Tilly had installed on Róisín's phone.

After Róisín had left the castle, Lawlor had tracked her. First home, and then out on a long run that didn't end until the sun came up. An hour later she was on her way into work, calling her ex-husband to say she would drive down to see him before lunch the following day. Lawlor had stayed on her, dozing in his rental car, and waiting for the ping. One of the phishing emails he'd launched in Los Angeles had finally hooked Johnson. Now Tilly's program was crawling through his personal files.

When the lights went out at Róisín's flat, Lawlor had driven out to where Johnson lived.

Now he watched as Róisín's Mini breasted the small hill in front of the big old house, wan sunlight glittering like a cheap firework on the car's rain-spattered paintwork. She pulled up beside the front door, and Johnson stepped out to meet her, squinting into the sunshine. He wore jeans and a dark green sweater. Róisín was wearing the same coat she'd worn at her meeting with Lawlor. She and Johnson talked for a moment, and then went inside.

Lawlor dug into the pocket of his coat and took out a burner smartphone. He fitted an earpiece into his ear and plugged it in. He opened the phone and activated the app on Róisín's phone, and the earpiece hissed into life.

They were in the hallway. Lawlor could hear them talking, but couldn't make out the words. He watched the big windows in the front of the house, hoping to see them walk into the living room, but they didn't appear. The sound in his ears dropped to a low murmur, and then went silent.

He cursed. He pushed the phone into the pocket of his parka and began walking up the hill towards the house.

There was a large pond in the center of the lawn in from of the house. As he passed it, the sun suddenly burst through the clouds, blinding him for a moment. When he blinked his eyes clear, a young woman was standing on the gravel in the driveway, halfway between the front door and Róisín's car.

He held up a hand. "Hullo Andrea. Remember me?"

She made a face, half frown, half scowl, like she didn't remember, but didn't want to admit to it. She had her mother's hair and figure, and her father's deep blue eyes. She might have been pretty, but for the tight mouth and the look she gave him, down her long, straight nose.

"Gary Lawlor," he said. "I work with your mum up in Belfast. Or I used to, anyway."

Her eyes narrowed. "I remember."

He grinned. "I must look a bit of a state, eh? I was just after knocking about in the woods there."

"Doing what?"

"Oh, I used to come here a lot in the old days. Back when your mum and your dad and me we were all in Special Branch together."

She hesitated. "Why are you here now?"

"I'm staying in the town, and thought I'd walk over. I took a wee shortcut. There's a gap in the hedge. A bit cheeky not using the gate, I know, but I'm sure your dad won't mind."

She hugged herself. Glanced at the car. "He's with Mum."

"Ah well, then. It'll be like a reunion."

There was a scraping sound, and then Róisín's voice, clear as glass in his ear: "I've got a bone to pick with you, Dennis."

"Oh aye?" Johnson's voice. They were in the kitchen. Lawlor

heard the sound of someone tinkering with tea things: pot, mugs, kettle. "You want tea first?"

"Do you've low-fat milk?"

"No."

"I'll have it black, then."

They fell silent.

Andrea was leaning on the Mini now, arms crossed like a schoolteacher. Lawlor pointed to his ear. "Sorry. Conference call. How's school?"

She shrugged.

There was a piercing screech in his ear, as the kettle boiled in the kitchen. And then the sound of liquid pouring.

Johnson's voice: "Go on, then. What have I done now?"

"Gary Lawlor came to see me." Róisín's voice was sharp.

"The man's got some balls. There's a lot of people looking for him."

"He told me he saw Rab Harper, over in America. Harper claimed he was set up by someone in the police. Someone watching out for a hairdresser called Paolo Moretti."

"A hairdresser? Okay."

"Harper said someone else put the device in Gary's car. Bobby McEwan."

"McEwan. Right." Johnson chuckled. "That fat bastard couldn't make a cup of instant."

"You remember him, then."

"And why wouldn't I? He was a player. It was my job to know who he was."

"Well, Harper said McEwan just planted the bomb. But someone else made it for him."

A bang, like someone slamming something against the table. "What's this bollocks you're feeding me, Róisín?"

"What was that package you gave me to deliver to St George's Gardens, Dennis?" Her voice was cool.

"I don't know what you're talking about."

"I told everyone I was away that weekend to see Dad. I didn't want them knowing I was down here with you. Not that we got up to anything. You were in that bloody workshop most of the time. And then on the Sunday, you told me you weren't feeling well. You gave me a package in a Stewarts bag. You said it was for a mate of yours, who wouldn't be in, but could I leave it on the step behind the pot plant there." Her voice was rising now. "28 St George's Gardens, Dennis. Bobby McEwan's house, it turns out. Who, two days later, plants a bomb under Gary Lawlor's car and ..." She began sobbing, barely able to get her words out. "Tell me it wasn't you, Dennis. Tell me you didn't use me. Tell me you didn't murder those two beautiful boys."

Lawlor pulled the earpiece loose. His hands were shaking. Andrea was frowning at him.

"Sorry about that," he said. "Shall we go on in?"

52

He pushed the back door open. He stood back to let Andrea in first.

"Oh, hi love." Róisín's voice was unnaturally bright.

"Where's Dad?"

"Your gran rang that wee bell of hers. He went upstairs to check on her."

"Whatever." Andrea slumped on the kitchen counter. "Your friend's here."

"What friend?"

Lawlor stepped into the doorway. His heart was thumping hard in his chest. He could feel the sweat on his palms. "Hello again, Róisín."

The kitchen was a medium-sized room that hadn't been updated since the sixties. Whitewashed walls. Two paintings. A Constable print and the Queen. A big old-fashioned dresser, arranged with a collection of china plates, each decorated with a hunting scene. A big wooden farmhouse table dominated the room. Róisín was sitting at one end, facing the window, her cheeks bright red and smeared with tears.

"What are you doing here?"

"I came to see Dennis." Lawlor walked around the table.

"I've some questions for him, too."

"And what if I don't want to answer your questions?" Johnson was standing in the doorway to the hall. He was holding a double-barreled shotgun loosely at his waist, broken so that Lawlor could see the glint of the cartridges in the breech.

Andrea's eyes were huge, skipping back and forth between them.

"He was in the woods, Daddy," she said.

"Is that right?" Johnson's eyes were like two pale blue marbles. "For how long?"

"Don't know. I just saw him walk up."

"I wasn't asking you."

Lawlor dragged his eyes away from the gun. He forced a smile onto his face. "Let's say I had the chance to walk about a wee bit, Dennis. Sorry to see you had to sell the land. What happened?"

Johnson stared at him for a moment. "The horses got sick. Vet's bills were huge. Then we needed a new roof. And new wiring for the house."

"That's all?"

"What else would there be?" He was very calm. "Now I've answered your questions. And it's time for you to leave."

A tinkling sound, like a spoon on a glass, came from deep in the house.

"Is that Mammy asking for her wee boy?" Lawlor said.

Johnson scowled. "Get out of my house."

"Not until you've answered all of my questions, Dennis."

The bell rang again.

"Go and check on your gran, Andrea," Róisín said.

"I want to stay." Her voice was a whine.

"I'll not tell you twice, now." Róisín warned.

"Daddy?"

"Do as your mother says, Andrea. Now."

They waited in silence, listening to the sound of Andrea's shoes on the hallway floor and the stairs.

And then Johnson snapped the breech of the gun closed.

Lawlor felt as though his stomach had liquefied. His breath was sharp in his throat and loud in his ears. The gun was a 12-gauge box lock, the barrels shiny with a patina that spoke of great care and frequent oiling. Which indicated frequent firing. Johnson had balanced the gun on his hip, pointed slightly upwards, so Lawlor was looking directly at the muzzle. At two black holes.

"Now you listen to me, Gary Lawlor." Johnson's voice was low. "If you don't get out of my house by the count of five, I'll give you both barrels and cut you in half."

Lawlor was mesmerized by the twin tunnels of the shotgun. His mind was split, part of him fighting his panic, the other part wondering which kind of shells Johnson had loaded the gun with. If they were buckshot, they would indeed cut him in half. Bird shot would just tear a large hole in his chest. It was academic. Either way, at this range, he'd be dead.

"One."

"Dennis." The same warning tone Róisín had used on her daughter.

"Two."

"Dennis! Put the fucking gun down!"

Róisín's voice was like a lash. It cracked off the walls of the kitchen and broke the spell cast over Lawlor by the gun. Lawlor stiffened his knees, and lifted his eyes to meet Johnson's. He felt suddenly weightless. Somehow separated from himself.

And inexplicably calm.

"Three."

"Go on ahead and shoot, Dennis." Lawlor stared into Johnson's eyes. "Go on. Finish the job."

"If you shoot him, you'll have to shoot me, Dennis," Róisín said. "You know that, don't you?"

Johnson ground his teeth. He let the muzzle of the gun dip towards the floor. Lawlor felt relief wash over him.

"Right." Róisín sounded like a teacher addressing a class. "Now answer the man's questions."

"And then he leaves."

"And then I leave." Lawlor nodded. "Let's start with Paolo Moretti."

"Never heard of him."

"No? Never ever?" Lawlor pushed down the urge to step across the room and punch him in the face. "This is the first time, right now?"

"Yes."

"How about Brian Coyle?"

Johnson's face was suddenly pale. He shook his head.

"How about Michael Foley?"

"No."

Lawlor snorted. "Come on now, Dennis. You were in a meeting with him just a few weeks ago. I was there too, remember."

"Aye, okay. I was in his meeting with the Chief. But I don't *know* him."

"What about Bobby McEwan? You know *him*."

"No."

"But you know his name."

"Of course. He was a small-time player in the UVF. Died in

a house fire in the 90s."

"That's right. A house fire. You remember the address?"

"No."

"28, St George's Gardens. Do you know that address, at all?"

"No."

Lawlor looked at Róisín. Her face was pale with anger. He took the burner phone out of his pocket, despising himself.

"I'm sorry, Ro."

"For what?"

He took a deep breath before answering.

"There's an eavesdropping app on your phone. I used it to listen to the conversation you and Dennis had, just before I came in."

She stared, her eyes huge in her face.

"You put it on my phone? When?"

"A friend did it. Last night. While we were talking."

"Last night..." Her eyes flickered as she thought back. And then she blinked. "Jesus Christ, Gary. I trusted you. I helped you."

"I know." He felt something shrivel inside him. He pushed the feeling away. "You wouldn't have helped me with this, though, would you?"

Her stare was like a hammer blow. He took a step back, and leaned against the dresser. He kept one eye on Johnson's face, and the other on the twin barrels of the gun.

"I had a wee look around the old stables last night, Dennis. That's a very impressive workshop you have there." He turned to Róisín. "You said he spent the whole of that weekend in there?"

"Fuck you, Gary."

"I had a poke about. He's got a whole whack of electronics

stuff in there. Fuses. Wires. An old soldering iron. Everything you'd need."

"It's my hobby." Johnson snapped. "I build remote control cars."

"Sure. I remember." Lawlor smiled. "You know who else used to build remote control cars? Rab Harper."

53

They stood around the old, scarred table, looking at each other. A clock ticked in the hallway.

Róisín was trembling, fresh tears on her cheeks, her eyes skittering back and forth between the two men. Johnson was smiling slightly. Lawlor felt bile in the back of his throat.

"Who's Brian Coyle?" Róisín's voice was flat, and edged with anger, but Lawlor could sense that her fury at him was tempered by her desire to get to the bottom of what had happened, twenty years ago.

"You remember Foley's visit to headquarters?" he said. "That was just before he resigned as Secretary of State and announced his run for President. Coyle was the scruffy one in his entourage. He's Foley's fixer. The guy who makes trouble go away."

"What kind of trouble?"

"The kind that carries warrant cards and asks awkward questions about hairdressers in Ballycastle."

Róisín transferred her stare to Johnson. "You spoke to him in the car park. What did you talk about?"

"Nothing," Johnson said.

"He poked you in the chest. You told me he was making a

point."

"It was just something about …" His voice faltered. "We didn't have some materials that he wanted for the briefing. He was angry about it. That's all."

"You're lying again." Her eyes narrowed. "Did you talk about Paolo Moretti?"

Johnson blinked.

Róisín turned to Lawlor. "So it's Foley who wants Moretti protected. Why? What's the connection?"

"Did you know Foley used to be in the CIA?"

"I've not checked his fucking Wikipedia page, no."

Lawlor held up his hands. "Okay. Sorry. Foley was an administrator, really, but he was ambitious. He was supposed to be just a liaison guy, but he decided to widen his portfolio and develop a contact in the Republican movement."

"Moretti," Róisín said.

"A man of many parts. Hairdresser. Sailor. IRA man. Gunrunner."

"And informant."

Lawlor nodded. "Foley is a very clever man. He got the idea of following the money that used to get collected in all those bars in Boston and New York back then. His guys in the Agency tracked it to Hungary, where it was used to buy weapons, and then they tracked the guns to Moretti. Foley could have given Moretti to MI5, but Five would have busted him, and the IRA would have found another way to get the guns in to the country, and Foley would have been back at square one himself. Instead, he got some dirt on Moretti and turned him."

Johnson was staring into the middle distance, a pulse in his jaw where he was grinding his teeth.

"Can you guess the rest, Róisín?" Lawlor asked.

"Moretti's computer was one of the nodes we picked up in our sweep. He's a pedophile." She thought for a second. "But he's not a newcomer. That was the dirt Foley got on him back then. That's how he turned him."

"You got it in one."

"But in order to turn him, Foley probably had to pretend to be one of the lads. Or maybe he *was* one of the lads. And maybe he was a wee bit careless. And Moretti got a little dirt on him, too. And when the Good Friday Agreement happens, the script gets flipped. Foley's leverage against Moretti doesn't amount to much anymore. But Moretti's leverage on Foley? Jesus. The further up the pole Foley climbs, the more valuable it gets."

"Right again. And Moretti's no fool. He lines up a wee insurance policy, to be sure Foley won't whack him. If he does, the kompromat gets leaked. And Foley's no fool, either. He knows Moretti's a liability. So he finds a way to keep an eye on him."

"By getting someone to put a flag on Moretti's name." Róisín stared at Johnson. "So if anyone starts sniffing around him, for any reason, there's a man on the ground to take care of things. To make sure no copper ever chaps Moretti's door. Not even for so much as a parking ticket."

Lawlor laughed. "I hadn't thought of that. Five gets you ten, if you run his records you'll find a few tickets wiped."

"Jesus Christ, Dennis." Róisín's voice broke. "You are a fucking disgrace."

The clock in the hallway began to chime. Above them, a floorboard creaked. Lawlor glanced up, but Johnson didn't move.

"One thing I'm not entirely sure about, Dennis," Lawlor said. "How did Foley get his hooks into you? Was it the same way he got Moretti?"

Johnson's eyes focused. "I'm no bloody pedophile."

"No, I don't think you are. But you do like a wee flutter, don't you? Poker, blackjack, baccarat. Something called teen patti that I'd never heard of before." He looked at Róisín. "Very popular in India, apparently."

"You bastard." Róisín was staring at Johnson. She sounded as though she had something stuck in her throat. "Five years without a bet, you said. You swore. To the lawyers. To the bloody judge."

"I didn't lie to them," Johnson muttered. "I told them I've not set foot in a bookies or a racecourse. Or any of the clubs. That's the truth."

"Aye, but only half the truth," Lawlor said. "You left out the bit about your VPN and your bitcoin account."

Johnson glared.

"Yeah, I phished you." Lawlor smiled. "You remember a fundraising email from the Police Federation last week? That was me. When you clicked on the unsubscribe button, you gave me full access to your PC. I had a wee look at your financials. Two mortgages? You must know the bank manager very well. Or maybe they just want to do the peelers a favor."

"Two mortgages?" Róisín's cheeks were bright red, as though she'd been slapped. "Jesus, Dennis. How much do you owe?"

Johnson's jaw was working harder now, his nose flaring. He said nothing.

"That's how Foley got you, wasn't it?" Lawlor said. "You were the Special Branch liaison to GCHQ back in '92. You were transferred back to Belfast in August. Foley was posted down to GCHQ in July, for his Balkan briefings. Not a lot of crossover, but more than enough for a guy like Foley to hook you and reel you in. What was it? High stakes bridge in Mayfair? Or big hand poker in some East End warehouse?"

Johnson said nothing.

"Dennis!" Róisín snapped.

"Newmarket. A couple of times." Johnson's voice was dull.

"The horses. Of course. He covered your bets, I suppose. How much were you into him for?"

Johnson shook his head. "It wasn't him. It was a mate of his. Or so he said. A bookie."

"For God's sake, Dennis!" Róisín sounded as though she was about to cry. "How much?"

It took him an eternity to answer.

"A hundred grand."

Róisín reared backwards, as though she'd been slapped.

"Jesus. A hundred K in 1990s money? That's like a quarter mil today." Lawlor shook his head. "So what happened? Foley offered to make it go away, did he?"

Johnson was staring at the floor. "The farm was a mess. We had two horses die. No money coming in. And then Dad got sick. I couldn't ..."

"What? Sell some land?" Róisín sneered. "No. You wouldn't want to disappoint your Daddy, would you? Jesus, you're weak."

"You're not a stupid man, Dennis, so you must have expected Foley to call in his marker sometime," Lawlor said. He had kept a lid on his anger, but once again he felt it beginning to stoke inside him. "I hope he took you by surprise, though, telling you to kill me. I hope you refused. I hope he had to put pressure on you. A lot of pressure. Like maybe he hadn't bought the debt from that bookie after all. Like some very nasty people might come round and burn your house to the ground with Mummy and Daddy inside it. I really do hope that's the kind of threat he made, to get you to do what you did, Dennis. To me. To Róisín. To the man you thought was Bobby McEwan. To my two boys."

His voice caught, and he felt tears spring up behind his eyes. His heart was pounding so hard it was difficult to breathe.

Róisín looked as though she was frozen, her eyes locked on to Johnson's face.

"Bobby McEwan," she said. "He could barely wind his watch."

Lawlor nodded. "And yet, somehow, he managed to get himself out of the province and into the wind, without anyone getting a sniff of him, for twenty years. New name, new address. He couldn't have turned into John Grogan of Newport on his own."

She was silent. And then she turned towards Johnson. "How's your prostate, Dennis?"

He wouldn't meet her eye.

"About a month ago. He went across to London for three days. To see an oncologist, he said. An emergency."

"When, exactly," Lawlor asked.

"Wednesday." She was suddenly deathly pale, the skin drawing tight over the bones of her face. "The same day I heard about Sean."

"He'll have kept an eye on McEwan the same way he kept tabs on Moretti," Lawlor said. "He'll have set up a flag at GCHQ. The moment anyone ran a check on Grogan, he'd know."

"Oh Jesus." Her voice was a whisper. "Dennis. No. Not Sean."

Johnson said nothing. He was staring into the half distance between himself and the table, the shotgun pointed down towards the floor.

"You bastard." Róisín's voice was a screech. "You absolute fucking bastard. He was a kid, Dennis. Twenty-two years old. A child."

She stopped, hiccuping as she fought for breath.

"Did you do it?" she said. "Or did you send someone to do your dirty work for you?"

"Your daughter would know," Lawlor said.

Johnson looked up. "You leave her out of this."

"I'll bet you if we call her down here now and ask her what her daddy was up to on the 24th, she'll say he was out that night."

"On operations." Róisín's voice was hard. "Or out with the lads."

"Shall we call her down, Dennis?"

"You will not." Johnson turned slightly, weight on his front foot, and raised the gun.

Lawlor felt his insides hollow. The room around him shrank to the twin holes of the shotgun's muzzle, pointed directly at his face.

"You going to shoot me, mate?" It was an effort to breathe.

"You broke into my house." Johnson's eyes were as hard as marbles.

"Put the gun down, Dennis," Róisín ordered.

"Yes, Dennis. Put it down. You think Róisín will back you up if you shoot me? Or are you going to shoot her too? And what about Andrea?"

"Fuck you, Lawlor. Leave my family out of this."

"What about my family?" Lawlor had the feeling his heart

might punch its way out of his chest. He could see nothing but the black tunnels of the gun, and Johnson's face behind it. But his rage had swept his mind of fear. All that mattered was what he had come for. "You have to answer for what you did to them."

"Not me." Johnson's voice was rough.

"You made the bomb. You gave the order."

"Dennis!" Róisín was shouting now. "Stop this, for fuck sake."

Johnson's eyes closed for a moment. "I'm sorry about your boys."

"Andrew and Tommy. Those were their names."

He shook his head. "They didn't live with you. Your ex-wife had them."

"Most of the time. But I got them every second weekend." Lawlor had the feeling that if he leaned forward, he might fall into one of those dark tunnels, and never come out again. "You didn't do your fucking homework, did you?"

"I'm not a bad man."

"Not a bad man?" Lawlor laughed. "You murdered two children. You murdered Sean Grady. That poor bastard who was in Bobby McEwan's house. And then McEwan himself. You're a serial killer, Dennis. You're the fucking angel of death."

"Dennis! No!"

Johnson let out a sound, half roar, half wail. His eyes bulged, and the gun lifted slightly, as he pulled the butt into his shoulder and steadied his aim. Lawlor looked into the twin black tunnels of the barrels. He felt inexplicably calm. He closed his eyes, and saw his boys, frozen in time - Tommy opening the front door of the car, Andrew running up the path.

He had left one of his shoelaces untied.

"Daddy!"

Andrea's scream shattered the vision. She was standing in the doorway. Johnson's eyes flickered. The gun twitched as he went to turn towards his daughter.

And then he fired.

54

"Jesus Christ, Dennis! What have you done? You've killed him!"

Róisín's words seemed to come from a long way away, like they were echoing down a hallway. Lawlor wanted to reassure her that she was wrong, that he wasn't dead. But he couldn't speak. He couldn't move.

His faculties began to return. Hearing first, and then sensations. At first he welcomed them. Until the pain came. The back of his skull. The dead weight of his left arm. He could feel his face, but he couldn't open his eyes. Was he blind? He tried to hold the panic back, but it swept over him, like a dark cloud, and he cried out.

He felt Róisín's hand on his shoulder. Heard the relief in her voice as she began issuing orders. Fetch water. A cloth.

He was lying half on his left side, half on his back, twisted against the dresser, with his face towards the ceiling. He felt liquid on his forehead, the press of material, and then, suddenly, he could see.

"How bad is it?" His voice was a slur.

"You need a doctor."

"Aye, no kidding. How bad?"

She shook her head. "I can't tell. There's a lot of blood." ' '

"I need to sit up."

She protested, but he pushed himself up, gritting his teeth when pain shot down his left arm. He leaned his back against the dresser. There was smashed crockery all around him. The left shoulder of his coat was shredded, and soaked with blood. But the fingers of his left hand were working okay, and he was able to flex his elbow.

He braced his arm across his belly. His shoulder throbbed. He felt tired. Shaky. Vision graying around the edges. Shock setting in.

Róisín was squatting beside him, sponging blood off the back of his head.

"There's a couple of pellets in there," she said. "Not too bad. But your shoulder's a mess."

A shape loomed over him, and looked up to see Dennis Johnson, handing him a mug.

"Four sugars," Johnson said.

Lawlor took the mug. The hot, sweet, milky tea was like an antidote, shot directly into a vein. His vision cleared and he felt the shakes dissipate. He forced the rest of the tea down.

Róisín rocked back on her heels. "I've done the best I can. But the ambulance'll be here in a minute."

"No, it won't," Johnson said.

They both looked up at him.

"He walked in on his own. He can walk out."

"He needs a doctor, Dennis." Róisín was outraged.

"I'm sure he does." Johnson sounded smug. "But I'm not about to help him any more than I have to."

"I'll be fine," Lawlor said. "No major arteries in the shoulder, so I won't bleed to death. And I can understand

333

why Dennis here doesn't want any record of an ambulance coming to his house. Not to evacuate a man with a gunshot wound."

"I'll drive you." Róisín's voice was cold.

"No. I'll call someone to pick me up."

"Not with this, you won't." Johnson tossed the burner onto Lawlor's lap. The phone's screen was smashed. The SIM card was gone. "I deleted the recording."

Lawlor chuckled. It hurt.

"What's so bloody funny?"

"For someone who's so good with electronics and VPNs and crypto and all the rest, you're not the sharpest, Dennis. It didn't just record onto the phone. It went up into the cloud as well."

Johnson's eyes seemed to shrink in his skull as his mind reeled backwards. "I didn't say anything about anything."

"You said enough. In both conversations."

"Hearsay." Johnson sneered. "You've got no physical evidence. Nothing that'll stand up in court."

"You're right." Lawlor pushed himself up to his feet, his arm pulled tight across his belly, his shoulder screaming at him. "But I don't want to prove this in court. Having you nicked and jailed won't help me. It won't bring Tommy and Andrew back."

He steadied himself, shards of fine bone china crunching under the soles of his boots. His head swam, and he had to grip the dresser for a moment.

Róisín was frowning at him. "So what's the point of all of this? If you're not going to make a case, what's this all about?"

"It's about telling people who he really is, Ro. His mum. His pals at the rugby club and the Lodge. All his old colleagues.

I want them to know the truth. About what he's done, and why."

Johnson gave a hard laugh. "Good luck. I'm a respected man. You walk into the Lodge yapping that rubbish and they'll whip you out of the place."

"Aye, well I'm not going to actually walk into the Lodge." His head ached, and his shoulder throbbed, but he was beginning to think he might actually be able to make it out of the place under his own steam. "I'm just going to send them the file I've worked up on you. Them and everyone else I can think of, from the chief constable to your church warden. CC, so they all get to see who's in the know."

Johnson sneered. "They won't believe a word. Fake bloody news."

"Maybe. Maybe not. But they'll read it, you can be sure of that. And they'll talk to each other about it. The reporters on the list'll start asking questions. And there's plenty in there that'll stick. One or two people will probably see grounds for an investigation. I'm thinking about Kilpatrick, now. He took a bit of a shine to young Sean Grady. The Chief won't want to do anything, of course. She'll want to bury this as deep as she can. She'll suggest you resign, nice and quiet, maybe with a bit of a bonus, but no farewell do. And word will spread from there. People will stop buying G&Ts for you down the golf club. And the rugby club. And the cricket club. And the Lodge. You'd better get used to being a pariah, Dennis, because there's not going to be any clubs for you. Not ever again."

Johnson's face was crimson. "Screw you, Lawlor. You can't do this."

Lawlor tossed the broken phone back, but Johnson made no move to catch it. It bounced off his stomach and clattered on the floor.

"Sorry, mate," Lawlor said. "I already have."

55

Róisín had made Andrea pack a bag, and got on the road as quickly as she could. She felt jittery and edgy, and the scar on her leg screamed at her the whole way. She kept imagining herself, pulling to the side of the road, putting a towel under her leg, jamming the car key into the ridged flesh, letting the hot blood seep over her thigh.

"What did you say, Mum?" Andrea was sitting up in the back, her face a pale smear in the mirror.

"Nothing, love. Go back to sleep." Her knuckles were white. One by one she took her hands off the steering wheel and flexed her fingers, letting the blood flow back into her hands. She glanced in the mirror again, and felt herself calm. Just twenty-five miles to go. She could hold it together for that long.

"Do you believe it, Mum?"

It was a while before Róisín answered. "It doesn't matter what I believe, love."

"So you do believe it."

She had no idea what to say.

"Well I don't. I don't believe a fucking word that bastard Lawlor said." Andrea turned back to the window.

When they got to the flat, Róisín made her daughter a hot

chocolate with marshmallows and put her to bed. Then she sat at the tiny table in her tiny kitchen and made a list. A bed. A mattress. A television. A kettle. She would go to the lawyers to talk about a new custody agreement. She would find a bigger house. She would move Andrea to a school in Belfast. Everything would have to change.

Her phone buzzed. An unlisted number. No prizes for guessing who. She let it ring, feeling the anger and the shame simmering inside her.

The buzzing stopped. And started again.

She picked up. "Hello."

"It's Gary."

"I know who it is."

There were metallic, humming sounds in the background, like he was in a factory of some kind. "How's Andrea?"

"How do you think?"

"I'm sorry, Ro. I didn't mean for it to go like that. And I'm sorry for bugging your phone."

"You're a cold bastard, Lawlor. I should have shopped you to Kilpatrick the very first time he asked."

"Why didn't you?"

"Well, I was covering for you."

"I don't need your help, Róisín."

Her stomach turned. "Apparently not."

He sighed. "What did Kilpatrick tell you?"

"Not much. Just that he wanted you in custody. That you were a security risk. He wouldn't say why. He made it seem like he didn't know either, that someone had ordered it and he'd been told to get on with it and get you in the bag, as quick as possible."

"Did he say anything else?"

She got up and closed the door to the living room, then sat back down again. "He read me your file."

"Which bit?"

"The childhood stuff. The boys' home. All of that."

"Ah."

She felt a wave of anger. "Why didn't you tell me?"

She could almost hear him shrugging. "It wasn't ... relevant."

"Jesus, man."

"Something like that, it's so much baggage. It's like, everyone sees you in a certain way. I didn't need that, so I just made a point of never answering questions about that part of my life. Not directly, anyway."

"I started thinking you might have been abused yourself back then. Or you saw someone there, someone who's a senior cabinet secretary now, or something."

"You see what I mean? That's exactly what I'm talking about. But to answer your question, I never saw anything. I heard rumors, sure, and I knew one of the people who came forward last year, saying he was abused, but I was never caught up in anything like that."

"Thank God for that."

He said nothing.

She laughed. "You made me believe you went to Campbell bloody College, you sod."

"You made yourself believe that. I never said a word about it."

"I felt a right bloody fool when I found out."

"Uh huh."

She sighed. "Okay. I suppose I asked for that."

The clattering sound on the phone drowned out Lawlor's

voice for a moment.

"Where are you?" she asked.

"Somewhere whoever's pulling Kilpatrick's strings can't find me. Was that all he told you?"

"Yes. Why?" The worm in her belly, writhing again. "What else is in your file? Why do these people want you in a box so badly?"

"I don't know. It's nothing that a dozen other people have in their backgrounds. Maybe they liked having me where they could see me. Now that I've dropped off the radar, they're worried I might start telling tales."

"What kind of tales?"

"Nothing that would make them look very good. But I've no plans to tell anyone anything, and you should tell Kilpatrick that."

"Seriously?"

"Sure. Tell him I called you and I told you that. I'm not going to write a book. I'm not going to tell any tales. I'm just going to drop off the map and disappear."

"And what about Dennis?" She had her thumb on the inseam of her jeans, right where it crossed the scar inside her knee. She leaned on the thumb, and felt a cold needle of pain lance up her thigh.

"What about him?"

"That file you said you made. What are you going to do with it?"

"Why do you care?"

"He's Andrea's father."

"He's Tommy and Andrew's murderer."

She closed her eyes. "It'll kill him, Gary."

"No it won't."

340

"How do you know?"

"I know because if I've learned anything these last couple of weeks, it's that Dennis Johnson has learned to survive, no matter what the cost." There was a pause. "To him or anyone else."

56

He sat in the cabin on the narrow bunk of the truck, listening to the sounds around him. The roar of the engines at the rear of the ferry, the shouts of deckhands, the slamming of doors. The cabin was seven feet by four; the bunk just a foot narrower. But it was clean and comfortable; the truck almost brand new.

The phone vibrated in his hand.

"How's life on the ocean wave?" Tilly's voice sounded sharp in the cheap speaker of the burner.

It was a moment before Lawlor replied. "You're not on board?"

"The port was crawling with cops. I'll wait a day or two until things calm down."

He had walked out of Johnson's house with his arm in a makeshift sling, and called Tilly from the end of the drive. She had driven him across the border, to a clinic in Castleblayney. A hunting accident, he told the doctor, who had smiled and shaken his head as he dug a total of fourteen balls of shot out of Lawlor's shoulder, and three out of the back of his head.

Lawlor had no idea what Johnson might actually do, or who he might call. He needed to disappear. So they hadn't hung around. They took the back roads to Portlaoise, Carrick and finally Cork, and the ferry port for the crossing to Spain.

Santander was Tilly's idea, ferries being easier to stow away on, and Spain being easier to enter. She made one call, then another, and they met a thin, weathered man in a car park and gave him an envelope stuffed with euros.

"I usually take people the other way." He grinned, teeth like gravestones, and ushered Lawlor into the cab of the truck. The mattress of the bunk lifted to reveal a coffin-sized space, and Lawlor had to take several deep breaths before he was able to fold himself inside. The last thing he saw before the mattress snuffed out the light above him was Tilly's face.

"I'll call you when we're at sea," she said, and dropped the burner on his chest.

Now he sat on the bunk, his shoulder still throbbing, despite the painkillers. He ran his fingers over the cheap cotton of the truck driver's duvet cover, trying to quell the feeling of panic swelling in his throat. "Did you do it?"

"I sent everything. Just like you said." The line crackled. "What do you think he'll do now?"

"Johnson?" Lawlor shook his head. "Other than drowning himself in cheap whiskey, I'd say nothing at all. He can't afford to have anyone sniffing around Paolo Moretti, or Coyle will send one of his lads over and that'll be the end of it. So Dennis is going to go very quietly. He'll retire. He'll grant Róisín full custody of Andrea. He'll resign from every club he ever joined. He'll cut himself off and he won't say a word to anyone."

"I can't see Róisín letting him get away with what he did to her guy, Grady."

"I told you. There's no evidence. Johnson was right about that." He pressed his thumb against his temple. "There's no hard evidence about any of it."

"So the man who killed your boys gets to die peacefully in bed?"

"If by peacefully you mean him withering away, drunk and alone in his dusty old house, I'll take it."

"What about Coyle and Foley?"

"What about them?" He had slept for six hours in the hole under the bunk, but he was still exhausted. "I can't go after them now. And even if I could, what would I do?"

The phone crackled, scrambling her words.

"You're breaking up," he said. "Say again?"

"I said you're unbelievable. Your kids were murdered because of them."

"No. Not because of them. Because of Johnson. In L.A., Fermin was told to kill me. To him that meant two in the chest and one in the head, made to look like a drug murder. Clean and simple. Zero collateral damage. Johnson should have done the same, twenty years ago. A bullet through each of my knees and one in the head. To make it look like an IRA punishment shooting. But he was too much of a coward to do it himself. So he outsourced it, to an amateur. That was what killed Tommy and Andrew. Not Foley. Not Coyle."

The ferry heeled over slightly, and there was the sound of things shifting on the shelves of the tiny cabin. Lawlor leaned into the movement.

"I'm not condoning what they did," he said.

"It sure sounds like you're giving them a pass."

"I'm being a realist. People like them do what they feel they have to do, to acquire power and hold on to it. They lie, they cheat, they steal and they kill."

"And that's alright?" Tilly's voice was flat.

"No, of course not." Lawlor was crouched over, the phone

344

clamped to his ear. "But what do you want me to do? Go after all the corrupt politicians in the world?"

"How about just the ones who put hits out on you?"

"Now who sounds like a gangster film?"

The boat shuddered as it hit a wave, and the phone crackled again.

"I'm losing you, Tilly," he said.

But she was already gone.

THE END

About the Author

Paddy Hirsch writes thrillers and mysteries, including the *Lawless New York* series, set in early 1800s New York. When he's not writing fiction, Paddy works as a Murrow award-winning business journalist for NPR's Planet Money and Bloomberg News. He's also the author of *Man vs Markets*, a best-selling, tongue-in-cheek guide to the darker corners of the financial markets. He likes hillwalking, rock climbing, surfing and baking tasty things.

You can connect with me on:
🌐 https://www.paddyhirsch.com
❰f❱ https://www.facebook.com/paddyhirsch101

Subscribe to my newsletter:

✉ https://tinyurl.com/4vsv7u5n

Also by Paddy Hirsch

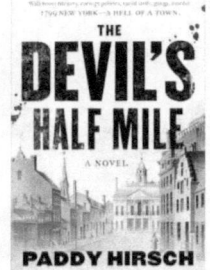

The Devil's Half Mile

Publisher's Weekly starred pick.

Journalist Hirsch makes his fiction debut with a superb historical whodunit. In 1799, after four years studying law in Ireland, Justy Flanagan returns to Manhattan in search of the truth about the death of his father, Francis, a stock trader who reportedly hanged himself when Justy was 14. Convinced by new evidence that his father was murdered, Justy wants answers from William Duer, a "reckless speculator" and former ally of George Washington and Alexander Hamilton, who was Francis's business partner before the 1792 financial crisis sent Duer to debtors' prison. But when Justy goes looking for Duer in Manhattan's New Gaol, he learns that his quarry is dead, and when he reunites with his uncle Ignatius, a powerful landowner who funded his education, he's met with skepticism about his theory. Justy persists, nonetheless, and Hirsch effortlessly incorporates the political and economic background of the time into the mystery.

Hudson's Kill

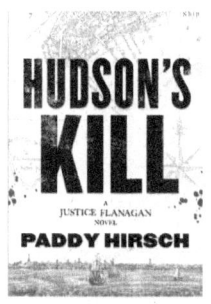

Publisher's Weekly starred pick.

Hirsch's stellar sequel to 2018's *The Devil's Half Mile* finds Justy Flanagan serving as a marshal in Manhattan in 1803. Crime is rising in the expanding city, but upper class residents, who can afford to protect themselves, oppose a permanent police force, fearing the equivalent of a standing army, and politicians object to the concept as an English idea. When Kerry O'Toole, a former pickpocket to whom Justy has given a chance to lead a law-abiding life, comes across an unidentified teenage girl in an alley who shortly after dies of a ghastly knife wound, Justy investigates. Tattoos on the dead girl's hands suggest that she's a Muslim, which, along with her dark skin color, makes identifying her and catching her killer a low priority for Justy's boss. Justy persists, however, and his inquiries take him and Kerry to Hudson's Kill, the home of a significant Muslim community, whose members aren't entirely cooperative. Hirsch makes the most of his setting and has a rich vein of potential future plots to mine. Historical mystery fans will be enthralled.

Man vs Markets

Man Vs. Markets is economics explained, pure and simple, for the layperson who wouldn't know a "bond" from an "option," and who believes that a "future" is when we'll all have flying cars. Here is an illuminating, insightful, and wonderfully witty journey of discovery through the often confusing financial markets, offering clear, relatable explanations and definitions of the system's various instruments, yet less simplistically than the popular ...for Dummies series. Man Vs. Markets is a must-read handbook for everyday investors, serious students of finance and economics, and everyone who wants to understand what they're reading when they open their newspapers to the business section.